LEAH BOBET

ABOVE

ARTHUR A. LEVINE BOOKS
AN IMPRINT OF SCHOLASTIC INC

All rights reserved. Published by Arthur A. Levine Books,
an imprint of Scholastic Inc., *Publishers since 1920.*
SCHOLASTIC and the LANTERN LOGO are trademarks and/or
registered trademarks of Scholastic Inc.

Library of Congress Cataloging-in-Publication Data

Bobet, Leah.
Above / by Leah Bobet. — 1st ed.
p. cm.
Summary: When insane exile Corner and his army of
mindless, whispering shadows invade Safe, a secret,
underground community of freaks and disabled outcasts,
Matthew, traumatized shapeshifter Ariel, and other misfits
go to the dangerous place known as Above, where
Matthew makes a shocking discovery about the
histories entrusted to him.
ISBN 978-0-545-29670-0
[1. Fantasy.] I. Title.
PZ7.B63244Abo 2012
[Fic] — dc23
2011012955

Book design by Christopher Stengel

10 9 8 7 6 5 4 3 2 1   12 13 14 15 16

Printed in the U.S.A.   23
First edition, January 2012

Produced with the support of the city of Toronto
through Toronto Arts Council

For all the people who
made Safe for a prickly
bee-sting girl, and were
steadfastly patient until
she learned to be kind.
I love you all very much.

My last supply duty before Sanctuary Night, I get home
and Atticus is waiting.

It's half past three already, and nobody awake except
for Hide and Mack and Mercy and me, unloading our
week's ration of scuffed-up bottles and tins into the broad-
wide kitchen cabinets. Most supply nights that's all there
is to it: the swish and thunk of stacking tins, the slow
quiet of faucets stopping, pipes sleeping, water mains
humming lower as the city Above goes to bed. The air
moves slower with everyone laid asleep; gets dustier, goes
back to earth. There's a light by the kitchen, run off a
wire drawn down off the old subway tracks, and the rest
is feel-your-way dark until morning, when Jack Flash
lights the lamps with a flick of his littlest finger.

Jack's got a good Curse. He might have made it Above
if not for the sparks always jumping out of things to kiss
at his knuckles. Me, the only thing good 'bout my Curse
is that I can still Pass. And that's half enough to keep me
out of trouble.

But tonight it's not the half I need, because there's Atticus, spindly crab arms folded 'cross his chest, waiting outside my door. His eyes glow dim-shot amber — not bright, so he's not mad then, just annoyed and looking to be mad. The glow's enough to light up the tapestry on my door: the story of Safe as far as I know it, in bits of paint and pictures, carved so everyone knows the Teller lives here. Atticus blinking makes it flicker like firelight.

"Up late," I say, stretching the knots out of my arms and pretending I'm not a little scared. Atticus's eyes have made grown men cower and run for the sewers. I carved it myself on his twice-thick board-wood door: Atticus standing tall and pale-armed, his eyes the brightest red I could scrounge up. There's no reason for that blink-glow, that flicker of Atticus's eye.

"She's got out again," is all he says, and shifts his weight to his other foot.

Every ache in my shoulders catches and double-knots tight.

"Oh." I can't even get upset anymore. I was upset the first time, and the fifth — afraid she'd run into the bad things in the sewers or the tunnels, that she'd make it Above and get caught by the men in white coats; not afraid enough of what scares Atticus, which is the Whitecoats following her back and finding Safe. She's run away too many times for me to believe that anymore.

"She's your responsibility," Atticus says. His claw-hands snap until the echo sounds like a hundred running feet: a sure sign he's annoyed.

"She's Sick," I say faint. I'm not usually one for talking back, but it's half past three and my mouth tastes sour and the ache in my back is a night's bad work, and I know Ariel's my responsibility. I stood up and swore her protection before everyone.

I've asked-told-begged her to stop running.

Now Atticus's eyes flush red, and I gotta clench both fists to keep from going *I'm sorry I'm sorry* like a little kid. "Teller," he says, calling me so instead of *Matthew* to say it clear: that I owe him my life, the food in my belly, the tin roof and plank walls and tapestry-carved door of my home. My Sanctuary. "She's your responsibility. And you're responsible to Safe."

To keep Safe. To do my best for Safe, so there's a place for people like us always.

I know.

"I'll find her," I tell him, and don't meet his eyes.

Atticus doesn't have to say *You better find her.*

I start fast down the footworn path, clenching and unclenching fists to get my body moving again. No time to stop at the kitchen for provisions, but I still have all the other things important for heading out of Safe: matches in my pocket, an unlit brand at my back, and twenty-five dollars tucked in my shirt. What Atticus calls emergency money; in case you have an emergency, he says, but really it's if you use it, it had better have been an emergency.

Maybe I can sneak a dollar to buy her a chocolate. Maybe if I do that it'll make her want to stay.

"This is the last time!" Atticus calls after me, his voice dry and hoarse-quiet from the things the Whitecoats put down his throat back before there was anywhere like Safe. Atticus can't shout anymore, but when you're Atticus you don't need shouting. People shift in their sleep, rustling like roaches ahead of the sound of his voice.

The last time, I think, and shove fists in my pockets where the matches are. *Oh, Ariel.*

"All right," I say out loud, and head back up the tunnel that goes Above.

It's cold Above. The first time I went up I thought it'd be warmer, with all that stone and dirt and loose history trapping the cold into Safe. 'Course, I went up first in the middle of winter, with snow patching the dead lawns and thin scruffy ice on the sidewalks, and it was colder than anywhere in the whole of the world. I shivered under the beat-up jacket I thought was going to be enough and thought no wonder people were so cruel up here, if the wind bit your bones all day and the sky stared you down into nothing with stars.

I know about things like winter now, know them as

more than a Tale, and even still the cold starts on me the second I leave Safe. I keep my hands in my pockets once I open the big barred door and cross the Pactbridge into the old sewers. My toes prickle through my shoes and start to scrunch up. I straighten them out and walk faster.

It's eight steps, nine steps, ten before the big door shuts behind me.

I carved the big door too, on the inside, not out. Not Tales; just faces. On the big door is where we put our martyrs.

And outside it, the old sewers. Dead-dry, and cold. Footsteps echo here, no matter how soft you shoe along the ledges. The new sewers are louder, warmer, and damp, and I get to the new sewers before I settle my head down to think where the hell my Ariel's gone.

I don't know Above like most of them. Most of them ran from there when they were young, made it down to Atticus and Corner and made themselves a home. But I was born in Safe; the only one 'til this year, with Heather and Seed's baby yet to come. There's nothing Above in my bones.

So I can't say if going up was worse for me or better. I don't have the fear like Violet or Scar, who can't bear light even after twenty years in Safe, but I've heard all their Tales. I spent my first supply run looking over my shoulder for Whitecoats and policemen, watching every sprawled-out lump on the sidewalks for a needle, a grin, a knife. I jumped so bad I almost didn't Pass, and Whisper had to tell some starer in a suit how I was her little second cousin who'd never seen the city.

It was on my second run I found Ariel.

She wasn't Above. It was on the way back we found her, huddled down in a corner that was halfway fallen in, down in the old sewers where most people don't ever get. I wouldn't have seen her except she was shaking just the tiniest bit, vibrating like sharks or bee's-wing; moving because things that don't move fall to the deepest depths and die.

I thought of that bee's-wing thing before I knew her, I swear. That's how I knew it, the first time she changed. That I'd understood somehow. That I can make her Safe again.

So the roster crew got their brands off their backs and lit the matches, because you can't trust things you find in the old sewers, not things whose names you don't know. Whisper nudged me — another test from her, *handle it, Matthew* — and I crept forward with my own brand to see what I could see.

She was curled up small, wearing sweatpants and a dirty white T-shirt that hung loose and smudged to her knees. Her hair was tied back — I remember her hair and I think I will until I die — and when I held up the brand to see if she flinched, it sparkled honey-golden, brighter than Atticus's eyes. Brighter than matches.

She backed up and straightened out a little, and I saw. She was . . . well. A girl.

Girls don't make it down here, through the rattly old subway tracks, along the vent that goes to the sewers, past the twist you have to be looking for to find. Not many make it down, period, and even less are pretty girls. And none had ever had those long-fingered hands, or that tilt to the chin. That spark of light caught in their eyes, their hair, that lit like the first lamp switched on come morning.

"S'all right," I called back to the supply crew, who were shaking and stamping with nerves, and to put her at ease as well. It's scared things that bite, scared things cornered. She looked scared but not like I'd ever seen it, not like people did scared in Safe when they had nightmares about the needles, the Whitecoats, the knife. She just watched me, not moving one bit except for the shivering; waiting to see which way I'd move.

"S'all right," I told her, and tried to smile. It came out bad. She made me nervous, with her flower-golden hair. "We can take you somewhere warm."

We picked her up. Her eyes got big when she saw Seed's horns and Hide's skin with its twisting, spattered colors, and she hugged her big black book so tight 'gainst her chest that her arms shook. But she kept herself quiet and didn't squeak or run, and we took her across the Pactbridge, through the big door, and into the cavern: into Safe.

We brought her into my house — I'd just got my house then — and settled her down with wash water, and it wasn't until the rest were gone to get Atticus that I found two things. The plastic bracelet on her wrist was the first, scratched-up with initials for things only Whitecoats understood. I cut it off with my second-best carving knife and picked it up with a rag. It was dirty. Whitecoat things aren't good to touch.

The shrunken wings falling out of her back were the second.

I was bad. I stared. One of the first rules of Safe was not to stare: not at Violet's twitches, or Scar's marks, or Chrys's apple-peeling skin. I turned away quick, but not quick enough: Her face went an ugly, terrible grey. But *one of us*, I was thinking all the while, dizzy and strange and trying hard not to smile. *She's like us. She can stay.*

"It's all right. We won't hurt you," I said.

"Yes you will," she whispered. Her eyes were pupil-big with worry.

"I won't," I told her, and put down her wrist. My hand brushed lightly her hand. "I swear."

"She's Sick," I told everyone once they straggled into the common to make council. I'm no doctor, I don't know from Sick, but I held up the sliced plastic bracelet and the circle shied from it like it was fire. "Sick's the same as Freak Above."

I didn't mention the wings.

The ones who'd been in the hospitals, heard the screaming and heads banging against walls until the Whitecoats rushed in with needles and straps, they looked at each other in the bitty bit corners of the dark. Atticus crossed his arms and his eyes were dusty sunlight, the color they don't get often. That's the color they get when he cries, instead of crying.

The light caught her tangled-up hair; it sparkled. She scuffed one foot, dragging, on the torn rubber and gravel of the common floor.

They let her stay.

You take your own names here, down in Safe. Ari couldn't pick one the first week or two, and after that she didn't want to and wouldn't tell us hers. So it was me who named her Ariel, after the girl caught in the tree in Atticus's best-loved bedtime Tale. And she answered to it, and she stayed. And after three weeks her nightmares went quieter and she got to talking, and would smile here and there at things I said, and morningtimes I'd wake up sometimes with her head tucked on my shoulder and all the worry lines 'bout her mouth unraveled. But I could barely ever, almost never get her to talk about Above.

So I don't know Above that well. I know the safe-houses and the supply drops, the five doors down to the right sewer line to get myself quickly home. But I don't know Above like Ariel.

I don't know where she might have gone.

So I wait. I stand at the door between the old tunnels and new sewers like it's my sentry duty, because the new sewers are the most dangerous part, and if she comes back, she shouldn't run them alone. The old tunnels are different dangerous, Atticus's kind of dangerous. People wander down in the tunnels sometimes: workers or explorers from Above who somehow *know* we're tucked here hiding. But you hear footsteps coming back through the sewers late at night, and who's to know if they're from people living or things not people at all. We find bodies there sometimes, set up to trip over, one hand reaching out of the dirty water to whisper 'cross your ankle as you pass.

There are things in the sewers that don't believe in Atticus and Safe. There are shadows that watch you there, too-still and solid, that don't move with the light.

I have a brand. I have twelve matches. I make sure not to pace, and I listen.

I don't know how long I wait. Time in the tunnels isn't a set thing, like it is in Safe with its hundreds of clocks, like Above with the sun and stars staring down at you accusing from the sky. I lean against the wall after a while — check the old bricks first for wet or bugs or traps — and think, drift off into the darkness. 'Bout the tilt of Ariel's head when she's sleeping; the steady sweep of her hand the day I mussed up three times drawing the curve of Beak's sharp chin and she just said *here, gimme that* and sketched it in perfect, four quick lines; the charcoal-dark fingerprints she left on my shoulder afterward. The heavy sound the paper of her writing book makes when she turns a page, pages full of things she won't let me see. 'Bout *last time* and the last time I heard those words, and what I might say to make her tell her hurts to me instead of paper. What I might say so she'd stay put for good.

So I don't know how long it is before I hear the footsteps.

It takes a second to realize; they're light, quiet, patter-quick. I straighten up — I've been half-asleep, and that's stupid, dangerous-stupid — and squint into the dark.

"Hello?" I call out quiet, knowing a second later that was also stupid and I shouldn't have said a thing. It echoes *hello-lo-lo* through the tunnel, and when the echo's gone I shift my weight one foot to the other and there's no footsteps no more.

Hello? I want to say again, and bite down hard on my tongue, remembering everything Mack and Atticus ever said about traps, tricks, fire; the pale gleam of dead fingers poking up from the water. The way there was so little attached to those fingers when we heaved and pulled them out, and the laughing after, coming deep dark from a mouth we couldn't see.

There are things in the sewers that don't believe in Atticus and Safe.

I reach for the brand at my back.

"I know you," a voice says too close, thin and dry and too close, and I whip around.

The tunnels are always dark, but I know from dark. Right now they're darker than they ought to be, the outlines of things gone blurred and strange. I put up a hand to my face; my fingers wiggle vague, black on black. The skin around my eyes is tingling, numb.

I can't tell if that was an arm I just saw. A sleeve. A face. *I can't see.*

"You're Narasimha's boy." The voice rustles the hair 'round my ear; rasp and darkness and the edge of something foul. I strike out at it with both arms, flail, hit nothing. "You're the Teller."

"Who calls?" I squeak too loud and reach out again. Nothing's there, nothing but air and the slightest breeze, but I can smell somebody now, feel them: the difference between old sewer and old sweat. A flicker of something living and warm.

"You are the Teller then," the voice says. Dry, short, bloody. I can't tell if it's girl or boy. And in the other ear: "Then I'll ask you a Tale."

My breath's coming too fast. I fumble a match, drop it between the twisted old tracks; it skitters into a crack and vanishes forever — *damn.* Fumble another and I can hear the catch and hiss as I strike it bright, but I can't see nothing, not a thing.

"No Tales," I manage as it flares and burns out, and my voice rises and cracks like rockfall. Match to the sandpaper, pull once — nothing — twice —

The brand's yanked full off my back, hard enough to pull me stumbling backward. I shout, and the echo of it mixes with the clatter of my one good weapon, tossed somewhere away. The voice breathes laughter on my face.

"What color were Atticus's eyes when he exiled the first Beast from Safe?" The words come hot, dirty, filth and waste and dead things rotted through, and I can't find it anywhere, not anywhere.

"Corner," I say, stupid, stalling, and the name's been forbidden so long it feels like licking mud. "It was Corner he exiled."

"What color?" it spits at me, burning on my cheek where I can still feel. "Teller, what color?"

The burning on my cheek shifts, turns into pressure just below my eye, and sharpness, a nail —

"Red," I choke out.

The pressure falls away; a poke and it's gone. I back up panting, free hand up high to protect my face, thick with panic. "All right, Teller," it whispers, whispers like worms; the little breathy laugh that follows is the opposite of real laughing, colder than winter Above. Something damp pats my cheek. "Go on home now." I feel it turn, feel the terrible weight of *something*'s attention lift away from every breathing bit of my skin.

And then a long-bodied honeybee comes screaming out of the darkness.

It stings and stings at the air, buzzes furious figure eights around the tunnel, past my hair, down low to the tracks. That awful voice calls out in terrible, muffled surprise, and the feeling rushes back into my face like it's me the match set afire. I hit the floor, press both hands hard against my face to block out the rush of nerve-prickle pain. The buzz gets low, heavy, and that attention suddenly scatters, clatters down the tunnel, little light footsteps that I don't dare and can't bear to see.

I blink against it, against the pain. Open, slow, my eyes. The blurred shape of my skinny fingers, twitching, tight, swims in front of me.

Oh thank god thank god.

I don't dare look up until the shapes come clear, until I know that I'm seeing what's there for true. When I finally do, the bee is drifting back toward me, floating, tired. It circles once around my head, tickles my ear, and lands in my outstretched hand.

"Oh, Ari," I whisper, because she won't let me call her anything sweeter. I close her in my trembling palm and the stinger hovers, pressed to my lifeline, for one long, long moment. And then I open it and she goes long again, wider, firming up into legs and arms and bone. I open it and she turns back into a girl with honey-colored hair and eyes that're red from crying, tucked in the skinny circle of my arms.

The wings change last. They go long with her and then fall out plucked, fall to the concrete like petals. We used to save them, hang them on the walls until we lived in a hollow that was veiled with glittering wings. We ran out of places to put them after the first three months. Ari runs away a lot.

"I heard you shouting," she says, and wipes her eyes. Her voice shakes worse than my hands. I can't help it. My arms tighten around her even though I know she's skittish, know she doesn't like to be held 'cause someone hurt her bad Above, so bad she still wakes me up some nights with crying.

"Came to save me," I say to cover her stiffening, to talk out what I mean even if I can't show it. I'm not good with her this way. I don't know the right way to move. "What was that?"

She half shakes me off, trying to sting without a stinger. The wings shudder and bend against the floor, refracting dim tunnel-light against the walls. There's a soft crunch as one snaps.

"Ariel," I say softer, even softer.

"I hate you."

I don't answer. I pet her bloody-golden hair until her chest stops heaving with tears.

"I'll get you a chocolate next time I'm up. Or a peach, you'd like a peach," I murmur, rocking her clumsy in my arms that're still learning touching. "I'll get you little bee clips for your hair."

"I don't want," she whispers, hiccupy, but she's not crying anymore.

"Come home," I ask into her ear, and she finally, eventually nods.

I take her hand. I listen for the footsteps.

It's grave-silent all the way home.

We don't get back 'til morning. The lamps are flickering on one by one through the cavern, each a different color from the rainbow of lampshades that Jack Flash bids stolen every fifth supply run. Half of everyone's already awake, and they watch us stumble all the way back to my house on the west wall, blind and time-muddled and tired. The clocks aren't chiming — morning bell must have already rung. That late out; later than anyone's stayed out in years if they planned on coming back.

It could be a Tale if I wasn't so tired. It'd be told to the young ones in the school Atticus and Whisper keep, recited singsong on the common. I'd carve it on my sill: the big door pushed open, my back straight instead of hunched over like the old tunnels make you do. Our arms around each other, framed against the tunnels and everything that's outside, everything that's bad. I could carve my Ariel beautiful.

Atticus is by my door again, or never left, his arms crossed like a statue. "Back late," he says. He doesn't look worried. His eyes are amber, though, fading down to nothing fast. Just another light by daytime.

"There was . . . trouble," I say, and swallow.

Ariel takes my arm and holds it tight. I glance back and her eyes are narrow, warning: *Don't*. But Atticus is watching, waiting.

I tell him about the voice, the smell, the questions. I tell him like it's a Tale: *Once upon a time there was a monster in the tunnels that struck me gasping blind, and it asked 'bout your eyes, and it knew all our names.* Ariel's hand digs into my arm and then, just as quick, pulls away. I spare a glance and she's drawn herself back, hiding behind her hair. Her mouth is tiny and sour.

Atticus's eyes light up switch-flicked when I get to the part with the tingling 'round my eyelids, the dimming, darkening pain; the question. I drop my head, not 'cause I'm scared, but shamed of it, dizzy and shamed. I told Safe things to something outside. A sewer-thing. A monster.

That's not keeping Safe. It's not doing my very best.

"Mm." Atticus grunts once all my polished story-words run out. "You kept yourself whole." He pats me awkward on the shoulder and it turns me absurdly proud,

proud like when I was a kid and I'd done well at my lessons. "Just don't tell this around."

"Sir," I say, breathing better now that he's forgiven me the whole of it, backtalk and telling and Ari running and all; *Sir*, like I called him when I was a kid with no mama or papa, sleeping foster in his house. "What was it?"

"What happens when you let unsafe things in Safe," he says, which is no answer at all. And then: "Last time," Atticus repeats, looking at me and then Ari with his molten-amber eyes. I put an arm around her, tighten my hand on her shoulder. She ducks away from it, one ugly jerk, and I drop it back to my side. She won't look at me.

Atticus's right claw is tapping against the left, *rat-tat*, *rat-tat*, open and close. He's not looking at us either; he's far away somewhere else and pacing. Atticus is nervous. Atticus is *upset*. He stalks along the gravel and tile, *crunch crunch* past his own door, past the scuffed-up furniture and chattering breakfast line in the kitchen and into the north side of the cavern. I count steps; he pauses at Whisper's clutter-house cave. Taps on the door, and waits 'til she lets him in.

Ariel watches tightly after him, her hands in fists stuck hard in her pockets. "You shouldn't tell things like that," she says, so low I can't quite believe it.

I blink. "What d'you mean? It could be dangerous —" Stupid; it *is* dangerous. It pressed sharp against my eye, and it knew all our homes and names —

"Don't you know what *happens* —" she starts, and then bites it off. Her eyes are clear and hard and emptier than the sky.

"He's just going to talk to Whisper," I say. I reach out for her hand, but she pulls away.

"What'd he mean, 'last time'?" she asks, half-challenge.

Ariel wasn't here for the time with Corner. She doesn't know what those words mean. "Don't worry," I say. I'm too tired to tell her now and set her crying, risk her running right back for the tunnels. Tomorrow, or tonight. After we've slept and she's done hating me again. "We should get to bed," I say, and open up our door.

When I turn to close it behind us, Jack is there too, leaning quiet against one of the rough-cut pillars that keeps our roofing up. Listening. Maybe all along. He pushes off it and pats me on the back with his scrapy grey glove. "Good work," he says, out of Atticus's hearing and everybody else's. "Kept your head."

I feel my face warm down in the dark. Jack's rough with praise sometimes: He talks a crateload when you do something wrong, and that makes his kind words kinder. "Thanks," I murmur back, tight so the sound won't carry. And this I can tell to Jack, and not to Atticus who's like my sterner pa: "I didn't know what to do."

"S'all right," he says, and pats my back again. His gloves are like padded sandpaper, rough as his black beard, and wrapped round and round his fingers with duct tape and insulator. "There's things out there that none of us know what to do with." A pause. One that's got knowing in it, but when I raise my eyes to his, he looks straight elsewhere. "I'll look around."

And like that I feel better, less dirty, less beat. Jack gives me another stone-crack smile and he's off across the common, soft gravel and shredded-up rubber tire crunching under his boots. Jack's tough, but he's good. He runs the wires so the city don't see us sucking power off their littlest electric toe and come down with work crews, looking for what we might be. Jack's not afraid of Atticus either, and for real; he don't need to save up backtalk.

Where he goes, the lights come on.

I rub my eyes with the back of my hand and look down at Ariel's watching face, the dark circles under her own eyes. "Bed," I say quiet, and follow her back inside to our own Sanctuary. To the house that's hers, hers and mine, all broke up with wings.

I'm writing to you as myself. They say writers, especially of memoirs, shouldn't speak in the first person. Atticus told me that's because they don't know what they have to say for themselves yet, but I'm pretty sure I know what there is to say about me.

I was born here. My ma had scaly gills down the sides of her neck and my pa had the feet of a lion. When I was three my ma died of a cold that didn't get better. When I was ten my pa went up on his supply shift and didn't come back, and I was given as foster to Atticus.

I don't have lion's feet, though they're big and have claws instead of nails. I can't breathe underwater. But I can Tell, and I can Pass.

JACK'S TALE

Once upon a time, Jack was born. His name wasn't Jack then, and he didn't spark yet. The sparking came later, when he moved to the city from his little backwoods town, past the forest and up the highway from the city Above.

Jack had a ma and pa and they fought a lot. Both drank (Jack had to explain this to me, along with forests and towns — I thought the first time it meant water, 'cause Atticus forbade anything harder). This wasn't a big deal 'cause most of the mas and pas in Jack's town drank, and the kids went out into the back fields to stay away.

The back fields went on until they met the roadway and the woods, and the boys in Jack's town dared each other nightly to see how far they'd go from home, into the dark, before turning around and running back. One day when Jack's ma and pa were yelling up a storm, he went farthest of all and stayed there until it got dark and the other boys went home for supper. Once they were gone he went farther, and then farther than that, and realized (with a strange glow in his eye when he tells this, like

Atticus's rubbed off on him) that he could go as far as he wanted until he fell down. That nobody would make him stay.

He went far.

It started raining after a bit, and Jack thought *they really did yell up a storm*, shivering wet in his T-shirt along the roadside that nobody drove on 'cause the town was so far from everything. It thundered like tractor engines over and over and he got scared, thought about finding somewhere to hide 'til the storm got done. He never thought about turning back, though — he's careful to say that every time: *I never once thought to turn myself back.*

But he hesitated, stopped for a minute on the flat roadway in the flat land, where he was the tallest thing for a little ways.

And the lightning kissed him bone to bone and he wasn't there for a while.

He woke up in the hospital three towns away, hurting bad from lying stiff (stiff like a body, he showed me, arms and legs all straight and locked and a weird blank smile on his face). His ma and pa had noticed him missing and come looking, but it was too late for that. A man and woman in uniforms (*Whitecoats?* I asked the first time, thrilled with terror, but he shook his head *no*) had come too, and they interviewed his parents and then him for a long time, and found out that his parents drank. When they let him out of the hospital the man and woman said he would go to the city with them instead of home with his ma and pa.

Once he was in the city, in a house full of rowdy boys and girls who didn't have parents no more either, the sparks came.

They had televisions in the city, and he couldn't turn them on for breaking them. They had microwaves, and he couldn't warm up food 'cause they'd spark and smoke and the firemen would have to spray down the house. They had stoplights, and the stoplights flickered and died dead when he touched the buttons to make them change. The man and woman took him to the city hospital for testing. They ran tests. They prodded him and took his blood away.

They couldn't keep him in the hospital. He broke all their machines: Tubes and wires leaned out to brush his fingers, a spark and then dials going wild everywhere, flashing lights, alarms. They took him out of the Normal-people hospital and to their Whitecoat place, a building by a park with big barred windows and different machines, ones that clipped on to his arms and legs and chest with little sucking sounds and measured the spark under Jack's skin. The sucker-clips left marks like bruises.

Nobody cared, he puts in at this part, that the Whitecoats did things that hurt him. He didn't have a ma and pa anymore to fight for him (*like yours would have for you, Matthew*, he said with a little twisted smile), and he was from a town back in the rocky brush that nobody'd ever heard of. It's not just Beasts that are scared of the city Above; not just us who live under.

Young Jack was clever though, like he is now old. The lock on his door only opened from the outside, but it was a lock with numbers instead of a metal key kept hid away. He touched his fingers to the back of the door late one night and hunted deep bone to bone for his sparks.

He set his jaw and leaned into the door, and when it hurt he pushed the hurt farther, out from the pit of his belly where he kept his oaths safe.

Dragged light to his fingers, and cried as they burned.

They sparked and sparked, and when the door swung open he crept out into the hallway and then into the street and ran as fast as he could. Ran far.

And how did he find Safe? I asked him the first time, because my job is to tell the story about Safe.

Jack smiled his crooked smile at me and told me Safe is the farthest far of all.

TWO

Ariel sleeps 'til Sanctuary Night, and that's fine by me.

Sanctuary Night's exactly what it says. Everyone lines up before Atticus and he reconfirms their Sanctuary: their right to live in Safe. Nobody's ever turned away, except for Corner eight years back when it all came out about Jonah and the killing, and after that it couldn't have stayed and shared our plates and homes and duties no matter *what* Atticus said 'bout it.

There are stories that they loved each other once, that the Whitecoats took them as much for their loving as Atticus's eyes and arms and Corner's bloodtouch hands. But nobody ever told those loud enough to make a carving, and Jack once said it's better that way. "Keeping histories," he said actually, his voice all popping with sparks, "is as much about knowing what needs forgetting as what ought to be remembered."

That's something that sneaks up on me when it's darker than the normal dark. I almost asked him to explain once what he meant, but his face was too serious, too hot with lightning when he said it, to ever bring it up again.

When the clocks strike night, I finally wake her up.

She's muzzy but her eyes open right away, big and scared like they always are if anything touches her sudden in sleep. "It's me," I whisper careful, not moving fast or talking loud. She relaxes, muscle by muscle outlined under our thin blue blanket, 'til I can stand up without towering over her. You learn a lot about how not to make people vulnerable when you live with Ariel. You learn a lot about making Safe.

You learn a lot about what makes a person vulnerable too. I remember those things, each little bit that makes her flinch. I'm saving them up in case one day I meet whoever made my Ariel hurt.

She sits up and stretches out, looking for the clock through the layers and layers of wings hung from the rafters. She hated that I hung them at first. Ariel likes things Normal. "Sanctuary Night," I tell her, and she shakes her head a little, like the thought needs settling.

"Gotta wash my face," she half-asks, quiet, and brushes through the wings to the basin when I don't reply. They rustle after her, dry and unbending, catching what bit of light comes off the bulb in the ceiling and spreading it soft: white on white on white getting gentler through every shed wing. In the morning, when Jack lights the lamps, the house glows like your mama's arms: sourceless light and iridescence.

I read that word in one of Atticus's thick old books once. When I went to Jack to ask what it meant, he held his hands out and they glowed so gentle I thought they might kiss the air, and since that day I wanted a place that was *iridescent*, that lit without burning. Being in love is sort of like that, when it's real. When it's true.

It's like that to watch Ariel smile.

And when she burns, it's not her fault. She's Sick, and if I'm soft, soft and unsharp and patient, it'll all turn out right.

She splashes in the corner. The sound's compact and quiet under the chatter outside the door: people carrying their offerings into the great empty circle between the houses and the kitchen to exchange them for Sanctuary from Atticus. Not Atticus the man, but him as the founder — one of the founders — of Safe. He takes it in for the whole of us, whatever token we have to show what's ours to offer, and then he touches you on the head with his heavy old claw and you can stay.

My offering doesn't get carried. What I give back to Safe is my arms for lifting, my hand for carving, my ears for listening sharp and careful, and my face, my Passable face. What I do is listen, and at the end of the night I Tell before everyone who went first and second, what they offered, and what it meant. I Tell them the Tale of themselves, and that's how I prove I'm a good Teller. And then Atticus puts his claw on my head and we go to the kitchen to feast.

Ariel comes back wet-haired, smelling strong like the flower perfume I found, tossed away half-empty in a curbside box, for her birthday. "You have something?" I ask. There's no hanging back on Sanctuary Night, not if you're able. She wasn't when she came down, so they let me take responsibility for her once, just that once. But it's been eight months, and that won't stand on Sanctuary Night.

She holds out her hand. There's a little stinger balanced on her palm, shiny-black with chitin and whatever bees sweat when they're caught up with insect rage. "S'what I'm offering," she says shy, like she never yelled or said she hated me in the sewers while she cried, and I lean down close to look, breath held so I don't blow it away.

Under her other arm is her big black writing book, and I know what that means. It's all that stubborn inside her, hiding, wrapped tight under her fear and Sick. The tough I've always known was there; a spark of light caught in her eye. Her Curse, her secrets. Her Tale.

It doesn't matter anymore if Atticus said *last time*. Sanctuary's a promise to keep Safe.

It's her promise not to go.

"It's good. A good offering," I tell her, and smile; I can hardly breathe from the falling-down relief of it. But she don't smile back; she looks away from me as we brush aside the long wing-curtains and open the door of the house.

The path out to the center of Safe takes us through the middle houses, all cut-up concrete and salvaged metal and boards, the oldest houses in the whole cavern; far enough back to be private and not so far as to hit the cavern walls. Back when Safe was founded there were even less people than now, and nobody wanted to stray too far from the fire that burned all night in what turned into the kitchen and common and stores.

It's not like that anymore. Word got 'round, even Above; more people came down. Things got bigger. Now there's electrics and a skinny pipe for clean water and no fires built inside for years, and the newest houses slope like subway tunnels against the rocky ceiling where it curves gentle down.

The oldest of them all is Atticus's, cemented-tight pieces of shattered slab that he took down with his own hard claws. The concrete's snipped like fingernails, ragged-edged where he cut and then moved his claw and cut again. You can see the glow of his eyes through the cracks arcing slab to slab, and you know when to stay away. We come out past it to where all of Safe is fetched up waiting, gathered half-circle across the spiraled, soft-swept common.

We're late, near the last: Hide is already shuffling back-forth back-forth on his little patch of ground, and

Heather's fingers are tapping 'gainst the arm of her wheel-chair, the one that used to belong to Reynard before he died and we put him in the ground. Seed's hand's caught her other, fingers tangled together, talking broad-smile low to Jiéli's ma, Kimmie, while the little girl squirms and fidgets and makes her singing noises in her mama's arms. I count heads: near the full forty-three people who shelter in Safe. Forty-three Tales in the back of my head; forty-three offerings to make a Tale of tonight.

For now everything's all chatter, the kind you get on special days; bits of bright new clothes first worn and washed-up hair. The tins of pears and sweets are lined up on the kitchen cabinet-top for the meal we'll make together after, and the little refrigerator we use only a few days yearly 'cause it's so much noise and strain for Jack is humming with cool cream inside. Everything's ready, set for Atticus to begin.

Except Atticus ain't here yet.

I look around for Whisper and she's all the way to the back, cradling the old Polaroid camera she hoards in her velvet-and-redbrick house that's more a museum than somewhere people live. There's one picture of every Sanctuary Night, dim and slick-papered, on the inside back of her door: all the people of Safe growing older and bigger and more plentiful year to year.

It's for Violet's sake they're back there, back where the light don't half reach. Violet's behind her where it's dim enough for her to bear, holding tight to Whisper's free hand. Violet used to mend clothes, dust tabletops, separate the cans and packets that each supply duty brought down to make fair-share meals for the rest of us, but it's been more than six full years since she could open a jar without dropping it or not stick herself with sewing needles from her twitch. Now Whisper speaks for her, and Whisper makes guarantee of her Sanctuary.

"Teller," she says formal when we make our way over. Not from any sort of trouble; tonight I'm Teller, calling back the Tales once Sanctuary's given. She don't give greeting to Ariel. People stopped after the first month, when she wouldn't speak to them back.

"Where's Atticus?" I ask, giving them the greeting back: a nod of the head to fuzzy white-haired Whisper in her beads and layers, to greyer, faded Violet with her crooked jaw.

"N-n-n-not," Violet manages, and pulls a rueful face between the lip-smacks and twitches and tangles. Today it's bad. Whisper will have to give her Tale too. "Notout," she rushes in one breath, and sighs.

Under the sounds that are nighttime in Safe is always the ticking, steady and strong, of seventy-one hanging clocks. The nearest one says ten to the hour, and Atticus is never, never late. "Should be out," I say, silly and obvious.

Whisper's hand catches at her skirts and skirts and skirts, showing green and red and tatter-brown even in

Jack's dimmer nighttime light. "He should," she says. There's a scrap of frown, pulling down her face just so. "Matthew," — and not *Teller* — "go fetch him out?"

Me, and not Whisper. Not 'cause Whisper's scared of Atticus, like some. She's more than useful; she's a founder of Safe too and has the ghost-talk and knows halfway all of Above, and she's the one Atticus talks to besides when something's tough or tricky. But I'm the Teller and lived foster to Atticus for six long years, and I can interrupt him in the middle of something important without causing a giant public row that'd spill out and blight our Sanctuary Night.

"Ma'am," I say, proper like you talk to Whisper, and turn for Atticus's great stone doorway. Even though Whisper didn't say nothing 'bout Ariel she trails along behind me, book balanced 'gainst her waist and her right hand careful closed, walking in my footsteps so's to leave no mark. We round the corner, onto the path, and shuffle-walk to the door.

There's red light spilling through the doorframe on the dirt. There's red light and voices, and I can't help it, even though I got taught by the first year I could talk that eavesdropping's a grave wrong. I can't help softening my footsteps, looking back warning at Ariel, leaning down low where the door hangs bad and you can see right in if you crouch just right. To listen.

And: "What do you want?" Atticus says, eyes on fire, brighter red than any paint I could get and hot enough to give off sparks. But he's not looking at me; he's looking at someone long and too-skinny, long and pale and tattered. Someone I can't number in the forty-three Tales of Safe I carry 'bout in my head.

"Sanctuary," whispers a dry boy-girl voice, and my gut chills like the worst winter night in the history of Above, because I remember that voice. *What color were Atticus's eyes when he exiled the first Beast from Safe?* it whispered in my ear with a finger over my eye, sharp and poised for scratching.

Ariel remembers it too, because she freezes. But not before she pulls me *down*. I stuff my hand in my mouth so I don't shout — it tastes like stone and old soap and wood shavings — and go down quiet as I can. The ground outside the doorway presses nubbly against my belly. Ariel's face is cold and her eyes are cold and she's leaning forward 'gainst the ground, she's listening so hard. Listening with every inch.

"Denied," Atticus says, and steps back, claws ready to snap and slice.

"I'm Beast," says the darkness, and it follows him. It's nothing but a silhouette against the bright of Atticus's eyes: a hand, a sleeve, a bony worn-thin hip. Atticus turns to the corner, back again, tracking it with one claw. "Beasts get Sanctuary."

"We should get fire," I whisper. We should get fire, Jack, Whisper, everyone. I don't dare look away for a reply.

33

"You were exiled. Killers don't get Sanctuary." Atticus's eyes are changing colors so fast I can't keep track: anger-fear-rage-grief-pain-memory, orange-red-yellow-cooldown brown.

"Never Killer," it says, rough and odd, and Atticus bares his teeth.

"Don't lie," he answers poison-hard. "Don't lie to *me*."

The quiet between them is terrifying.

"What's *you* anymore?" it backtalks right in front of us, and that thin, starve-jointed hand reaches out, hesitates. And though it don't move, Atticus yanks his arm back, claw flailing high, and for a second I swear his eyes are golden. "What's *me*?"

"I won't have Killers in Safe," Atticus's voice stutters. His claw draws in, hugs to his chest; scrapes soft against the armor of his other arm.

Corner. I bite my lip to keep from yelling that dirty name across the cavern into the cheerful, chatty crowd. I grope for Ari's hand — *get fire* — but she doesn't know what I mean or ignores me, doesn't care.

"That's how you tell my name, then. Killer?" The voice sharpens, deepens down, and the muscles down in my back get thick with true, real scared. "No more founder? No more lover —"

"Out," growls Atticus, and all the murmuring on the common dies dead.

"You can't do that," it says, dangerous and shattered. The hand flicks up, and Atticus squirms back, chest and then shoulders and neck. He clacks his claws when it reaches his throat. "You lock one thing out and then it'll be another, and another, and you won't be any better than they were."

"I stopped," Atticus rasps, stone on stone. "It's not me who doesn't know when to stop."

"Oh, Atticus," it says soft, and the softness is scarier than the rest in its sorrow. "I'd have done anything you asked. I'd have been your sea and sky."

Ariel's shaking. She's shaking and her jaw is closed tight, fists hard like I've never seen them before. The back of her shirt bulges and I squeeze her arm tighter, whisper "No, Ari, no," as clear as I dare, as clear as I can be without letting Corner know we're out here.

It's in looking at her that I miss it. I take a moment to look away, and that's when the knife slips under Atticus's raised arm.

Finds home inside his throat.

I was wrong, I realize, as the claws go up, claws that can't hold his own good blood in. Atticus's eyes in anger weren't the reddest thing I've ever seen. He falls, ankle-twisted, to the floor. The light of his eyes turns golden, yellow like sunshine. Goes out.

And: "Fire!" I finally scream, choking, scrambling to my feet. "Fire to Atticus's door!"

There's a shout, and it's not others taking up the call. It's Jack, booming out louder than he's ever done, "Arms to the big door *now*!" Ariel's up in a flash, flailing, running, wings humped and unfolding, streaking toward the big door.

"Ari!" I yell and set off after her, tripping around the corner through the darkness.

The door is open. The big door is open and the Pactbridge is swaying, stuffed full with shadows, all two arms two legs and a head dark as your third wrong turn at midnight. More shadows than we've ever seen, more than I thought the old sewers and new could hold. They howl empty on the Pactbridge and shake it with their stomping feet. And between them and me is Jack Flash, hands sputtering light, burning from nothing but the lightning in his bones.

Corner's brought them, I realize, sudden and sick. *Corner's come for Safe.*

"Arms!" I call, and scramble to the kitchen for something that'll burn.

The brands are in storage, lined up careful on our shelving beside food, gear, clothes, everything else we smuggle in from Above; tucked away tight against prying hands. They're not close by for an emergency. There's never meant to be emergencies in Safe. I shove through boxes and bags and rows of rope and empty bottles before

I find them, a stack of split wood and old fabric, and yank down as many as I can carry to the door.

Fire in Safe is dangerous. There's not a lot of air where we are, even with the tunnels and vents that the founders dug night after night to funnel good air down from Above. But I burst into the common and nobody hesitates. Nobody stops Seed from grabbing a brand from my cradled arms and readying a match.

Every clock in Safe strikes the hour, cacophonous hour, and the shadows burn darkness through the door.

I've never seen shadows straight on before. Nobody's ever seen more than a foot, a finger in the tunnels, or couldn't describe more than that after, not even for a Teller and a whole stack of founders doing their level best to ask the right questions instead of thinking *monsters*. Seen straight on they're tall and spindling-thin, muscled even stronger than Heather's wheelchair arms, and darker than nighttime, darker than sleep. They've got no eyes, just dips and dents where the eyes should be; no wrinkles or creases or hairs or bumps all down the chest and into their tough runner's legs. They run compact like rats and just as nasty, and puddles drip into their footsteps, slicking the ground deadly.

I drop the brands, all except one, and kick them back behind me. Seed's match flares for a moment against the shadows, *iridescent*, and I swing.

My unlit brand passes right through the first body.

There's no trail of dark, no drag following my swing; the tendons of the shadow's neck just go paler, translucent, and swallow the brand like black water. The shadow laughs like metal cutting into bone: It's fingernails dragging down a million chalkboards, across an eyelid, down my spine. The color leaks back into it like ink into water, turns the curves of its face and fingers solid again. It looks down at me, weighty, heavy, and raises its hand.

"You need fire!" Seed shouts over the noise that's suddenly everywhere, and touches his lit brand to mine. I swing up into the shadow-fist, trail the smoking beginnings of fire through its chest and neck.

There's a smell of damp things burning. The shadow stumbles back, bats at its smoldering, vanishing arm.

The laughing stops.

"Thanks," I say faint, and Seed jogs my elbow: *C'mon. Let's go.*

"Form a line!" Jack hollers, his voice a pop and crackle, but it's too late: The shadows are across the Pactbridge. They tread like giants across the kitchen cabinets, knock down jars and cans and heads that all smash the same, *shatter clunk smack*. They lean quivering into the concrete, somebody's throat between the rag-ends of their fingernails.

"C'mon," Seed presses, and we scoop up the fallen brands. I shove them into any hand I see, any hand that's skin and bone and not variable dark. Behind us come the gouts of smoke, bloody firelight. Shadow-screams.

"Where's Atticus?" Mercy shouts, hoarse and coughing in front of the Sanctuary Night canopy, five feet or a million years or the end of the world away. I'm out of brands and can hardly see; there's too much smoke in the air, too much unpeeled dark.

Gone, I think, and stab fire into another shadow until its lean belly catches and burns. *Gone. Corner's killed him.* It's not one second before another, broken black teeth and giggling murder, pushes forward to take its place. There's hundreds of them. There's more of them than us.

"Teller!" Seed calls, and I turn just in time to see him sprawled flat on his back on the churned-up common floor. The shadow above him has delicate, long-fingered hands. It would make a good carver, I think, as it raises one black rope-muscled foot and kicks Seed in the belly. Seed is looking at that foot. There's blood on his mouth. He's looking at me.

"Hey!" I call, turning heads elsewhere, every head but the one I need to: the one craned down intent like the fastening of a strap. "Hey, shadow!" I choke, and stumble toward it with my brand out like a flag.

It watches me one full second, whuffing and trembling with held-back power, before it brings the foot down.

Seed's head breaks below the horns.

He makes a noise, a terrible strangled noise as his skull

hits floor, bounces, and hangs broken in a way it never ought to be. The second stamp breaks the horns in half, blood coming everywhere and painting the floor terrible bright colors, and then he don't make no noise at all.

My scream comes raw, a formless nothing next to those bent toes and slick arches and the ankle flexed to kick. The shadow looks up as I rush it, screaming hard and wild and *wrong*, and shove the torch into its fat grinning mouth. It ducks and pales, trying to disappear, but I shove it there and hold it 'til the fire takes its wicked head clean off.

"Seed?" I croak when it's collapsed into ash — no, into nothing, a tidy stack of nothing and I've got no time to think about that now. I ground my brand in the gravel and kneel down close, feeling automatic for pulse, for the rise and fall of the chest just like Atticus taught us. Wet soaks through the knees of my pants. "Seed?"

His eyes aren't brown no more, but big and stained bloody. He don't breathe, and he don't answer. My brand tips over, totters onto the floor and smokes out.

Heather, I think as its smoke blobs and thins. She's strong but she can't fight fast, not from her chair; not heavy with Seed's half-orphan child. I've got to find Heather.

I've got to find Ari.

Seed's fallen brand sputters high as I stand up, look around. There's fighting around the common and to the door, between the banged-up metal storage shelves, on the Pactbridge where the smoke is pouring out. A shadow bursts into flame, wailing train-squeal high, and the Sanctuary Night canopy steams and catches. I can't see Heather anywhere, and I can't see —

The hand 'cross my throat brings me down before my tearing eyes even track it.

I hit the ground hard, back and ankles and the back of my head, everything gone bright white for one second too long. The brand bounces out of my hand, and when my eyes clear up, the last thing in the whole Tale of my life I see is an outstretched arm, five delicate carver-long fingers, a pair of shadow-eyes, terrible and sparking and *sad* —

And the tiny sting, coming down.

It screams.

The shadow screams and hops and shakes. The sting lands again and again, stinger ripping that dark away from the inside, punching through it like paper ashing outward from the spot where a lit match head's touched. The shadow, realer than real, unwinds bone by ridge by joint into the smoke.

I blink. My back's wet against the ground. My legs are wet, and I don't know if it's sweat. Ari's bee circles me, once, slowly. Her wings beat once and she starts to sink from the lack of motion, and then she *runs*.

"Ari!" I scream again and stumble up, running after her through the bodies and the wreck and the blood on the smooth-graveled floor, across the Pactbridge. Into the old abandoned sewers.

I run light-blind. I run hands out in front of me, eyes shut, choking because it was the last time and there are shadows in Safe and I can't let her get away, not now. My shoes slap against the cold ledges and my toes don't even try to curl against them. *You're running away*, I realize halfway down the tunnel that splits the old sewers from the new, stinking and scared and listening for the buzz of wings over the faded noise of fighting and bleeding and dying. *You left them.*

I try to turn around and my legs shudder *no*.

I keep running.

I catch up with her after the cramp in my belly's arrived, shifted, and settled, after my dark-vision comes back and then doesn't matter for the sweat stinging my eyes. She's sitting back to the wall like the very first time I found her: curled up tight in the remnants of bloody-edged wings.

Everything's burning. Everything's burning bright.

"Hey," I whisper, not to be gentle but because there's no more voice left to me. Her chin comes up like something hunted.

Behind us, far and faint, there are footsteps in the sewers.

Can't stay. I reach out, teetering, and she hugs her

arms tighter. It's her book. She's hugging her book like a baby child. "Ari?"

She's shaking. "You saw it," she says. Her voice is taut and frightened and harsh. "You all saw it. It was *real*."

"It was real," I say. It comes out more like a cough. I've been breathing smoke. My voice won't work.

She shudders again, one thick terrible one, like earthquakes.

I brush her shriveling wings with my fingers. They flutter like curtains. We can't take them with us. They're too big to carry, and if we leave them they'll show our trail for sure.

I take Ari by the shoulders, light and slow. Turn her to face the wall. "Don't look," I breathe, smoke-mouthed, aching, and then I stomp them. I stomp 'til they break, tear apart their thick-paper membrane, dump them in the sluggish wend of sewer water — and thank you, thank you that nothing reaches up to receive them. No shadow-things left in the new sewers tonight. They're all away in Safe.

She flinches as they sink out of sight, and I'd stop, I'd stop to hold her but there's no time for it now, not with the shadows behind us. I can hear their giggles coming up the tunnels. I can hear their rustling in the dark.

"Gotta run," I whisper, and she nods, clinging to my arm.

We run.

We're in the new sewers when Ari stumbles to a halt and I do too, legs shuddering and stomach tight, everything silent except the slow-moving water and the sound of us breathing like waterfalls. "They're gone," she says, and they are: Those scraping hoots and giggles aren't behind us anymore, and the smell of rust and rot and cold dirty fingers, shadow-smell, is all drowned out in people-smell and refuse and living things. Above things: all the smells that mean life and breath and light and terrible, terrible danger.

"Where are we?" I ask. Ariel turns a blank and hopeless face on me, so smeared with damp from running it looks like her hair's been shedding tears. I squeeze her shoulder — I'm scared, but she *needs* — and squint at the walls. If this is one of our pathways, I'll know it; if it's on our marker maps, there'll be a sign on the concrete: paint, or clay, or circles chiseled deep pointing *danger*, or *fallen path*, or *this is the way back home*.

There aren't none.

I search the walls twice. My sweat cools. By the third time Ari's not going to believe me if I miraculously find something, so I stumble back to her, making real sure to put each foot in front of the other. "We'll find somewhere to hide," I say. "We can rest, figure things out." There are places, dry places, with doors you can bar and good air and soft darkness: the four safehouses we hold outside of Safe.

"Not in the sewers. They sleep in the sewers." She's picking at her palm. There's something in her right hand, dark, like a shadow-tooth. I pluck it out, brush away the blood that comes after it. The stinger, her own stinger. Her offering. She looks down at it and goes quiet, shrinks into herself. "I've seen them."

I go still. Careful-still, the kind I've learned to make people forget I'm there while they Tell the most real nightmares they've ever lived. "When? Where?"

She shrugs, uncomfortable. Ariel doesn't like being the center of anyone's attention, good or bad. "A couple times. Where the ceiling's fallen in. The Cold Pipes."

Nobody goes down to the Cold Pipes. Not even with fire. Every sign that points them out reads *danger, fallen in, do not go*. If we had a sign for *monsters*, it'd be carved in there two feet deep. "When were you at the Cold Pipes?"

I can't keep the strain out of my words. She ducks away from it; hides behind the fall of her mussed-up sunshine hair. "It was only the couple times."

"A couple times?" and my voice is rising now, fright and echo and all those things that don't make a person feel Safe. "Ari —" I say, and then we both look up 'cause we hear it.

Another voice.

It's a little mutter on the air, *rightwise or left, look in for me*, all on one note like the scales've been cut out of its throat. My back seizes up, terrified, but just a second after, my Teller-memory kicks in: I know that kind of song-talk.

It's how you talk to ghosts.

"Whisper?" I breathe. "That you?"

"Teller?" Her hoarse little voice comes out of the dark.

"Whisper!" I call as if we're not in danger, feeling through the dark for her. I make contact too hard, wrap both arms around her. "You're all right, you —"

She doesn't hold up her hand like Atticus might or shush me or nothing: She just lets me babble out the panic 'til I'm out of breath for true and shivering. "Something's happened to Atticus," I finish, broken down, beaten. "Corner killed Atticus."

"I know," she says, pinched. "My folks showed me." Whisper's folks are her ghosts; the ones that're always about, whispering her secrets about everything.

"Who else?" I manage, but she shakes her head.

"I've a pain in my side, Teller." I can barely hear her on the stuffy air of the sewer. "I need some medicine."

There's medicine in the kitchen, in the carefully counted stores that Atticus keeps for emergencies: painkillers like you can only get in hospitals Above, bandages and gauze and tape and splints, little sick-sweet lozenges for the coughs that come every wintertime. *Not any more Atticus*, a little voice in the back of my head whispers. I close my eyes tight and see it all over again:

shadows in the kitchen, throwing our medicine to the ground.

"I don't think we can go back," I say. Dirty words.

"Nuh-uh," she agrees, and steadies herself one hand on my shoulder. "It'll have to be up."

"Up?"

"Above," she says like it's repeating herself, and Ariel makes a little noise from her corner. Whisper looks at us both, and her mouth hardens like she's not to brook any arguing. I reach down for Ariel and help her to standing.

"We don't know where we are," I say, all my calm run halfway home now that someone elder's here.

Whisper shakes her head minutely, makes that keening noise again. "They'll lead us," she says, and strains her neck forward like she's listening for beautiful music.

We follow her through the slippery new sewers, over pick-foot catwalks and pitted rock, holding hands in a chain to keep together. *Above.* I've never gone without provisions, two days' good rations and matches and wood, sacks and a crew and Passing clothes. I've never gone without warning. Nobody ever goes up *alone.*

Roach-feet skitter on the walls, the tunnel roof. A rat tail curves around a corner and plops into the flow, and Ariel lets out a little moan. I squeeze her hand tight. She doesn't shy away this time.

Whisper turns a corner and finally stops, head stretched up like a mouse feeding on the air, her stringy white hair falling like emergency rope and wires. "Thank you good friends always," she murmurs into the dark, and then reaches out for the ladder.

It's rubber-runged so we don't fall off, but still slick and deadly cold, and for a moment it's like all the cold of Above is being forced through the palms of my hurting hands. I lift one up and get a good look at it. I was holding the brand too tight. It's pocked red with splinters.

"C'mon," whispers Ari behind me, quiver-shake and shivering, and I put down my aching hand and climb.

Whisper pushes the top of the world aside with a metallic stutter, and the light, oh god the light comes pouring in. And then I'm breathing droopy heat and there we are, there we are, dizzy and sick with running and strange air and stars.

Above.

There are Whitecoats and there are Doctors. Doctor Marybeth was in medical school when she helped Atticus and Corner go free. Doctor Marybeth saw me born and sewed up my mama afterward, and one of the first lessons I learned about Passing was telling the difference between a Doctor and a Whitecoat. Whitecoats never smile, Atticus told me back in those days when me and Hide and Seed, who was a teenager but hadn't had much school on account of his horns, learned at his feet in the afternoons. That was how you could tell Whitecoats; you knew them by the smoothness of the corners of their eyes.

Doctor Marybeth has wrinkles at the corners of her eyes, wrinkles from smiling, but when she opens the door of her little old house there's no smiling on her. "Matthew," she says, looking over my shoulder, face paling the color of road dust.

"Atticus is dead," I blurt, and Doctor Marybeth looks at me, at Ari and Whisper. Opens her mouth and shuts it again.

"Inside," she says like I was hoping she would, like good people always say in Tales when you tell them there's bad, bad news. I stumble through the door, tugging Ariel behind me by her limp little hand.

"S'okay," I tell her. She's gone big-eyed and still again. "Doctor Marybeth's a good doctor."

"Doctor —" Ari mumbles, and her hand spasms in mine. I hold it tighter, insisting, 'cause it's hot to sweating here and my back's prickling and I can't take one more person leaving me tonight. She follows me slow, crouch-kneed, like something cornered. Whisper stays tight behind her, making sure Ariel doesn't run, and she don't say a word about it. I thank her in my gut for that and hope she can hear it like ghosts.

Doctor Marybeth's kitchen is polished wood and tile, too bright even though the wood is pale and the placemats a soft-glowing purple. I cover my eyes with my free hand. They sting even in the shade.

"What happened?" Doctor Marybeth says. She looks ready to be sick.

"I lost Violet," Whisper gasps, and it's not the whistle of singing no more.

Doctor Marybeth's face goes even grimmer. "Shh. Don't talk," she says, and takes out her stethoscope.

I hold Ariel's hand.

She listens to Whisper's heart, Whisper's breath, and her round brown hand makes Whisper look even skinnier for being there. "Tell me," she says, hooking one rubber-tipped prong out of her ear. Her hands move, ceaseless, 'cross Whisper's back and wrists and heart.

I tell her, 'cause that's what I'm there for. Telling the bad news. Telling 'bout death. *Once upon a time on Sanctuary Night there was a fight between Corner and Atticus.*

But I can't tell it far before I'm hiccuping and Whisper's crying, harsh little inhales like a sock-foot sliding along stone. "Shh," Doctor Marybeth says, and puts her soft hand on my back. "You're safe here. You're safe."

You're Safe here, I translate without thinking, fever-scared, splinter-palmed, and even though Ariel's watching, that's when I start to cry.

ATTICUS'S TALE

Everybody knows Atticus's Tale, but I asked for it anyway. I told him it was because we wouldn't all be here
someday, but really Atticus's Tale was all tangents and
whispers and I wanted it for real. I wanted Atticus to tell
me his Tale true.

Atticus measured me all up with his eyes and then
nodded quiet; sat himself down on the chair that was
made, like everything he has, to not be snapped to cinders
by his claws. He sat straighter than straight and took
three deep breaths before he started Telling.

Once Atticus looked and walked and talked just like
the other people Above. He had a ma and pa and brothers, and a girl he took to movies on Saturday nights. (Jack
had already explained movies, and I was afraid to interrupt.) He worked in a shabby bookstore that was crammed
every crack with old things, and his job was to straighten
the books that people brought to get rid of or trade or sell.
He liked to read the ones that nobody came for; he didn't
understand all of what they said, but he read them just in
case. He liked the way they made the world tilt different
ways in his vision.

One day Atticus was putting boxes and boxes of books
on the old shelves of the bookshop and the world tilted a
way he'd never seen before. The world went dark and he

saw fire, fire at the center of everything, building and yanking itself upward into a mountain of light.

Then he fell down off the ladder and cracked his head.

They took him to the hospital, and a nurse felt him all over for broken things. They put him in an X-ray machine (and here he explained X-rays, the whole experiment where they were discovered, how they made shadows out of your flesh and brands out of your bones). They kept him sitting an awful long time, and then another man came into the waiting room with pictures of his arm bone, of a shadowy bulge latched on to it, made of bits and scraps of his own body gone wicked. "We're sorry," he said. "You're Sick."

They took off his arm at the elbow, and the Sick kept coming. They took it off at the shoulder and gave him a plastic arm whose fingers didn't close right. He had to quit the bookshop and be full-time Sick. The plastic hand wouldn't turn the pages of a book.

"We may have to try some new drugs," they said, and injected liquid amber burning into the crook of his shoulder. It made him toss and shake and throw up 'til he could only eat soup and water for seven days, and at the end of that week he started to change. His arms stretched and grew, and it was the worst hurt he'd ever felt, the claws growing in, shell taking shape, blood flowing through.

(*So you weren't always a Beast?* I asked, and Atticus shook his head with his golden-eyed sad smile. *I was always a Beast*, he said. *It was always inside of me to have my real arms.* I wanted to ask if he'd ever cried tears, not light, but he went on talking and the chance never came again.)

Atticus's doctors saw the crab-arms and were scared.

"We're going to have to take you in for more study," they said. They brought him to a brick building with big lawns and high hedges, gave him a room, and locked the door. The crab-arms were still soft. He was afraid to pound 'til they let him out. They drew his blood, and it shifted red-orange to gold in their needles, like liquid amber burning.

They came back again and again for it, and Atticus didn't know where they'd spent the last. His arms ached from needles. They ached when the crab-arms hardened and his Normal-people muscles stretched against the weight. The Whitecoats gave him books. His claws cut the pages to shreds.

At the night desk was a student named Marybeth. She was just as old as he, and when the crab-arms got strong enough to *bang bang bang* on the door, she was the only one who heard him. She looked through the double-plastic windows and saw the books with cut pages, the words opened up at the belly and spread on the floor. Student Doctor Marybeth put down her needles and tubes and took a book from her pocket. All night she read it to Atticus through the crack of the locked-tight door.

(And he didn't need to say what that was, or what it meant. Because here, his eyes glowed like sunflowers.)

She brought more. She read against his door until dawn every night for months, and the Whitecoats muttered to themselves and wondered why he slept so late daytimes.

One day (he said quiet, after a long stop that made me think it was time to tiptoe out), Student Doctor Marybeth said she was leaving. Her time in this hospital was done, and she had to take her examinations and then she would be sent to other hospitals. "They're not gonna let you out," she whispered through the tray slot on the door.

"Yes," Atticus told her. "We know."

"Good luck," she said, and slipped the locks open.

He wouldn't tell me more. The story of flying from the Whitecoats down to the tunnels, from dry place to dry place until they found Safe, was a story I could get from the others. His story ended there, he said, with the slip of the lock.

Atticus used to be one of them, he said, leaning forward hard, and his eyes were fire like I'd never seen them. He used to be one of them and then it didn't matter, when his arms grew back Beast. They cast him out, his ma and pa and brothers and friends, and none of them were sorry, not one bit.

And that's why we have to be careful, and sharp, and stick together and uphold Safe, he finished. That's why we work together. Because even if we're strange and Cursed and Beasts, the people Above are monsters.

THREE

I wake up in the morning in a wide bouncing bed, warm and soft and safe — until I realize how bright it is. There's light in my eyes, hard, wingless light; light that does you burning. I turn over and it's still no good: Everything under my eyelids is red. Red and long-fingered and slicked in blood, and the curve of a broken horn —

— and I open my eyes not to Safe, but Doctor Marybeth's white ceiling, Doctor Marybeth's soft blue drapes over her glass-paned window, Doctor Marybeth's yellow-painted, slope-roofed attic room. Hot, damp summertime air. It's thick like the new sewers but hotter, hot like it never gets in Safe, where a season's nothing more than a bit of warm or cool, the pipes freezing slower or running quicker than before. The air's sweet with the smell of coffee and toast: Safe things. Morningtime things.

This is how Normal people wake up, I realize, fuzzy-headed, tired. This is how I've imagined it, some cold and sleepy nighttimes, when I told myself made-up stories where I wasn't Freak. Not that I go 'round wanting that. It's just foolishness to spend your time wanting not to have a Curse, and that was my pa's lesson, not Atticus's. But just imagining it. What if.

I lie still three whole breaths. I drift alone in a little shell of myself, floating, and nothing in the world makes a difference where I am, between half-asleep and awake.

Then something moves in the corner.

I reach for a brand but there's no brand, just pillows and soft things. I throw the blanket between me and it, me and every shadow in the sewers come to take my blood, and it *squeaks*.

I stop. Let down the blanket, slow.

It's not shadows.

It's Ariel, curled up in a patchwork quilt in the big green plush chair on the other side of the room. Her eyes are big and frightened, fist tight around a stubbed yellow pencil, reared up to strike. There's sunlight tangled in her hair.

I lift my hand, careful. The bed's warm and a little damp next to me; warm like another sleeping body, smaller and softer than mine. I close my hand to keep that warmth in and try to breathe slow. "Ari?" I say, and sit up the rest of the way, slow and safe and careful. "What time's it?"

"Dunno," she mumbles, cheeks bright red. The pencil comes down, tucks into a fold of the quilt. The rumpled pages of her book crinkle somewhere beneath it.

I look at the nightstand, a rickety white-painted kid's thing with one chipped drawer. No clock there or on the walls. The walls are full of paintings instead, clumsy-brush things like the first I ever did back when my pa stole a set of acrylics for my sixth birthday party. In Safe there were always clocks. The clocks chimed the hour, every hour, a shout of bells echoing against the walls. You always knew what time it was.

I don't know how many of us made it free.

Suddenly the Normal air is terribly hard to breathe, but Ari watches me like it's just the damp, the heat, a tickle of the throat, no expression on her pale pointy face. "We should wash up," she says. There's something in her eyes I've never seen, can't name. "There's soap. I looked."

"Okay," I say, slow-brained, slow-ache, rubbing my chest with one hand to make the hurt ease up. "You go on." She hesitates. "I'll keep watch."

Her shoulders unwind just a bit as the quilt comes off, as she pads across the floorboards to the bathroom door in clothes that are ripped and layered one atop the other to keep the good heat in. Warm is what matters down below, in Safe, where it's cool and dark even in summer. In the full light of morning, Above, they look wrong. Ari, who works so hard to look Normal, looks Freak.

She goes into the washroom. I wait until she shuts the door behind her before I bury my face in the bed-sheets and breathe her smell in deep: sweetness, flowers, spring.

● ○ ●

The shower runs cold. I grit my teeth underneath it and rub soap between my hands as fast as they'll take; scrub armpits and ear backs and myself wide awake. Where I'm cut up it stings: palms and elbows and knees. There aren't band-aids in Doctor Marybeth's medicine cabinet, so I leave the scrapes and scabbed bits bare. Then it's towels and clothes again, heavy with damp, and all the warmth of the bright new morning's gone.

The coffee smell in the bedroom's turned bitter when I open the door again. Ariel's at the window, looking down into the street. Her hair's clean and golden, brushed back from her face in a long, mussed braid. She's found a rubber band somewhere and tied it 'round the end. I scuff my foot on the floor a little to let her know I'm coming. Still, she sits up tenser the minute I get near.

I try not to let that hurt.

"Ready?" I ask, and hold out a hand that's still stinging. She doesn't take it, but she follows me downstairs.

They're in the kitchen. Whisper's chair is wedged back to the wall, facing watchful the door. Her white hair's tidied and pinned up in the way she does for Passing: what she calls her Society style. Doctor Marybeth sits across from her in her light green doctor shirt and slacks, elbows on the round wood table, cradling her coffee cup like it's the last match in the pack. There's cold eggs in the pan, white and curdled yellow, everything bright and sunstruck like colors get Above. My eyes water from the cream wallpaper. It sparkles hard between the patterned flowers.

I squint against it and then let out a shout, 'cause leaned back in the dimmest soft corner, scabbed and scratched-up along his old, hairless arms, is Jack.

"Good morning," Whisper says. She's wrapped up in a long shawl with holes in it, soft sky-colored crochet. She pronounces every letter. Whisper never skips words 'less she's whispering.

Jack levers up from the wall and squeezes my hand. His gloves scratch my fingers. "Glad you're living," he says. I can't tell if it's to me and Ariel both, or just me and she's a nuisance. But I nod and smile much too big at him, squeeze his hand back, and go pour myself a mug of coffee.

"Ari?" I ask, and she shakes her head bee-tiny.

"Do you prefer tea?" asks Doctor Marybeth, fixing her in smiling regard, and I wish I could have told her not to, not to give Ariel hard attention or put her on the spot. Ariel just stands there unmoving, big-eyed and wet-haired and half behind my shoulder, and the quiet stretches long enough to swallow once, twice. Doctor Marybeth seems to get it quick, though. She turns her eyes down to the crook of Ariel's arm. "It's in the cupboard. Help yourself," she says, softer, and turns back to Whisper, cross-legged in her five-spoked chair.

I fill two plates up with eggs and toast and two rare, dear strips of bacon each. There's two chairs left in the kitchen, what with Jack standing back to the wall like he's got watch duty 'gainst the encroaching sun. With a look that says *oh please* I ask Whisper to move over, put our plates on the table side by side, and sit.

"Who else?" I ask into the silence.

Jack lets out a breath and shakes his head. *Don't know.* Or at least I pray it's that, *don't know* and not *nobody, nothing, that's it.* "Those things are still in there. Shut the door behind themselves this morning." He pauses. "I didn't meet anyone else on my way up."

I can't help but picture it: shadows in Safe. Shadows in my house, spreading darkness not soft or loving through my Ariel's shed wings.

Corner, in my house.

"What're we going to do?" I ask hoarse.

Whisper squints from Jack to Ariel's faded red sleeve, sticking out beneath another one that's black and just as moth-chewed. "Whoever else got out wouldn't just come here. We need to get some Passing clothes and check the safehouses before we get to choosing about anything."

The safehouses: Mack and Atticus made everyone in Safe memorize them, in case we ever got stuck Above. One in an old warehouse down by the lake; one through a door from the tunnels that'll lock from the inside, and a seven-day stash of food and water there; a homeless people shelter on a busy busted-up corner that don't ask no questions so long as you can Pass good; and here. Doctor Marybeth's. And but four of us here of forty-three Safe-sworn.

I stare at my plate and the food stares back.

"Mm," grunts Jack, and that's when I notice how far he is from the coffeemaker, from the electric stove Violet once said she'd give up her house and everything in it for, from the panel on the wall where the kitchen light turns on. The lights are off, the back door blinds open. His fingers flex and close in the left asbestos glove. "Get Passing clothes with what?"

Whisper's mouth firms up tight. "The emergency money."

"How much?"

"All," she says, and Jack straightens with a wild look in his eye.

"How'd you get the whole stash?" He's pacing a little circle on the tile, one step in each direction, tucked away from the glimmering machines.

"Atticus gave it to me," she says, every word crisp. "Yesterday morning."

My hand goes still on my heavy table knife. Yesterday morning, when he said *last time* and walked away from us, and went into Whisper's house more upset than I could ever remember seeing him but once.

"All but twenty-five dollars," she says.

I put down the knife and reach into my pocket, feel the crush of bills inside. "I have that," I say, face hot and prickly. "I went out on duty and forgot to put it back." Keeping duty things is wrong. It's near-stealing, but I was so tired, thinking of nothing but getting Ariel back in and falling into bed. The feel of something cold and numb up against my face. Any other day I'd have caught such trouble for that: Atticus's eyes brick-orange and his raspy voice precise, going *and what if there had been an emergency?*

Good thing there was an emergency, I think, and tuck my chin to my chest to keep in the terrible laughs.

Whisper pats my hand. Her skin's soft, like wing-light. "Well, it's where we need it now, isn't it?"

"Ma'am," I murmur, and bend back over my breakfast. Bacon's a privilege. I shouldn't waste it.

"Irresponsible of him," Jack rumbles after a moment, and I cringe. "No, not you, Teller. Atticus. We don't know who else made it out." Or where they are. Or what they're doing for food and shelter while we eat Doctor Marybeth's toast and coffee.

"Who do we know didn't make it out?" Whisper asks.

The toast and coffee stick in my throat. "Seed," I say.

"Kimmie," Jack adds, subdued and dark. "Mercy. Maybe Scar."

"Heather?" I ask soft.

"I can't say, Teller," Jack replies.

The sun flutters through the long lavender blinds. Heather and Seed's baby comes due in not two weeks. If she's alive. If the child inside her still is, on short emergency rations somewhere, knowing in the way babies do that its papa isn't ever coming back.

Doctor Marybeth frowns. "I have a friend who works the street patrol. I can ask him if anyone's come in."

The old-woman lines in Whisper's face deepen. "No."

"They won't be far in the system. Most times," Doctor Marybeth says, speaking delicate around foul medicine-taste words, "they just disappear again."

Ariel is still beyond still. I reach out my foot for hers. Hold it there. She twitches for a moment, shies away.

Whisper sits back in her chair, hands flat on the dainty purple placemat. "Atticus told me to take care of Safe when he's gone, and he wouldn't want anybody put into the system. He wouldn't want anyone looking for us."

Jack stops in the middle of his circling. "He told you that?"

Whisper doesn't answer. She just looks Jack in the eye.

"We don't know that —"

"He's dead, Jack," Whisper says, her lip shaking a little. She reaches into one of her million pockets and pulls out a picture from her precious Polaroid, white-rimmed and slick on its special picture paper. The shapes don't make sense for a moment: round center, a splash of color, darkness that rights into two open eyes. I turn it so it's watching me straight.

It's Atticus, bleeding amber, with a knife in his throat.

"Oh," I say, and set it carefully down. My fingers tingle hot where they touched it. This year's Sanctuary Night picture.

Doctor Marybeth's mouth opens, then closes, and she puts down her coffee cup and pushes out the chair fast enough to make Ariel flinch. "Excuse me," she says, sharp and short and like a Whitecoat after all, and stalks to the bathroom where she closes the door.

The egg bleeds yellow onto my toast.

"Poor woman," Whisper says after a moment.

"Poor somebody when we find the others," Jack says. His eyes are on the photo, and they're lightning-sharp.

"Jack —"

"The big door only opens from the inside."

Whisper frowns at him, fierce upon fierce. And a little cold hand pokes into my belly, taking away the last of the morning's quiet, the smell of mellow honey and wax that I took in from the pillow and held close to keep me warm.

"Everyone inside swore to uphold Safe," I murmur, and Jack and Whisper look over like they've just remembered we're here. "Every one of them raised me from ten."

"Teller," Jack says none too gentle, "someone opened the door."

"*Jack —*"

"Corner," Jack says, "had hands in Safe."

Down the street from Doctor Marybeth's is the Salvation Army. "Full of clothes," Whisper says, and parts my hair with the comb to make it look like I belong here. "Let's go get us some disguise."

I used to play in the disguise chest as a kid, back when my pa was still around; Atticus didn't allow using important resources — *disguise is a resource, Teller* — for a kid's toy. Disguise clothes are clean and neat. My second run Above was a disguise run: I kept watch in the see-your-breath cold while Hide's pa Mack broke the lock on a frost-covered metal bin and we filled up three garbage bags with everything inside.

"We don't have a pry bar," I point out, and Jack laughs.

"We're already in disguise," he grins, and taps his nose in the way he does when he means something's hush-hush. "We've got money."

If disguise is a resource, money's twice as much. Whisper and Jack count the money at the table: five hundred dollars in creased old bills, stained from pocket-sweat or sewer water, packed together in a sealed sandwich bag. Not including the twenty-five still tucked in my pocket, which I can't offer up with Ariel watching, her eyebrows drawn down like wings. A peach can't be that expensive. And a chocolate is only a dollar.

Doctor Marybeth has to go to work, trouble or not, and I clear the dishes quick while Whisper hustles Ariel upstairs with a measuring tape in hand. "I'm not going for clothes twice," she says, Ariel looking over her shoulder like I'm gonna disappear if she lets me out of sight.

Jack keeps on pacing while I wash up, running the hot water over the plates again and again 'til my fingertips pucker. His mouth doesn't move one bit, but I can see some dark argument rip and spit in his head. "Turn off the lights on the way up, Teller," he says when I switch off the water — a hot faucet and a cold on the sink, and part of Passing's knowing what that red and blue mean. "I think I'd like a shower."

I hit every white-panel light switch I can find going up the stairs, snuffing Doctor Marybeth's dangling glass lamps one by one. Jack never comes up on supply duty, or patrol duty, or any duty outside the big carved door and the Pactbridge. Nobody ever asks why, because Jack lights the lamps and you need him downstairs. I don't know why I never realized how that couldn't be the all of it.

Even if he wore his sleeves down to cover his snow-flake scars, Jack's never, ever gonna Pass.

"Hold still," Whisper's saying in the buttery sunshine bedroom, pinching the measuring tape around Ariel's waist. Ari squirms like she'd love to grow wings then and there, her head down to the side, staring down at the floor away from Whisper's tugging, smoothing hands.

"I know my size," Ari mutters, inching away from the tape. Her eyes are small and angry.

I step in fast. "What size?" and she gives me a look so full of scorn that I'm ready to promise her peaches all over again.

"Eight on the bottom," she says, with a strange and stolen pride. "And a small on the top."

"And the inseam?" Whisper snips.

I don't know what an inseam is. Neither does Jack, I think, who I hear come up the stairs tiptoe, pause, then decide to stay out of it.

Ariel flushes, strawberry-red cheeks. But Whisper withdraws her tape and rolls it up, sharp little jerks. "It'll be you hemming those pant legs, missy."

Ari glares all the way through Whisper fixing me up to go: a tidy pair of jeans Doctor Marybeth's left us, the cleanest of my dirty shirts, then lifting my shoulders with her own two hands 'til I stand like we're in houses and not tunnels that hunch.

"Forty minutes," Whisper says, to Ariel and Jack both. "Be ready. We're leaving again as soon as we come back." To visit the safehouses and find our missing. With food and water and clean Passing clothes.

A splash of red, terrible red flickers at the corner of my eye. I swallow. *And matches.*

67

"We'll be back soon," I tell Ari, not like she wouldn't know it. It makes her feel better when I say it. Like a promise.

She turns to the window. Away.

"C'mon, Teller," Whisper says, her voice a little funny. There's a crooked sad look on her face that I suspect is all for me.

I hate it.

We get moving.

I'm not scared of the sun. There is — was — never enough light in Safe to see the ceilings anyway, so it may as well be sky, dark starless sky. But I still don't like feeling daylight on me Above. It's harder to Pass, for one. Daylight shows what you really are: beast beast beast beast beast.

Just remember, I tell myself, *you belong here. You grew up here. You're nothing else but Normal.*

Thinking it hard enough lets down my shoulders. I swing my arms a little more as we hurry past the woven-wire fences and the lean, muttering trees, breathe deep instead of in little puffs; inhale the rare, sweet scent of living dirt 'til it crowds out the smell of the dead kind. There are pigeons in the greyed-out gutters, beaking at nothing and fat with feathers. No rats, which is good: There's no brand over my shoulder. I feel in my pocket, though, and there are still matches, bent but dry; nine whole heads left in the pack. I close my hand around them, snug and tight.

"Teller," Whisper says, four steps ahead.

Normal people don't think about fire. I put the pack away.

The Salvation Army doesn't look especially like salvation. It's a brown, squat brick building with a huge black-topped lot for cars. They have metal boxes outside, the kind we take pry bars to, but Whisper breezes right past them and through the hard glass-and-metal doors.

Inside it's the opposite of Passing: The plasticky floors make my shoes squeak, and the lights are bright and sharp. They show every splotch of brown on my sneakers. My neck gets the tight feeling right at the back as the girl at the counter looks up, but I keep my head down, shoulders up. Follow Whisper. Nothing behind you, I tell myself. Nothing but Normal here.

Whisper drives her hands into racks of clothes — red and blue and green and orange; more clothes, I realize, than I've seen in my whole life — and pushes them here and there, feeling fabrics, peeking at tags, fluttering like a fussy old Above lady. She pulls blue jeans and faded shirts and socks off shelves and bounces to the next stack, and it takes me a full four racks to realize what the change in her is, what's making her walk like a stranger.

Whisper *likes* it here.

"Here," she says, bent over a plastic bin now and fishing out some prize. "Put these on." It's new sneakers, thin at the soles but scuffless, tough. She knows my size. I wonder how many sizes Whisper knows. I tuck my thick-nail toes deep into their socks and tug my sneakers off, slip on the new ones fast and sharp. They fit.

The old ones sit abandoned on the white tile floor, chewed-laced and muddy. I blink; off my own feet, they look like throwaway. They look like something stained and bad.

That's not mud, I realize, catching the smell of them off my fingers, cold and dead and metallic. The sick comes up through my chest, and I manage to stop it in time. Sicking up's bad Passing. I wipe my hands careful on my jeans.

I can still feel where the blood on those shoes touched me, every inch.

"That's you and me, then," Whisper says, already off across the whole massive hoard. I rock back on my feet and think about balance, muscles. The new shoes bounce different. I want to bounce in them, find all the springy spots, but I don't know if people Above bounce. "What's your girl's favorite color?" she asks once I catch up, her fingers deep in a round pants rack.

My head's full of Tales. A whole book of them: every grief and joy and trouble that ever crossed the Pactbridge. None of them are about Ariel or if she has a favorite color.

I never asked.

Whisper looks at me with her white-grained eyebrows up, skeptical as you please. And I don't rightly know what

I say, but I mutter something and scuff my toe and flee outside into the quiet, the paint-stripper light and thick, choky air of Above.

The concrete stairs of the Salvation Army are hot in the sun — *afternoon*, I think. Maybe. I should go back inside, ask if the Salvation Army has wristwatches. I can't count minutes steady in my head, and there aren't clocks here like — *like I'm used to.*

It's too late. The picture of Atticus bleeding swims up behind my eyelids, then Seed, Mercy, Beak —

"Ready then?" Whisper says sudden behind me, arms full of plastic bags with dirty red slogans flaking off the sides, and I jump. She passes me one; it's packed so full the handles sting the insides of my knuckles.

"They don't have any wristwatches, do they?" I ask, and she shakes her head. So: "Yeah," I mutter, and kick a rock down the steps with my brand-new worn-out shoe. The shoes are soft blue fabric. They wouldn't last two nights in the new sewers.

She don't say nothing 'bout my bad temper, just sets off down the steps to the browning grass.

Doctor Marybeth's left the back door unlocked for us, since it's too dangerous to leave one's front door open Above. Whisper opens it brisk as you please, though we've likely not been gone that whole forty minutes. "Jack?" she calls as she steps into the cool kitchen. "Let's go!"

Jack doesn't answer.

Whisper's eyebrows draw down until her whole forehead frowns along with her mouth. "Jack?" she says again, and starts for the stairs. The door's wide open behind me; *bad tactics*, Mack would say. I close it snug as a voice rumbles low under the upstairs door. Jack's. And angry.

I take the matches out of my pocket.

Whisper shoots me a glance when I catch up, halfway up Doctor Marybeth's winding steps. "Houses burn, Teller."

I don't put them back.

Whisper's shoes barely sound on Doctor Marybeth's soft green carpet. I know to walk quiet too, but behind her I sound like clumping. "Don't tell me *nothing*," Jack says on the other side of the door, close enough now, coming into focus. "I heard you not one minute ago."

There's a mumble; a buzz and a mumble.

"Who were you talking to?" he says, and the scuffed metal doorknob arcs with blue light.

"Jack?" Whisper says, softer than she steps.

"Don't open the door —" he booms, and then Whisper turns the doorknob.

"Fuck!" Jack shouts, glove-shed and furious. He's twisting like the lightning's caught him again, his hair wet and clumped and his white undershirt damp, the whole of him strangely undone. "Fucking mother*fuck* —" and something shoots out past us, something small and dark and bright at the same time. Something about the size of a bee.

Ariel.

"Jack!" Whisper snaps, rushing to him.

"She was talking to someone, I swear to God —" he spits, lightning in his eyes, sparking and singeing his tiny little eyelashes into smoke. The bathroom light flickers. Doctor Marybeth's bedside lamp rocks, sputters, and dies, and there's no Ariel. There's no Ariel anywhere. "That little bitch *stung* me —"

"Don't you call her that!" I yell, searching the hall frantic for yellow and black against yellow walls, short steps, green green carpet.

"Teller, she's spinning us some bullshit," Jack snaps, and I half don't hear it. *Last time*, Atticus's cut-out voice is reminding me. I don't know who's living and who's dead right now, and I don't even know her favorite color.

Down. She went down.

I stumble down the stairs, yank open the front door, and reel into the naked street, scenting for bees.

I had it good in the tunnels, I realize, five steps down pavement that burns hot as brands through the soles of my new shoes. In the tunnels there were only so many places to go, and the sound of humming buzzing echoed long against the walls. In the tunnels she had to come back for food, clean water, rest.

Above, there is everywhere to go. Including up.

"Fuck," I echo, staring up into the pale aching blue sky, and taste the rough Jackness of the word on my tongue. It doesn't stop the rattling, shaking sob working itself under my ribs. I thought I couldn't be upset anymore. The rattle turns into a laugh, and it sounds fake and sick.

"Matthew —" I hear behind me; Whisper, high and sharp. Whisper *yelling*.

I look both ways down the street and catch a glint of —

— and run after it with everything I got.

The shoes bounce. They bounce good running down the rough sidewalk, running faster than you can in the tunnels without slipping. All the streets have signs and they're meaningless, the names of Tales I don't know. I ignore them all, ignore cars, ignore people; ignore the tiny differences in plants or roof tiles or paint colors that're the only way of telling Above houses apart. I'm not Passing. I'm looking for bees.

There are lots of leafy, hiding trees Above, garden after garden with the same incredible, windblown flowers. I run past them with my eyes moving, watching orange and purple and bright red petals for a bee cowering behind them. A bee who sits down still and just waits to see what you'll do to it.

I run right into the end of the road. I run over the white stone curb and onto grass, lumpy ground like I've never been able to keep my balance on despite how many trips Above, and I stumble, go down hard on my knees.

When I look up it's all flowers.

I blink. Rub my eyes. But no, it's sky-to-toes flowers, red and purple and yellow-sun-golden, all sweet enough, big enough to shelter whole handfuls of bees. It's a whole Sanctuary Night storehouse of flowers in tidy strips of dirt, baking in the afternoon sun. Any other day they'd be beautiful. Any other day I'd bring one home, press it between the pages of one of Atticus's books and hang it, spinning, from my rafters.

Park, I think. The word is park.

There are bees everywhere: fat and skinny, crawling along tree bark, nosing through flowers and moving to the next. The park is full of bees doing their supply duty, and none of them sing to me *Ariel*, even though I know I'd know her anywhere, I have to know her anywhere.

"Ari?" I say. "Ari, please?" and not one of them turns.

How many bees are there Above? I realize, throat tight and everything sweating, and then my chest aches and my eyes get hot with running and I don't know where I am no more, so I sit down on the prickly grass and let them cry.

She finds me inside a playground tube. A mini-tunnel, thick red plastic that changes the light coming through it; just small enough to curl up in and hide from the sunlight, the daylight, Above all huge and cut up with hate. I look up after five minutes or an hour and there she is, scrunched in next to me, her braid all mussed up. Enfolded in wings.

"Why'd you go?" I ask. I keep my voice soft, tunnel-soft to cut the echo. She smells like sweet and fear-sweat, like flowers. Real flowers.

I've never asked her that since the first time she ran. The first time, she cried and cried, and I let her get away with not answering. Her left wing brushes my arm. My skin's damp from running; it tickles, drags, and sticks.

"He was yelling." Ariel stares at her clasped hands. Her voice is hot and hollow, every letter heavy as the last.

"Ari, what happened? Who did he think you were talking to?" *Who* were *you talking to?* I stay soft. I am soft and edgeless and quiet and kind. She doesn't answer.

It could be Normal people, neighbors. It could be someone come in from Safe, shimmying up the drainpipe for god knows what reason. It could be herself, fake Tale-telling conversations like I used to have late at night, before I had an Ariel to talk to. But I know what Jack thinks.

Jack thinks shadows.

It couldn't be, I tell myself. It couldn't. She was with me, in our house, the whole day. She couldn't have let Corner in. *Except when you were sleeping, and thought she was sleeping too —*

I lean my head on my tucked-in knees, close my eyes. Light bounces and sticks out its tongue behind them.

Light won't leave me the hell alone. "I yelled at him. I ran," I say.

Nothing.

"They're gonna think I left 'cause I was mad." The space between my legs and my torso is dark and clean. My eyes don't hurt for the first time all day.

"Sounds like you did," she says, funny and tight.

"No —" and I look up, and the sunlight wipes that clean soft dark away. "Above's not like Safe. You can get lost here." I talk square at her pointed, skinny face so she knows I'm serious now, deadly serious. "There's dangerous people out Above."

Ariel looks at me a second. And then she laughs.

She laughs and laughs, leaned back against the inside of the red plastic tube, and it echoes so loud it's hard to tell where the real thing stops and the ghost of her laughing begins. "Oh, Matthew," she says, again and again. "Oh, Matthew —" until I start to get angry for real.

"Hey," I say soft, then louder. "Hey, shut up. I came for you."

She doesn't stop like a bulb going dark but slowly, in sniffles and eye-wipes and the occasional gulp. *Not scared of me*, I realize, and my heart does a little bounce. But *Above they laugh at you*, Atticus's voice said at lessons, his arms crossed, claws rattling each other with every shift of his weight. *Freak's for teasing Above. Don't ever stand to be teased.*

She never laughed at me in Safe.

"Don't laugh," I say, softer than I meant to, and her face goes slack and small and edgeless and she puts her hands on mine.

"Oh, Matthew," she says, real different now, and leans our foreheads together.

I breathe in spring. I breathe spring and gold and the smell of powdered honey, sweet as peaches on the back of your tongue. My eyes water. It's a thousand kisses in a breath.

Five minutes or an hour and she leans back against the wall, pulls apart that quiet mixing of breath. The quiet stays inside me though, in a warm and steady ball just above my heart. I breathe into it. It keeps me warm.

I don't know where we are. All the streets Above look the same, houses and houses and the blank blue sky, and the signs don't mean a thing and there aren't no walls or landmarks. I've broken the first rule of traveling Above: I wasn't counting right, running like I was. I've lost the turns.

"I don't know Above," I tell her, wiping my nose on the knee of my jeans.

Ariel tugs a thread from the sleeve of her shirt, holds it up to the light. It shines silver. Iridescent. "I do."

Ariel leads through the dying afternoon, and I follow.

We walk slow and steady through row after row of peak-roofed houses, green-brown lawns, shut blinds. My feet hurt after the first ten blocks and they hurt more after twenty, and the buildings, the streets, the sloped-round corners blur. There's no nuances to Above; nothing close or made of comfort. The buildings hunch each away from the other, not one house touching the next, standoffish with bricked-up suspicion.

It takes me too long to realize it: We ain't going back to Doctor Marybeth's.

Every step we take goes farther and farther from the bits of Above I know: the careful paths Atticus and Mack drilled us to remember in our sleep, sewer to supply and back again. Every step makes me more and more lost, and Ariel doesn't talk. Her back is straight and solid, even though in Safe she hunched down sad all the time. I don't know what to think about that. I follow her. I count the turns.

They'll think you ran away, I tell myself, strong beats down as my feet hit the raggedy pavement. *They'll* think! *You* ran! *A*-way! I close my eyes between the stirring weak streetlights — Jack-magic, those — and picture all this carved on Doctor Marybeth's solid white door. The curving arc of a bee in flight, running. Doctor Marybeth and Whisper and Jack, opening the doors of safehouses to dead bodies, or set upon by shadows, shadows that burn them into bones, or dust, or nothing; caught by Whitecoats with their needles and papers and cold eyes.

"Where we going?" comes out before I know it.

We ought to go back. We need to go back.

"Somewhere Safe," she says, and I follow, trip-footed, after.

The buildings get bigger. They lose their pointed roofs and grow to three stories, five stories, up. They get plainer too: Red brick turns into brown or white and smooth, the kind it'd take months of polishing to get for one cavern wall, and then they start melting together in rows. The road beside us is wider: more cars noise by like the sound of coming trains, and more people. *Don't touch me*, I think at them as they pass, chattering and weaving and heads upturned to the darkened sky. I can tell my breath's coming fast.

You belong here, I tell myself over and over. *You grew up here. You're nothing else but Normal.*

A lady with a rattling blue cart passes by, leaving a gap, a gasp in the crowd. I reach through it and take Ariel's hand. It's warm, dry. Mine is damp and it holds too tight.

She doesn't shake me away.

The streets have quieted and narrowed and settled again when Ariel stops, squares her shoulders, and takes me up a rounded, sloping walk to the double doorway of a towering brown building. There's washing hanging on the balconies, little hoards of goods and chairs stacked up those white box walls. *Apartments*, I think, holding tight to her hand. Atticus had an apartment once; people and people living stacked up like soup cans, locked together inside a giant kitchen cabinet.

Ari opens the glass door and slips inside a room smaller than Doctor Marybeth's bathroom: nothing but glass doors both ahead and behind, dark tile, yellow bug-stained light. It smells musty, like smoke and old food.

I slip a hand in my pocket. Find my matches. Hold on.

There's a button beside the second door: no, racks and racks of buttons, and names in a long list beside them. The light behind them hums and spits in the dark. I raise my eyebrows at Ariel and she just flicks her eyes over like I'm a kid who doesn't know right from left. She runs one finger down the list, kissing-distance away.

"Ari?"

"*Shh.*"

She does it until someone comes in with their keys, looks over at us and away again, and lets himself through the heavy glass door.

Ari waits 'til he's around the corner, then catches the door with her foot, quick as shadowfall. It lands loud and heavy on her shoe. I've known her long enough to catch the grimace.

"Ari —" I say. She doesn't even need to shush me this time. She just *looks*.

A few heartbeats later she opens it and slips through the gap between door and dirty wall. She holds it open for me, impatient, sharp like I've never seen her. "C'mon," she says through her teeth. She's annoyed at me, and I don't know why.

No; it's for not following the rules. Not knowing the rules of this, of here. *That ain't fair*, I want to say, but this isn't the time and it's not the place. I bite it down and follow into the soft, dim hallway.

We go up thin-carpeted stairs, seven flights that give under my shoes in a way so much more kind and even than the rubber tire and rock of the common. Ariel opens the thick metal door at the top real soft, and closes it even softer behind us. Leads me into a hall with dull green carpet, dull beige walls; doors and doors and doors. She goes up and down the hall twice, hands stuck into fists, lips trembling around some word I don't know the shape for. Talking to herself. Talking to someone else.

Who were you talking to? my mouth shapes, but no. Not now.

A little hump grows under the back of her shirt, and then she shakes herself, shakes it and my hand off her pale little arm and knocks, three knocks on one of the plain brown doors.

There's a shuffle, a mutter. The lock clicks from somewhere inside.

When it opens it's a girl with red hair, a deep fake-color red all standing up straight from the middle of her shaved-sides head. Her skin's almost Freak-thin, pale enough to see the blue, tired veins under her dark eyes. One hand's in her pocket. Where people keep their matches.

Her eyes don't look like Safe.

There's no brand at my shoulder. I don't have fire. *Get behind me*, I want to say, *let me handle this*, but I don't know what I'm handling, and the words stick like cold toast in my throat.

The girl doesn't look at me. She looks at Ariel, and her face is smooth and hard as crab shell.

"Bee," I think I hear Ariel say, blurry and small.

"Hey, baby," the girl says and takes that hand out of her pocket, rubs it tired along her skinny, nubbly scalp. "Welcome home."

Whisper's Tale

Whisper always whispered. From when she was small.

There were ghosts living (well, not *living*, she laughed) in the attic of her old redbrick house, and they toppled the umbrella stand, stole the silverware, kicked the pipes, and gossiped when she slept. Whisper's mama cried and carried on and got a prescription for female troubles. Whisper's papa denied he heard any such thing, but he spent most of his day at The Company and slept like a dead body himself. Whisper's big sister got quiet and grave and talked lots about windspeeds and coincidence.

Whisper was little, and Whisper heard voices. So Whisper whispered back.

The ghosts (she said, and smiled so her wrinkles folded and stretched) didn't expect any of that. They stopped their rattling, paused mid-kick, plucked air instead of pinches under the bedsheets at night. "I'll send you to bed without supper," Whisper scolded them, the worst punishment she knew, and after a month of prospector's silence they whispered back.

It was okay when she was a child. Little girls with imaginary friends were little girls who didn't need to be minded. When she was too old for dolls, she would sit with the phone to her ear for hours, and her sister and mother made suffering faces and let her talk to the air. But once she finished school and all her girlfriends were Missus Something, whispering got hard.

There were ghosts in the trees and ghosts in the alleys, but the shiny new apartments built for respectable young women did not have any ghosts, and the ghosts who were her best friends were firm about not leaving. Ghosts can be strong about their places (she told me) and sometimes don't even quit 'em when the house goes down. So she stayed in the old attic room, and that was what made the trouble.

There were no young men, you see. Young men weren't much conversation after years and years of ghosts, who swore and laughed and told you dark true things (and

I begged Whisper to tell me the dark true things, but she only smiled a little sad smile and shook her head). Whisper's father thought there ought to be young men; there comes a time (Whisper said, and the lines came out sharp in her face even by lamplight) when respectable young women need to be out of their fathers' houses for the good of all involved. He introduced her to the sons of neighbors and bought her tickets to community center dances and even had words with the shy young banker down the street.

So when he walked by her attic door that last night, he thought it was young men.

He beat the door open roaring, his face red like gunfire and fists ready for whatever young man his grown-up daughter was whispering to in that giggling, singsong voice. But it wasn't no young man, and fathers can't see the ghosts in the walls.

Whisper's father brought in the same doctor who had helped her ma with the female trouble. The doctor sat Whisper in his office, took her pulse and made her breathe into a tube, asked her about her dreams and whether she had boyfriends, and pronounced her Sick.

They sent her to the hospital that same morning.

Whisper was part of General Population: That meant that she was Sick, but not scary or a Freak or someone who couldn't be let out of her room. In General Population there were other Sick girls. They talked to walls too, except for her roommate, who didn't talk at all, but pointed to stray sentences in books and newspapers to ask you for the salt. They told her about midnight visits from angels and colors shifting bright inside the potted plants.

No, said the ghosts, who had heard of Whisper through a chain of whispering that stretched from her attic to the hospital in the park. *We don't think those things are really there.*

She met with the doctors twice a week. They didn't think the ghosts were really there. This made her wonder about the angel lovers.

"Go look," she whispered to the ghosts of Lakeshore Psychiatric, singsong in the group shower where the guard watched to make sure you didn't fight or slit your wrists. "Find me out what's going on, and maybe we'll know what's real."

The ghosts of the hospital were prone to making fuss. They had died in all the worst ways: hanging themselves in their Isolation cells, wasting away from turning down food, or under the electrodes on the shock table, back when they still shocked Freaks with lightning to see if it'd shock them right out of their Freakness. They sniffed out the blood and misery and to it they went, out of General Population to the Isolation ward.

There's a man there with crab claws for arms, they told Whisper when she was nose-deep in her roommate's copy of *Ivanhoe*. She chuckled and shook her head: They must be putting her on.

There's a thing that can reach and touch skin through the walls, they murmured during her doctor appointments, distracting her from playing firm and sensible with the doctors. That was clearly silly. Nobody could touch through walls, and the walls in Isolation, the ghosts delightedly informed her, were made of stone, cold and thick.

After months and months in General Population, where Whisper's doctors told her there were no ghosts and the ghosts told her there were no angels and she smiled her half smile at all of them and treated them just the same, the ghosts came to her in the middle of the night: *There's a little squaw girl doctor reading to the Freaks.* "Language," she told the ghosts out loud, loud enough that her roommate tossed and flounced a pillow over her ears.

The one who touches through the walls is listening, quiet quiet, and it weeps. The ghosts held their hands up to their chins praying, 'cause they threw their whole hearts behind anything that wept, and that's when Whisper knew that they were telling true.

There's folks here odder than me, she thought, and *dark true things* rolled about in her head, and (she told me, smiling wry) there was not a little of her that was bored stiff of doctors and quiet and pretending.

So she started trying to get into Isolation.

It wasn't as easy as you'd think. The nurses were always threatening it when the girls in General were bad and the doctors weren't around to hear. Whisper threw all the pillows around in the common room and shouted at the top of her lungs. She spat on the floor and paced and fussed. All this bought her were trips to the Quiet Room. In Whisper's doctor session that week, he asked why she was acting out.

"You're normally so well-behaved," he said. He was mild, like her father.

"I'm not going to make it," she told the ghosts, knees drawn up in her narrow bed at night. They shook their delicate heads. They thought you had to be crazy to want to be in Isolation in the first place.

Gotta hit someone, one said, proud. *Bite 'em. Piss on the walls.*

Whisper was a little woman. She made a little fist. It looked soft. "I certainly will not."

Her roommate muttered something; made soft kiss-noises in her sleep.

Then you're not goin' to Isolation, said the ghost.

That's okay, said another. *I think Isolation's comin' to you.*

Whisper slid her legs out of bed and tiptoed out into the hall. The nurse was at the other end of the ward, by the door: There was only so much trouble General Population could make inside the stacked walls of its little world. On the other side of the wall there was a shuffling. A moving of feet.

"Oh," Whisper said, and the opposite door opened.

The man on the other side wasn't a hitter or biter. He was lean and messy-haired and tall, and there was a trickle of light burning in his eyes that wasn't light reflected. It blinded her enough that she couldn't see the face of the even skinnier person behind him.

(I held my breath at this part. I closed my eyes.)

"You're the man with the crab claws for arms," she said.

Atticus's eyes — because of course it was Atticus, young and less muscled and shielding a straight-hipped young slouching thing with his thick arm — went dull matchbox red, and "Who're you? Who's told you 'bout me?" he asked.

"The ghosts," Whisper said, and he gave her that look like she was talking about midnight angels.

Those claws can cut locks, Whisper's ghosts whispered. *The other could touch through walls, and put the nurses to sleep. You should think about it.*

She tilted her head. She thought about it.

"Do you want to know the way outside or not?" she asked Atticus, and the ghosts plucked at his hair and pinched the crooks of his strange hard arms.

He blinked; spotlights fading. "Yes," he said after a minute. "All right," and Whisper smiled.

"All right," she said. "Let me just get my roommate."

Whisper's coming and going had woken her room-mate up. She opened one eye and looked up all reproachful, and said (which was rare, even when it was too dark for books), "Are-are-are you gonna be quiet now?"

"No," Whisper said, and pulled her camera from the bedside drawer; the photo of her mama and sister and her from its frame. "Violet, we're leaving."

The ghosts of the hospital led them, tumbling and giggling, through the grey service corridors and dusty, closed halls. They led them past the men's unit where Scar lived and joined with them; tiptoed through the offices to a window that could be broken. Through it, one by one, they tumbled into the night.

What's the moral of the story? Whisper asked when she told me this, and smiled a little at how I sat up surprised.

The moral of the story? I asked her, and she nodded. *That that's what's wrong with Above, that even your own pa would betray you?*

Whisper's smile went funny, and she shook her head. *That's Atticus's lesson,* she said, and before I could talk again: *The moral of the story is to always keep something up your sleeve. Especially when you don't think you need it.*

FOUR

Ariel's friend is named Beatrice. She tells me so once Ariel's asleep, curled up on a broken-backed old mattress under an emergency blanket that didn't start out grey. There's a pile of other kids in the bedroom, roused awake by us coming in and back to bed inside fifteen minutes. I can't count how many; they're all limbs, and my eyes are aching.

Beatrice closes the bedroom door almost all the way — just left a little open — and settles down on the cold wood floor, cross-legged, once Ariel's asleep. I sit across from her and wait 'til I'm spoken to. She's tall and walks quiet — heel-toe like she was taught it by Mack his own self — and thin around the wrists, but she's got eyes as cool and bright as Atticus's could ever be.

"You don't look like a runaway," she says after a minute, and the way she says it lets me know all at once what kind of place this is. Low and soft and edgeless. Making Safe.

This ain't the one that hurt my Ariel.

"M'not," I say, and keep my eyes down in deference. *Are so*, my head rebuts. I was with Whisper and Jack in a safe place and warm, and I ran. And I was with everyone who raised me up from ten, all of them getting hurt or killed or taken, and —

Okay. I ran away.

"What's a runaway look like?" I ask, because even when Atticus was cool and bright and sizing you up for something harsh like ten days of latrine duty, he never turned away a real question.

"Looks like a smart mouth." There's an edge to it, but I don't think she's mad: Her head's tilted back a little, not low like someone looking for a fight. "You're not hungry 'nuff. And you're way too clean."

I am. I can still smell Doctor Marybeth's sweet white soap on me, under a full day's sweat and tired and fear. And under that, edged and hiding, the hint of dead blood on my fingers.

I don't feel clean at all.

"We got rules around here," she says. Rubs her head again, but it ain't distracted. She hasn't stopped watching me for one second. "I don't let in just anybody."

"You let in Ariel," I say before thinking, and the quiet is hard as bright red light on wood.

"She's Sick," I say to break it. My fingers twitch for a hospital bracelet to hold up, to dangle dirty between my fingers. I shove my hands in Doctor Marybeth's jeans' pockets and keep still.

Beatrice looks me over again, taking the measure of me this time. "It's good you get that," she says carefully.

I nod my head, feeling all of a sudden like I don't get it at all.

"So. Convince me I oughta let you two stay here," she says, and leans back against the wall.

Ariel rustles on the mattress. Turning over, blanket drawn tight. *If not, the Whitecoats'll get us*, I think. *The shadows'll get us. I don't know where I am, and whoever's caught in the safehouses dead or scared or bleeding will starve from waiting and there'll never be a Safe to keep again.* None of that's reasons. None of it means anything to Normal people Above.

I swallow dry, and then I get what she's asking for. I can Pass, but I'm also the Teller, and I can Tell like nobody.

"There's a place for people like Ari and me," I Tell her, seeing it in carvings, seeing it in paint. "There's a secret place hidden away that my ma and pa and the other ones who were Freaks went to live in, and it's been invaded by trouble."

"Where?" she asks, not at all believing, hard through and through like a girl made of bone.

"I can't say. I can't. It's gotta be a secret to stay Safe."

The corners of her mouth go down. "Bullshit."

"It's not," I say. And against the wind and road-noises and mutter of people dreaming, I Tell in Atticus's cadences the story of the going down to Safe: Once upon a time there were four half-young people who were Freak and Sick and hated, and they went down and made a place for their own. I Tell it in his voice: the version painted-over, scratched-out. There's no Corner in Atticus's story; a hole he steps over, a blank place nobody reaches to touch. I leave it out.

I think she thinks I'm Sick. I *know* she thinks I'm Sick because she leans back wary, every muscle hips to crown, and then she asks me, "So what's your problem?"

The air vent in the wall hisses. Someone says something in the bedroom, to ghosts or air or nobody. I know every betrayal in the history of Safe: the way Whisper's hands flutter when she talks about her pa and Atticus's claws quiver as the needles go in and how Violet don't talk at all when it comes to the part where her lover called them in to take her away. She couldn't scream, she said. They stuck her full of needle-juice and took away her screams.

You can't trust people Above. People Above are monsters.

I take a deep breath. "You didn't send her away," I say. She didn't.

On Sanctuary Night the Cursed show their scars. My pa went without shoes on Sanctuary Night, and my ma let down her soft-wrapped scarf. Safe shows one and all their Curses, and Atticus looks on it and takes your pledge to the rest of us and lays one claw on your head and gives you Sanctuary.

I take off my shirt and shoes.

Here's the scales that run down my back, along the spine. I take her hand and have her touch them, the rough where they're scraped away, the slick where they're new come in; flicking bits of armor that don't prickle cold like my arms and chest. Her fingers through them are blunted and mute. Here's the claws, thick and dull, warping my toes but not my fingers. I clip them with old shears when they come in too long. They're better than my pa's. His were padded and bone-bent; his feet ached in the cold. I take her hand. I make her feel.

"I can Tell, and I can Pass," I tell her. "My ma had gills and my pa lion's feet, and 'cause of them Doctor Marybeth says I'll die young and leave no children behind."

That's what my problem is. That's my Curse.

I bend my head, and wait.

"What are you asking for here?" she says after a long time, while Ariel shifts in sleep that I don't think's really sleep no more, 'cause Ariel is cannier than to let me and her Bea alone. I lift up my head and look Bea straight in the eye, make her look at my Normal not–Freak person eyes.

"Sanctuary."

"Why?" Her voice shakes and shudders.

"You didn't send her away."

(Ariel does not stir. She stays small and still and quiet.)

"You saw wings, didn't you?" I ask. "Tall brittle bee's-wings, tall as a girl. Translucent. Iridescent."

She looks away. She nods her head.

"Okay," she says. "Okay. Just a few nights."

There are shadows in the edges of my dreams. There are shadows that I don't know if I just took from some Tale, because Tales are my talent if fish-scales and lion-toes and a short, small life is my Curse. They whisper through the night, echo-words I don't know the names of, between the noise of breaking glass and breaking hearts and the snap of muscle, of bone, all down into morning.

I wake to the bang of a bathroom door and footsteps in the kitchen; bundles of tangled clothes lugged back and forth. It's morning in Doctor Marybeth's house, morning in Safe: the move down to the latrines and the smell of oatmeal, toast, tea. Except the people washing and yawning here are all soft and perfect, two arms two legs one head and all the toes. Straight long skin-and-nails toes. Normal. It's Normal-people morning again.

This time I don't keep my eyes shut, drag it out, play my silly what-ifs about being Normal my own self. It's been a whole day now. Long enough for shadows to cut, or break, or count up who's gone missing.

So many things can happen in a day. And I'm responsible to Safe.

I claim the muggy bathroom once Ari's done and wash under spitting, lukewarm water. The shower's yellowed, streak-stained along the tiles, and the towel smells like other people's skin. My clothes piled up on the bright white toilet lid are near-wet from the steam. Whisper would scold; damp rots cloth. I flip over my puddled jeans and stuff one hand in the pocket. The twenty-five dollars are still crisp and dry.

I let a breath out, and it comes out foggy. I put on my clothes.

I stop before the shirt goes on. There's a big mirror in Beatrice's bathroom, bigger than the one in Doctor Marybeth's attic. I wipe the steam away with one hand and the wet, frayed towel; crane my neck over my shoulder to see.

I've only seen the scales once or twice. There aren't mirrors bigger than a grown man's hand in Safe. Whisper gifted me once with a picture from her precious camera, held to develop under the kitchen lights, but the mirror is clearer.

The scales are speckled black and a little silver on top of the brown hollows of my shoulders. They race down, layer on layer, halfway to my hips and stop. Trickle away.

And they shimmer. Iridescent.

Someone bangs on the door. "Come *on!*" I jump, yank the shirt on in three strong pulls, and head out to breakfast.

Beatrice's people hunch six around their square plastic table with some left over and sitting on the floor, holding mumble-conversation in the way that means late nights, bad mornings, long duties. "Morning," Bea says, and "This is Matthew." They all turn around and *look*. A drip of water wends down my shoulder, chill and itchy. "They're staying a few days."

Ariel shrinks down in the mattress-mussed corner. *Embarrassed of me*, I think before I bite it back, imagining my measure with all these Normal Above people: some jump-up kid who can't navigate one good street and weighs 'bout as much as a plastic bag, wet hair to wet hems of someone else's jeans.

Still. Nobody says no.

There's no coffee here, and no Doctor Marybeth telling us gentle where the toast and eggs are, but there's a box of open cereal and mismatched dishes in cream-painted cupboards naked enough to beg for carving; a half-empty carton of milk in the fridge. I fill a bowl for me, one for Ari, and set them down on the floor with the others; runaways, maybe, 'cause they're skinnier than me though just the same clean. The cereal crunches loud in the quiet.

"So what can you do?" asks a tall scar-lean boy out of nothing, and he's looking at me.

"Ah," I say. Look at Bea.

She shakes her head *no*.

"I carve," I say, voice small and shy in my throat. Ariel's knees draw up to her chest, her bowl to one side. The cereal looks soggy.

"Carve?"

Doors. Tales. The remembering that ends up in other people's heads. "Wood."

He bites off a smile that's not smiling; a smile that warps all the lines of his face into a naked baring of teeth. "Great. Fucking *artist*."

He ain't looking at me. He's looking at Ariel.

"Darren," Bea snaps, and he turns away. The bite goes out of the air with a little sigh. "That's fine. Matthew can go out on bottles with Cat tonight."

Duty. My shoulders ease down. I know how to do duty roster to earn my bed and board, and there's a long time between morning and tonight, time to visit four safe-houses if we're quick and careful about it. "What's bottles?"

"Getting bottles from the dumpsters to return for deposit," says a little girl who must be Cat. She's curly-haired like Seed — *smashed-horns, shadow-foot raising up to kick again.* "It's only good on weekends, 'round the university. Rest of the time s'all picked over."

Her hair's black as the night sky Above, and her eyes too. But she gives me a smile that puts lines at the corners of her eyes.

"Chick duty," Darren puts in, watching Ari again, cool and flat. "Fag duty," and then Ariel's on her feet with a rush of air. She crosses the room in three quick steps and tangles her fist in the front of his shirt, long pale fingers curling like stingers in the fabric, up against his throat. I'm the only one behind her. I'm the only one who sees it: the second when his face goes limp and scared.

Nobody moves.

"Babe," Bea says, low.

"Don't even," is all Ari says, and stomps away into the bathroom.

Underneath her shirt writhe stillborn baby wings.

She don't come out until they're all gone, a subdued blob of leather and broken-laced sneakers, and us left with instructions to not open the door for nobody. She waits five minutes for the quiet to settle in and then turns the brassy bathroom knob. It creaks loud enough to set me jumping.

She presses plucked-out baby wings in my open hand and stalks into the corner kitchen without a word.

"What was that?" I ask. We've lost half an hour of

good searching time already. No time to argue right now, but I can't, I *can't* have her run.

"You never asked *me* to touch them," she says, every word snipped short.

It takes me a second to realize: my scales. Bea's hand on my back, and Sanctuary. Ariel's never really mad about what you think it is. I move, but she won't meet my eye. She stares at the dangled-open kitchen cabinets for a few long seconds, and then slams them shut.

I close my hand around the tiny wings and they crumple.

"You never asked me to touch your wings," I say back, soft and even.

"Don't talk to people about your back," she says, her voice thin and strange again: *Don't you know what happens —*

"It's my back," I snap, even though she's right.

"Then don't talk to people 'bout my wings," she replies, and goes into the bedroom with her shoulders round and tunnel-hunched.

I tidy up the kitchen while she does whatever in the bedroom. The faucet's jerky here; one long crowbar-handled knob not labeled blue or red. I yank it until the water gets warm, never finger-wrinkle hot. The plastic plates clack in the draining board and drown out the noise of Ariel moving. All the while I'm biting my lip against the memory of fifteen hundred kitchen duties full of cold-water scrubbing: not enough cloth to dry, company to keep your hands from chapping cold; someone telling a Tale or a bit of music while we worked. Here there's nobody to tell the Tale to, nobody to listen, and when I raise my voice to sing the first lines of "Frère Jacques" like my ma sang to me as a little baby, they come out thin and wrong.

When there's no more dishes or excuses, I nudge open the bedroom door. She's sitting on a mattress under a wall piled with posters, back to me, hair across her face like wings.

"I'm sorry," I say. A hand maybe twitches. "She already knew." She shifts on the mattress. The tangle of blankets, red and blue and faded no-color, is shoved against the wall. A pillow hangs from the mess like a stained, dead hand. I sit down on the one chair, a busted one shoved beside a cobbled-together desk covered in half-empty mugs and bald capless pens. The metal seat squeaks with give. "Ari, why'd you grab him?"

"He doesn't like me," she mutters, and plaits her fingers together.

"Why?" But she just shakes her head, shakes it off once more. Like Jack. Like running. Like everything.

I almost ask her what her favorite color is.

"We've gotta go. We've only got 'til dark to find everybody else," I say. "They'll know what happened. We can make some kind of plan."

Ariel stops fidgeting. Her face has gone pale as the light on my first night ever Above. "Why us?" she asks, trying to make it sound not scared. "Why not Whisper and —"

"'Cause we're sworn to uphold Safe. We're responsible," I say, 'round the ache in my throat.

Her eyes go big. "That's not fair," she nearly chokes. "That wasn't my fault," and I don't know what the hell I said by accident, 'cause that sure ain't the thing I said on purpose. And then — oh.

"You think it followed us home." I still can't say it. I still can't say the name.

"You don't know that." She's still as a dead thing.

"It asked us Safe things," I stand too fast and the chair creaks like it's dying. My face is hot. It makes sense, terrible sense. This is all my fault, and hers. "It asked us, and I told, and it knew our names —"

"*It wasn't you,*" she says so forceful that I step back into the chair, half-thinking I might find her hands in my shirt-collar. She sees it somehow and backs down; falls into herself like her own shriveling wings. How many times can she grow them in a day? How much upset and panic and fear before the skin over her spine goes raw, chaps from mad, starts bleeding? "It wasn't you," she says again, and wipes her nose sharp on the back of one hand.

"What then?" I ask. "What do we do?"

"We're *here* now," Ariel says, dismayed and red-eyed and unlovely. "There's no monsters here. We don't have to go back."

My breath catches.

I ease forward. I step slow and careful, and push in the chair with a little lift so as to not scratch Bea's scuffy floor. My hands linger on the metal rods of the chair for a long time, until I can peel them out of fists.

"Yes, we do," I say hard and even, and walk into the big room, grab my shoes. One lace knotted up, two. My voice is shaking. My hands are shaking. "That is my *home*. People could be *dead*."

"Matthew?" she says, shocked, small. Tiny. "Teller?"

She never calls me that.

"Matthew, please —" and her hand's on my arm, tugging, light and useless. I turn around, ready to shake it off me. "When was the first time you saw the sky?"

She brings me up short with that, short enough that my hands forget all about being mad. "My first supply duty." I've told her this story before, singsong in the drip-rustle nights of Safe, to bring us both to sleep. It's my favorite of all the Tales, because the first supply duty leads to the second, and that's when I find my beautiful Ariel. "A year past. It was cold. And I thought no wonder people were so cruel up here, if the wind bit your bones all day and the sky stared you down into nothing with stars."

My eyes've slid shut. I open them after a minute of watching the stars glow behind my eyelids, and she's still watching me.

"You wouldn't miss it if you never saw it again."

The wind rattles the leaves on the trees outside. It's nothing at all like pipe-music. I think about it.

"No," I admit.

"Well, I like the sky," Ariel says, eyes pleading, sharp, *important*. "I need it."

"I'd be your sky."

It just slips out, quiet in the dark on soft-shoe feet. I put my hand up to my mouth, but it's too late, and Ariel's looking at me steady and keen like she'd never been close to weeping just five minutes before.

She looks at me and it's sad like Whisper's sad.

For the first time under daylight, the first time it'd ever count, I feel a hot and ugly blush come up like a blister.

And I run.

Through the door and down the hall, down the stairs to the ground, and I don't wait to see if she follows. I can't turn back, can't look her in the face now, not like that. I push through the button-studded doorway, shouldering past a lady with a laundry basket filling up both arms who calls me a word I don't know as I push the outside door open and let it swing free. The sun is hot and bright outside. It stings my face, my eyes.

That sadness cut hard enough when it wasn't on my Ariel's face.

I pause at the end of the walk and look right, look left. I don't know where I am. I don't know where I'm going, but I've got to get away. Somewhere I don't have to look her in the eye, or Whisper, or Jack, and see that hateful faraway sick-sweet sad face.

Somewhere Safe? snips a little voice in the back of my head, and all my angry shame turns sour.

I'm being selfish. Thinking of nothing but my own little hurts, and I made a promise to keep Safe.

People could be dead, Matthew, I tell myself savage, and bite my lip 'til it's sore. I can find them. There's more than one way to find a thing. There are ways that're dangerous, that could get you locked behind sharp metal doors.

This is an emergency.

I start walking.

The shelter that Atticus deemed a safehouse is at Queen Street and Bathurst — *QueenandBathurstQueenand Bathurst* he would make us repeat when we first trained to go Above. I know the way there from two sewer caps and the big food store where we steal most of our tinned goods.

I don't know the way from Beatrice's place, from no-man's-land. But I'm the Teller, and I can Pass.

Here's Whisper's other lesson: that even if people Above are monsters, they will point you on your way if you smile and meet their eye. So I do my best to look young and nothing-special and Normal, and I tilt my head and look them in the eye, bustling 'round ladies and kids waving fat chalk and men with no shirts on. They point and say *east* or *south*, and though I don't know from east or south I thank them and make careful, meticulous, my way. I watch the street signs and tell myself *QueenandBathurst*.

I walk with my shoulders down, watching feet, dodging the swift snips of music that leak on cool air out of the stores. After the first hour or two or year — who knows without clocks? — I can almost pretend I'm not upset anymore, can almost unsee the way her eyes went soft and shut and sad, but conversations still quiet as I go by: a different hush than the one that screams out *Freak*. I don't know how I look to make that so.

Selfish, I remind myself, and pinch the side of my leg. And instead I dredge up everything I know 'bout Corner.

Corner met Atticus, Corner of the bloodtouch hands, in the Whitecoats' house on the hill. The ghosts loved it for its weeping, loved it for the way its hands touched through walls, clothes, flesh.

Atticus stood before Corner like a shield, and Corner took that protection gladly.

After that there aren't really Tales about Corner. Corner founded Safe with Atticus, and Corner took care and gave Sanctuary with Atticus up until the year I was seven years old and they found Jonah struck dead in the tunnels, and then Atticus didn't give Sanctuary to Corner and called Corner Killer instead of its right name. My pa hid me behind his pant leg when they closed the big door against it. And then nobody told Tales about Corner.

(And here I catch the sign that says *Queen Street West* and mark the corner; turn.)

There's nothing in that little Tale to help me; nothing that'll tell me why Corner would come with swoops and waves of shadows and speak sweet and sad to Atticus, and then put a knife square center in his throat. Keeping histories is as much about knowing what needs forgetting as what ought to be remembered, and Corner's been forgot.

Maybe that shouldn't have been so.

The shelter at Queen and Bathurst is huge: swooping brown brick with an iron gate, and I don't know if it's a gate to keep bad things out or the kind to keep you locked in. A couple men are spread out on the steps, wrapped in layers of dirty shirts and the four-day beard I can't even grow in twenty. They watch everyone passing with bright rat eyes, eyes that go *bite or run away?* I keep good and wide of them as I go up the steps to the door.

You can't just walk into a shelter. They got rules about in and out Above, and a frowning someone behind a desk to enforce them. This someone's a wrinkle-faced man who sits crooked on a dim orange rolling chair, making faces at the papers on his desk like they hurt him. The walls are grey, but they're hung all over color; blankets and weavings like Doctor Marybeth has in her house. I wonder, quick, if it was her who found this place for Safe. If I stayed long enough, patient and quiet and Normal, would she come to fetch me back?

"Can I help you?" says the man behind the desk in a voice rough like first-cut carving.

"I'm looking for someone," I say; stumble, more like. "My cousin." Cousin's good. Cousin could be girl or boy, young or old.

He peers down at me through thick glasses. The scratches on them glint in the sharp, flickering, Salvation Army lights. "I'm sorry, son. You can't just wander in here." He don't sound sorry in the least.

I remember the metal of that gate, and the lock.

"You don't understand," I say, trying to sound young and small. I've got to Pass good. Mack could be in here, or Scar; Violet or Hide or Chrys, scared and waiting to be found — "They're Sick."

That ain't no good argument here. Here Sick's a thing to fear, to avoid and lock away. That's an argument for Safe, and I'm botching this up, and then I have to turn my head away so this Whitecoat man doesn't see my throat go all thick with failure.

He stands. I take a step back, brace my leg unthinking to give a punch or take one or run, but the look on his face ain't punching, and it ain't rats. He drags his own leg a little, limping 'round the desk. "Come on, now. No need for that," he says oddly, and while my mouth's still hanging open, he opens a stained brown door and lets me inside.

The shelter for homeless people is two dirty tile steps down into a big room set with folding chairs, spindly tables, and couches in different colors along the corners. There are posters on the walls, not pictures like in Bea's place but cramped writing: warnings and signs and rules. A slow fan turns lazy on the ceiling, making a breeze that's only halfway there. And everywhere there's people: young and old, dirty like Safe-people, tired-looking 'round the shoulders and sunburnt and grave. Some turn to look at me, mid-wise the rows of white-top tables. Some don't, huddled over food or drink, talking to each other or curled into themselves. I look around. Walk the rows, the Above man behind me every other step; hoping and hoping as I turn every corner.

No Mack. No Hide or Scar or Chrys.

Nobody.

"Not here, then?" he asks when I turn, and I shake my head fast, thinking 'bout busy streets. Thinking 'bout hospitals, and medical exams that strip out all your secrets.

"Nobody came in and was sent —" I ask, and this time I don't have to pretend to be small and scared and lost.

"No," he says, and the sympathy in his voice surprises me. "Do you want to leave a name and number?"

"No," I say, eyes blurred, head aching. They have to be somewhere. I have to *think*. "Thank you," I tell him quick, and hustle myself back out front, down the steps to the street. The warehouse next. Most of Safe can't Pass. Surely they wouldn't come here; they'd go to the warehouse.

One of the rat-men on the stairway laughs.

I take a few steps to the corner, look one way, the other, before I realize. I don't know how to get from one safehouse to another Above.

There's three breaths where I just panic, blind white broke-down panic, before it comes clear: *Then don't go Above*. I know the way from here to two whole sewer caps, and through them to the tunnels. And I know the way through the tunnels to the warehouse.

I let out a long, shaky breath. Cross the street away from that big rusting gate and bring up my map of the world backward, turned around: Beatrice's house to safehouse to sewers instead of the other way 'round. Count the turns.

The way to the tunnels is in a painted-wall alley, bright and narrow in a way that's comfort 'cause it's just as closed in as home. It's stopping there that makes my legs finally hurt, makes the tired catch up with me. I lean against the wall a second, Doctor Marybeth's jeans stiff 'gainst my knees, and swallow through a hurting throat. I've never walked this long, this hot.

I stick my hand in my pocket and press my twenty-five dollars between two fingers; they sip my sweat in. It could be an emergency to need water, even if I don't need it so hard I'll die. One bottle of water, clean and cold like water's made Above; I could fill it up again in Beatrice's sink. It wouldn't be more than a dollar.

No, I tell myself. Close my eyes tight and let my heart slow down. *Don't have time. Come on.*

When I open them I can stand on my own again, solid enough to put my eyes to the ground and look for the pathway down. It'll be a sewer cap, the kind that tops off our line: round brown metal carved with words and punched with holes. Two steps, three, and my foot comes down hollow on something half-buried in litter and wrappers. I brush it off with my shoe and yes, there it is: brown and stained, something I know from dealing with. From here it's into the tunnels, follow the sign, a quiet walk through the old sewers before coming Above again. Scar could be there. Mack could, and he knows everything about making it Above.

And if so — and if not — it's but twenty minutes along this line to Doctor Marybeth's.

Mack, Hide's papa, taught us to open a sewer cap blindfolded in the darkest dark; he stuck sock-scraps in our ears so we couldn't hear the clicking and had to tug and coax with just our fingers to make the locks give way. It's not much different from up top than below. The holes in the metal are small, but they let fingers have their way.

I lift the cover and peer down into the dark.

The smell of sewer comes up, thick, familiar. Above has grass- and dirt- and smoke-smells, but sewer is dark like life, like everything that ever lives and dies and bears a growing thing again from its waste. Sewer-smell is dark like home.

The tear falls into the tunnel with a trickle and a plop 'fore I even know I've shed it.

It echoes slow, quiet. And then a different smell comes up like an answer: It draws into my nose, trembles out my palms and the pores in my skin, thick and sweet and rough-fingered. It whispers like pressure behind your eye, whispers words no person child or grown stays clean for knowing. Metal, ruined and eaten, sour on the back of your tongue. It says *Teller Teller Teller. Down in the dark in the dark* —

I blink. My hands are cold. They're shaking. I look down and they're covered in black, strange, every crease and bend and hair drawn so sharp 'gainst the thin sunlight that even looking at them feels like it'll cut. Sharper than sharp; realer than real —

The grate slides down from my scabbed-up fingers.

Through my fingers the shadows come.

"Teller," they whisper, trip-tongued, in layers, pouring up from the tunnel like soft mud and sewer water. They puddle on the cracked asphalt, blotting out the fat green garbage bags and the oil stains and the sun.

I stumble back. I stumble, reel, scrub my hands against my jeans, the wall, anything. The bricks scratch my palms and the shadow-stuff leaves dark slug-trails 'cross the paint, but nothing makes it come off. Instead it stretches, lazy and wicked, into two legs and two arms; a thin and grimacing face with a small kid's nose and a smooth, blank space where the eyes should be.

The shadow steps off the wall, toward me.

Its footsteps sink through a scatter of stained paper and pavement, and then land firm, firmer as it darkens from thin grey to charcoal to black. I dodge sideways, angle for the mouth of the alley, for light and noise and the press of Above people, but too late. It's cut me off.

Not it, I realize, as I see the third foot land strong atop pavement, the fourth. *They.*

There's another behind it. Five. Six. Dozens.

"Narasimha's child," they whisper dead and loving, like the rustle of wings; like a voice in the dark that knows all your Tales and names.

I run.

They follow in my feet, my footfalls. They jump between licks of sunlight like kids jumping the sewer flow, gone and then there again in the next bit of shade. They don't breathe (and I'm breathing too hard). They don't trip or slow or mess up (and there's too much on the ground to keep track of, to scramble over, for me to not, sometime, mess up).

Smell something else, I tell myself, limping past bright-paint rolling doors and 'round guttery potholes and weeds. The smell drew them up. The smell of home, and my own crying. *Breathe something else.* So I think: *sky air trash bird wall*, and none of them clean me out, none of them stop the heartbeat-fast tramp of dark feet coming 'round the corner, joining and circling and parting faster than I can go.

When I see the wall at the end of the alley it's almost no surprise anymore. Dead end. The end.

Dead.

"Teller," the shadows whisper as I skid on something slimy and barrel into the wall. The concrete blocks hit my right knee hard, hard enough to draw out a swear. I plant my back to it. "Teller, I'llaskyouatale —" they rustle in Corner-voice, in echoes that belong in a tunnel with your eyes blocked out and not under the bright sky Above, and oh please tell me true that I don't hear one say *Matthew*.

115

They stop in ragged, mixed-up lines not ten breaths from my face, squirming solid to smoke like something hungry. They can't keep still. They fade in and out of each other, push through chests and legs and clip each other's ankles. They reach out as one with fingers extended; long knuckle-creased carver's fingers with nails to scratch, to press against the flutter-lid of an eyeball, and all I can hear is the rasp of my own breath, the scratch of the wall 'gainst my T-shirt. The catch of my own swallowing.

My hand goes to my pocket without thinking; the emergency money. I should've just used it for peaches, a bottle of water, or five thick pairs of good socks; books like Atticus's that we'd not read a dozen times before. I shouldn't have hoarded hard before the shadows hunted me to death and I didn't have time for any of it. My fingers close on that useless, stupid twenty-five dollars.

Touch the packet of nine matches between them.

I have fire.

I strike a match fast, throw it into one of the lidless metal garbage cans. It mutters, catches, smokes hot. Thirty or fifty or a thousand shadow-heads snap toward it, scenting, hesitant for just one second.

It's enough.

I shove the can two-handed, and clumps of smoldering trash spatter through the alley. The flames melt into each other like anti-shadows, climb atop the backs of old papers and twigs and start to burn. It's not a lot of fire:

It's small enough to step over. Small enough to stamp out on your Normal way by.

And it's enough.

The shadow-mass stops. Those arms come down slow. The fire ducks, pops, and they inch back from the smell of burning.

"Leave me alone," I manage. It ends in a cough. My throat's full of smoke, and my hands are shaking. My hands are half-burned from the hot, fire-touched metal.

"Hey," someone yells, down the alley, back in the world where there's sunlight and quiet and nothing's dead. "What the fuck?"

The shadows turn around: smooth pointed chins ducking, smooth hairless heads rising all at once. And then they spill back, fall back, sharp elbows pushing into bellies into thighbones into dark. They tumble into each other, crowding together like roaches, move like a river *away*.

They're running. Running from *me*.

All Atticus's *stay quiet*, all Jack's *quick and careful* can't stop me from letting a war-shout into the air. *That's right*, says a part of me that's red like Atticus's eyes, like blood spilled under firelight on familiar floor. I'm gonna hurt those who made my people hurt.

I run again. I *follow*.

They flee around the corner, under a fence, across underpasses stuffed with frightened birds. They weep and chatter through all the places Normal people don't go — through back alleys, past low empty lots grown fat with weeds — and I follow, legs numb, breath gone, knowing by rights I should be scared to be running full tilt through the death-empty parts of Above with nothing but a half-pack of matches. But I fix my eyes on them ahead of me like they're a golden braid bobbing up and down through the endless crowds, and this time, this time I don't mess up. This time I count the turns.

I follow right to another dead end, a beat-up black fence painted over and over with posters and papers, streaked white. They back against the fence and watch me, waiting to see which way I'll move.

"Got you," I croak, 'cause that's all I got, and then as one they shrink down low and slip under the fence planks.

I grip the fence slats and even though it hurts, close my hands around the wire loops. My foot slides and kicks, looking for a foothold, and then I find one and pull myself up to see.

The place beyond the fence is weeds waist-high, elbow-high, running wild and thick. The shadows are already halfway across, diving under the few stunted trees beyond, fleeing for a building that sits on the grass heavy and dark. A building the sun ought to touch by rights, but doesn't. Sunlight moves right past that place, whistling and carrying its watchman's brand as fast as fast can be.

Knocked-out windows, narrow and arching. More arches around the door, a portico screened by bricks not half as solid as the ones that people Above use to shore up their alleys. Grey concrete foundations, and then bloody red brick dripping up to the fallen-in rooftops. Everything's falling down here. Everything's broken.

I know this place. I've seen it in pictures, in Tales. I've seen its window smashed and my friends and loved and dead tumbling free into the night in my dreams, a thousand times. Lakeshore Psychiatric. Where the Whitecoats live.

Or maybe lived.

The Whitecoat house in the park stands silent, window-broke and windblown in the middle of the overgrown field. Empty as a bricked-off subway tunnel. The shadows flow into it, stripping the sparkle from the bits of broken glass. They puddle darkness on its rooftops like a growing sore: *Whitecoat place. Bad place. Abandon hope all ye who enter here.*

And then — they wink out. And gone.

I breathe in, hands raw, throat raw, legs shaking. *Sewer-things don't run for Whitecoat places when they're scared*, a nagging voice in the back of my head says. *They run for sewers.* Something's up; something's strange. Something's wrong.

I stop. Drop off the fence. I can't go in there alone.

I'm not no burning vengeance. I'm not something to fear. I'm small and smelly and worn right out, and I don't know half as much as I thought I did 'bout shadows.

I need Whisper and Jack. I need Doctor Marybeth, and there are likely still shadows in the sewers to bar my path. There's no passing through there; not for the twenty minutes through the tunnels to Doctor Marybeth's house.

I need help.

I drag in a breath, let it out.

"Ghosts?" I say, small and like a kid, swallowing down the way that makes me feel even smaller, shamed. "If any of you know Whisper, tell her Matthew's here. Tell her there's shadows nested up in Lakeshore and I'm blocked off from my way home."

The wind gusts. Back behind me, I hear a clatter. I turn right around, not sure if it's ghosts or shadows or what, hand wrapped 'round my matches to strike.

It's nothing. Some bit of wind. A crumple of newspaper blows and bounces down the sidewalk.

Nothing.

I let out a breath, wipe my palms on Doctor Marybeth's old jeans gone soft in the seams from two days' wearing. This is stupid. I need real help.

I need Ari.

She slides in next to me when the lights are out, my feet sore from running, my fingers sore from bottling three hours with Cat in the nervous, press-down dark. Four safehouses Above and there was still nowhere left to go for the night but back, back through the turns and blocks I counted careful to Beatrice's apartment — and I *promised*. I promised them a duty for their board and roof and Sanctuary.

I promised Ariel I wouldn't hurt her, and that I'd come back to her always.

So she waits 'til it's dark, 'til the lights are out, when I'm tight-faced and troubled with thinking. That telltale hump is under her shirt, and I can't tell if it's fear that's got her trembling or that constant pull to fly, to stay alive by moving.

You didn't come, is what she doesn't say. I feel it in every line of her held away from me, legs and arms and back all kissing-distance and refusing to let me touch. *You left and did not come back for me. You. Did. Not. Come.*

I didn't. I left and let that fight hang in the air all the long day. I stayed away, angry and hurt, and for once, for maybe the first time ever, I didn't come looking for her with soft words or soft hands to make one thing about it better.

I didn't. She didn't either.

But "I shouldn't have said that 'bout not going back," is what she actually says, tight and anguished. It jars me head to toe, jars me into looking at the space between my hands and her back, her skin and mine. How I'm already leaning forward, set for a fight.

I'm terrible. I'm cruel and bad and Beast.

"Ari," I say, and slowly, careful slow, put a hand on her back. She flinches just a little, just enough so I pull back from a second of sweat-damp T-shirt, of fitful, living warmth. "S'okay," I say, weak, even though it's not. "I'm not mad. Honest."

After an age of silence, two dozen lights streaming by through the window, a whole world turning over in sleep while she holds herself away from me, she says, "Doctor Marybeth said that?"

"Said what?" I blurt. And then I remember: my Curse. Dying with no children, and young. I never thought of Ariel wanting children. I try not to think 'bout her letting me close enough to get them on her. There's no good in aching for the things you can't have.

Awake and listening, then. I knew she was.

"How young?"

"Doctor Marybeth don't know," I say low in her ear. "Could be as many years as Atticus." I pause. "Could be less."

It doesn't make me cry anymore. It did once. Now all I feel is shadow cold.

"Matthew?" she whispers, edgeless, soft, sad. "Touch them?"

I touch her wings.

They're small, stiff, living. I trace the edges with one finger, watch my skin blur through their thinness like a light that don't burn.

They feel like Sanctuary.

ARIEL'S TALE

Once upon a time Ariel lived Above with other girls and boys (Cat told me, leaning into a blue glass-bottle bin; walking along darkened sidewalks, over the rattle of a shopping cart). They slept like puppies on the floor in rags and tatters and shared everything down to their skin. In the mornings they squared their shoulders in the way a body does when it's Passing, and went into the world to wait tables and clean bathrooms and lift heavy things and put them down again.

Ariel did not wait tables or clean bathrooms or lift things and put them down. She tried for a few days, each one, and came back fired or frightened or both, got into fights with the managers or just stared at the walls until none of the scarred-up boys and girls were willing to stick their necks out and recommend her for another job. So she stayed in the apartment on the seventh floor instead, and kept it passable clean. Sunlight came in through the windows. She put up sheets to mute it out.

. Cat thought she came from somewhere in the north end, past the gutted pothole street that separated the city from the suburbs. Suburb kids didn't know from feeding themselves, she said. They couldn't deal with want. So they went and took drugs and then couldn't pay for them, and the Dealers took them off the streets right quick.

(I didn't ask if Dealers was another name for Whitecoats, with their needles and their hospital in the empty green park. I didn't want to know.)

Is that what happened to Ari? I asked, thinking 'bout the bracelet sealed 'round her wrist, and Cat's eyes got confused and sad.

I dunno, she said. *One day she was just gone, and nobody knew where she had run to.*

CHAPTER
FIVE

"We have to find Whisper," I tell Ari in the morning, when the damnable sun is coming through the sheets hung over the windows and drawing a headache into my eyes. I've not slept enough, not had enough supper or breakfast. But it's been two days now, and two days is enough; enough time for a lot to happen if you're trapped in a safehouse, or in Safe with the shadows, or wandering, cold, the streets. Long enough to start seeing things and die without water, Mack told us when giving his strong lectures about travel in the tunnels and the proper supply.

Already too long.

Ariel bites her lip. I can see the *why?* in her eyes, though she's afraid to ask it; afraid I'll walk out again and break the delicate thing between us last night: my hand on the edge of her wingtip. Her head on my shoulder.

But I can't shake remembering the morning before it, and that sad, dry look on her face.

"I found the Whitecoat place," I tell her. "It's all broken up with shadows." And I tell her my Tale of yesterday:

empty safehouses, too-full tunnels, shadows running hop-skip through the dark calling and hollering my name.

Her hands go still like dead things, sink into her lap. She knows what that place is. I told her our Tales every night to let her sleep without screaming, to help her love the people who raised me up from a child. I don't know that it worked. But she knows all the Tales, beginning to end.

"We can't go in there alone. We've got to find Whisper," I finish.

"We can't," she says, sharp and immediate this time, and I see the scared in her eyes for a full second before she gets the chance to look away.

"What d'you mean? What'd happen?" I ask.

She's quiet for a moment, quiet like empty houses. "He won't let me back out if I go there," she says, and I know right away she means Jack. *Someone opened the door*, he said, and the burn of lightning in his eyes was the same as when she stung him, when she ran. The terrible words he said.

She's right. He wouldn't.

"Ari," I say, cool and soft and careful. "I think you better tell me why you were fighting."

She shifts under the blanket, just a titch. "He thinks I was talking to them," she says, toneless. "So he thinks I opened the door."

She doesn't need to say who *them* is: shadows, who could melt down a drainpipe, into a desk drawer, slink away. All of I sudden I realize what was so bad yesterday morning about *responsible*.

"Jack didn't say that —"

"I'm not *stupid*," she snaps, and when she turns around her eyes are huge and hollow. A cornered thing. "I know what he thinks."

I let out my breath. She never yelled at me before we came Above either.

"We'll just explain it," I say, and it sounds weak. "We'll tell him true what it was."

She just looks at me. She don't say a word. The sound of rustling bodies whispers out from the shut bedroom door.

"Who *were* you talking to?" I finally ask.

Her mouth curls up into a smile that's no smile at all, something dead and bitter. "Myself," she says, and her little mouth quivers and firms. "Nobody."

And then the bedroom door opens and spits the first of Beatrice's sworn out, foot-drag stumbling across the scuffed wood floors like a night of shadow dreams. It's the lean one — Darren. He's too tired to be hard-faced this morning, even when Ariel gives him a dirty, dirty eye. He just looks at us, hunched-up and blurry, and shuts the bathroom door behind him.

Ariel lets a breath out and seals her lips tight behind it, staring at the crack in that door, where sound travels clean and clear.

What do you mean nobody? I want to ask, my hands open-closing; I want to ask if Darren's the one who broke her apart, sent her down into the tunnels to shake like something dying. But she won't tell me nothing with other ears listening in. I know there'll be no answer.

So later, when Beatrice is taking out the trash, I pick up two fat bags and follow her, fixing for a few moments alone. Ariel's lips go even thinner as she shuts the door behind us.

"What happened?" I ask Beatrice, walking down the stairs with her to the dumpsters out behind.

"Mm?" she goes. Her black boots sound *thunk* against the steps, squeaking where there's no carpet laid down.

"Between Ari and Darren."

A corner of her mouth tucks in all ladylike, like a sheet out of place or a mussed-up hair. "Fight," she says, and rounds the corner with a sigh. *Fourth floor* says the scratched-up sign on the wall. "Not serious. I'd've kicked his ass out if he touched her."

Named him Killer, I fill in and nod, the knots working out of my restless hands. There's no fighting in Safe either, not with fists. Atticus wouldn't have it.

"It went down . . . two weeks before she left? They had a real goddamn screaming match, and he wouldn't tell me what the hell he'd said," and the tidy corners go down, down. "That's when I saw it," she says, softer.

Looking away from me, at the smudges and burns and scars on the brown plastic rail.

"That's when you saw her change," I say, because I know that look from Tales, the kind where people stare five feet into the distance for the Telling and you need to help to Tell them, like a hand light on the curve of the back.

She stops. Scuffs her boot on the landing. There are grey embroidered skulls listing along the ankle, gazing out hollow-eyed and grinning at the chip-paint walls. "She kept going at him," Bea whispers. "I thought she was gonna kill him. And he was swatting and I didn't know if he was gonna kill her either."

"What'd you do?" I ask gentle.

"Opened the window." She bows her head. Scuffs one more time, hard enough to leave a streak of black on the sticky plastic tile. "She booted it."

I lean back a moment, close my eyes. "You did the right thing."

"I should have stopped her," Bea mutters.

"The best thing to do is let her go." Light-shapes swirl and flutter inside my eyes. Inside them I don't sound like myself. Older. Hollow. "She always comes back."

She's quiet so long I open my eyes up and look at her, and she's watching me funny, watching with that curious sad look on her face that Whisper gets sometimes talking 'bout Atticus in the old days. About Ariel in the now. "She didn't come back."

"No," I say after a second, and look down at my old-new sneakers. "She came down to Safe."

She starts walking again. I walk beside her.

"There's a house on the hill," I say. "A big redbrick house in a park, with boards over the windows."

"The asylum," she says and rattles her hand along the metal stairway bars. I nod. *Asylum*, in books, means Sanctuary. Above it means Sanctuary too, because Above, knowing enough about *asylum* to tell the difference between the two is something to fear. But it's not Sanctuary; it's everything good in Sanctuary turned 'round hard and bad.

Beatrice shifts her feet, back-forth, back-forth. "Shouldn't go there. It's a squat. People disappear."

I don't know what a squat is. But I won't be asking now, with don't and shouldn't and oughtn't being pushed about. "Disappear how?"

She waves a hand in the air, explodes the fingers out like smoke, like flames going out. "Poof."

Poof, I think, and swallow.

We're five steps out the back door when I feel the first pinch.

I drop the garbage bags hard, go knees-bent and wary, hand in my pocket for matches. But there's no voice, no shadows or whispers, and the smell's green-cut lawn, not sewers. Two breaths go by. I stoop over and pick the bags back up.

Nobody cuts me throat to belly.

"You okay?" Bea is three steps ahead, her forehead crinkled and watchful again. *Sick. Freak.*

I let out a breath. I've not slept enough, not by half. "Yeah. Just — I felt something," and that just makes it look wronger yet. The crinkles don't go away.

When the second pluck comes at my sleeve, I bite hard to keep in the scream. I look around, beside, behind, but nobody's between me and the door, me and Beatrice, me and the fence she's edging around. Green grass turns to grey concrete 'round back of the building, and Beatrice opens the first garbage bin with a clang.

The place where my sleeve pulled is burning, cold and —

— *pinches under the bedsheets at night —*

— familiar.

"Ghosts?" I whisper under the clatter of Beatrice's garbage landing in the bins. Hold my breath for a long second, under the buzz of flies and a brown bird singing, sharp and harsh, on the fencepost.

The nothing tugs at my arm again. Three, then two. The signal for Safe people come knocking.

My stomach goes tight — *Safe people, dead and head-smashed-in and ghosty* — and then I think, slow down; no. That doesn't for sure mean they're dead. It's Whisper. Whisper's sent them for me.

It worked.

Bea tosses the last bag into the blue bin and closes the lid with a clang. "You coming bottling tonight?" she asks turning, dusts her hands on her pants.

I nod. Chill small hands are prying into mine, between my fingers. Yanking. "There's something I gotta do first."

"Your people," Beatrice says, carefully.

I flush bright red and nod. I've never been good at hiding things. *It's not a skill a Teller ought to need*, Reynard used to say, back when he was Teller and I was young, as if maybe he had some notion of what would eventually come to pass. But there's no harm in admitting it. Not if she already knows. "I'll be back before dark."

"All right," she says, and jerks her chin up sharp in a way I guess is meant to be good-bye. She walks 'bout twice as fast going back to the door; much faster than we managed coming down.

The chill hand tightens 'bout my own.

"I have to get Ari," I whisper under my breath to whoever — whatever — Whisper's sent the second Bea is out of earshot. The cold gets deep and scowling. *Tug tug* on my fingers, my pant legs, my hair. "It'll just be a second."

The shove comes from nowhere. It nearly takes me off my feet.

Now.

I glance up at the window where Ariel is as they drag

me to the curb. It'll be all right. I can find Whisper, sort it out with her and Jack so there won't be another fight.

I can come back for her.

"Hey," I call after Bea; "Hey! Tell Ari I'll be back before dark?" Bea pauses in the doorway, holds a thumbs-up high.

She'll be safe here. Just for a little.

I flip a little wave at Bea, an Above-smile that's fake as fake. Invisible fingers tug my sleeves, shove my back forward, *come on, come on.* My heart's going like a subway train, and I understand for the first time, real down deep, why Whisper's pa and the Whitecoats and the girls in General Population were so sore scared of ghosts.

I follow them down the walk and into the empty street. Away from my Ariel, to the people who raised me from ten; who I left, selfish, high and dry.

When'd you learn running, Teller? asks the little voice in my head, and I wish it was a person so I could snarl at it.

It's a full hour walking and trying not to trip, ducking 'round Above-people and stoplights and trying to keep the turns before I realize where the ghosts are taking me.

Lakeshore Psychiatric.

Whisper's waiting.

"They told me," she says simple, leaned back 'gainst the black fence that keeps the Whitecoat place from the world.

The ghost-hands light away, shiver off me like bee's-wing. "M'sorry," I say, and stuff hands in my pockets. My mouth tastes foul, and I'm all over sweaty.

She don't answer; don't say *when'd you learn running, runaway boy?* And I can't take a thing from her face, blocked as it is by the angry noon sunlight. "I taught you better Passing than to lose your way Above," she finally says, and sits down on a knocked-down newspaper box, shoulder bag sagging and skirts spread like a lady. Now that she's sitting down, I can see her face: like a Society lady, as always. Perfectly composed.

"I'm sorry," I say again, heart-flutter and a little helpless. I'm not the kind of kid who disappoints my teachers. Who curses, who runs.

Wasn't.

"Report." Like it's my first supply duty: Tell me everything you saw, and I'll tell you everything you missed. Every way those things could've put you away in a cell five by five with cinderblock walls, with nothing but ghosts about to laugh and babble and weep for your weeping.

I report.

"There wasn't no one at the shelter. And I couldn't get through the sewers, to the warehouse —"

"We went there." Her voice comes tight and sharp, and that's how I know there wasn't no one there either. An ache starts down in my belly. Two safehouses, empty as tin cans. "We couldn't reach the tunnels."

"No," I say, and squeeze my eyes shut. Soak in darkness. Open again. "There were shadows. They knew my name, and they went —"

Whisper nods; she knows. 'Course she knows: I told it to the ghosts, and they brought me here. Where shadows are.

In the outline of Whisper's bag, there's the edges of something hard and heavy.

Suddenly my throat is very dry.

"They were waiting for us at the sewer entrances. They knew we'd try to go back." Whisper's frowning, her hands in her lap where it's best manners to keep them, 'cause that's just the place where nobody ought to be staring, so nobody'll see if they shake.

"Whisper," I ask, and don't watch her hands for trembling. "How are we gonna get back home?"

Her eyes are sharp now, and not ghosty or faraway. "We'll destroy all the shadows in Lakeshore, young man," she says, and stands up smooth as a dancer. And I realize, sudden, why she's brought me here. What the heavy thing in her bag is *for*.

"We should get Ariel," I say, trip-voiced. If this is a raid we're running, we need her; her stinger that she was to give Atticus on Sanctuary Night. "She hurt shadows."

Whisper looks down her straight statue-nose at me. "Not today, Teller."

I bite my lip. "Why not?" It sounds bad: like tantrum

and not being Community-Minded, which is what Whisper calls keeping Safe. I firm my feet in place and make sure they don't shuffle. The edge in my voice is bad enough.

"She's not sworn to Safe," Whisper says, even, "and this isn't her story to tell."

And it's not. It's Whisper's and Jack's and mine. Ariel had to offer something up to Atticus on a Sanctuary Night before we might ask her into a Whitecoat place with us to do bloody, dangerous things; before she's responsible in that kind of way to Safe and anyone sworn to it.

Even me.

She was right. I'm responsible. She's not.

"She hurt Corner too," I say, weak and suddenly hurting. "She stung it in the tunnel and it ran."

"Corner's flesh and blood," Whisper says evenly, and holds out her hand. "Now come along. Jack's waiting."

Jack is waiting at the edge of the battered old sidewalk like it's borderland, not one foot over the concrete curb that breaks it from the street. "Teller," he says rough, my grown-up name. He don't clap his hand onto my shoulder, and he don't quite meet my eye.

"Jack," I whisper, and duck my chin to my collarbone.

We turn together, the three of us, to the wicked building on the hill.

The Whitecoat place is long with shadow even in the thickness of the hot sunshine Above. It folds into the sky utterly silent, not a wind or a rattle or a breath from it, and even in midsummer, at the top of the afternoon, night steals out through its windows to turn the sky empty. The fence isn't enough to cage it in: The streets are empty for a block around. Nobody, even Above, wants to get too close.

Shadow-place, it says to the world. Monster-place.

"We do this fast," Jack says. "Quick in, quick out."

"Then down to the sewers," Whisper agrees, and draws the heavy thing from her little pack: a long pair of clippers, beaked to cut wire. The handles are scarred and bitten where the rubber's fallen away. I don't recognize them: conjured up from some box or ghost or Salvation, and not from the tool chest in the kitchen in Safe, full of comfortable things. When they close 'round the old fence wire there's a *snap!* loud as a slammed door.

The day's quiet for a fat, thick minute.

Nobody comes.

Jack breathes, and then I breathe, though I hadn't even realized I'd caught my own breath back. He pulls away a board cautious with his gloved hands. *Snap! snap!* go the clippers, and Whisper and Jack cut us a hollow through the rust and bleached-dry boards. I stand back, hands in my pockets, feeling matches and emergency money, matches and money over and over again. I watch for the police who ain't coming, the dogs that aren't with them. I keep useful. I watch.

I watch all the way around to the slick-painted sign on the fence five feet sunwise, as faded down as the boards.

"Coming soon," I read aloud. "Another residential living project by CityCorp." Someone's painted scrawl over it. I can't read those words.

"They're taking it down," Jack rumbles.

"Good," Whisper says, and climbs on through.

The wires and boards prick my arms as I follow. I tuck in small, remembering every little thing Atticus used to say about rust cuts and tetanus, and keep my arms close for a count of three after the fence spits me out. We pull the boards back into place. Our feet dent the swamp of white-puffed flowers and clutter. "They'll know we were here," I whisper, toeing the holes my feet've made in the sway and pull of long, ghosty grass.

"They'll know *someone* was here," Whisper says, and creeps forward, heel-toe, to the broken doors of the asylum.

They used to be wood — good wood, and still — but they're hinge-broken, paint-spattered, scratched up under years of bad handling. Even though it's a place full of wickedness, it burns me up just a little to see good wood treated this way. There could have been Tales on this door. Now they're all left to roam loose in the halls, stealing the sunlight away with their untelling.

The doors swing open silent under Whisper's hand.

Inside stinks: dry air and sour and something that makes my nose tingle sharp. Hallways twist from a sweep of common area into the dark, and in front of us a great wood staircase crawls upward, beckoning and dirty, to two windows blocked up with boards.

This is what they saw, I tell myself to steady my feet as we tiptoe slow inside. *This is what they saw when the Whitecoats brought them in.* I gather up a split board from the floor, test its weight. Not a good brand — not wrapped and made ready — but dry. Dry enough to burn shadows out of our way home.

We creep through the entrance hall under a ceiling lofted high on beams solid like the roofs of train tunnels; solid in a way that tells you they were held and hammered in place back when they didn't build things to fall down. Something stirs atop one, flutters —

I shout before I think.

There's no chance to reach matches, call fire. Between one breath and the next, the beams are full of birds: pigeon-fat and startled, fleeing into the dark. Their wing-beats blur and crackle like a thousand trains hitting a thousand rails, echo loud enough to bring out tears.

"I thought it was shadows," I whisper when Jack looks down at me, my nose still itchy and miserable, and this time his hand pats my shoulder and brushes away.

Whisper holds up a hand, *wait*, ready for anything, but nothing comes for us down the wide wood steps. The board snugs tight to my hand, sends splinter-roots deep between the lines of my palm, and the building sighs. Whisper lets out a slow, slow breath.

"We roust them out, then," she says to herself, and tilts her head back to the eaves.

Her whisper is just a murmur at first, mumble-lipped, slow, but the great high ceiling captures it and takes it traveling: *Come come my friends my lonely friends who held my hand my head* —

Ghosts, I realize. She's calling her ghosts to lead the way.

The tunnel-beams rustle: birds coming back in, creeping back to their safe-built nests. *Come come down and bring me news I've missed you long and long.* My hand aches; I shift the brand to the other, not as strong and not as sure, and wring the hurt one to shake off pain.

When she breaks off it's like cold water to the skull.

"Whisper?" Jack says.

Whisper is pale in the bad, comforting light. "There's no ghosts."

The quiet gets deeper, falls different. *What do you mean, no ghosts?* I don't ask.

"They wouldn't go unless something went bad," she says, hands in her skirts now, old-lady skirts that still look Freak even after her lecture about dressing clean and Passing good.

"They don't . . . move on?" Jack asks.

"No." She sounds small. Scared like a little girl and that's enough to make me scared, because even when Atticus died and the shadows came into Safe, Whisper led us free without leaking fear into her step.

"We'll walk careful then," Jack says, and takes her by the hand. Whisper startles: It's his naked hand, full of shocks and sparks. Even in the dim I can see his markings, the ends of latticed snowflake scars. "Up the stairs?"

Whisper's hand closes around his. "No. Down," she says, and circles the staircase, runs fingers over the walls until they close on a handle smudged and rusted the same color as the staircase. "They'll nest down where it's dark."

Beyond the door it's darker still. The building breathes out up plain grey stairs. Cold, and must. Abandoned things.

The smell of shadows.

No ghosts, I tell myself, a calming hand on my back and a thrill of terror both, and follow Jack and Whisper down the stairs.

At the bottom the bird-smell fades down into dust and death and earth, the smell of the Cold Pipes where nothing flows and nothing lives. The door clangs shut behind us and then the quiet is absolute, dust tickling at my ankles like monstrous, long-fingered hands.

"Teller," Jack murmurs, "strike a match."

My brand's already down between my knees, my free hand on the sandpaper.

The tunnel shows grey under light; grey under the wash of fire that blinds me as it catches and flares. Light fixtures stretch long-legged along the narrow grey ceiling, low as any tunnel. One full wall is panes of glass, webbed with wire, dirty and empty and cracked. They reflect the light, reflect everything oily-bright.

"No shadows," Jack says, near-disappointed, and keeps walking.

Clump clump clump go our steps on the hard grey concrete floor. *Clump clump hiss* the walls whisper back as we bunch together, moving fast, tied to the circle of light given out by my one quick-dying match. Jack's sweating; gritted teeth and clenched-tight hands and a mumble that sounds awfully like a swear. "Faster," he says, and we go on tunnel-blind, sweating through our Passing clothes, and let him hurry us up two steep flights of cold grey stairs.

We tumble out into a room torn up so long ago that the dust's wrapped arms 'round the chaos, given it a warm blanket, and made it a home to settle down. It's ripped mattresses, ripped wallpaper; everything ruined and tattered and bent. The smell of shadow-must is gone. The building's silent as tunnels.

"They're not here," I whisper, then risk a noise, clear my throat. "Maybe they went out," which just sticks me thinking of all the things shadows might do gone roaming.

"There's been people here, though," Jack says, and points down into the dust to a lighter dust, thin rips and darns in the blanket of the floor. Footprints. He's winded, a puff of air hiding out behind every word. I lick my lips and don't talk for a minute 'til the stitch in my belly stops complaining.

"Bea said it was a squat," I say.

Jack knows what a squat is. And it's nothing good, because he pulls a twisted metal bar from a pile of hospital beds heaped in a corner and hefts it in his gloved left hand. "I didn't hear no one," he murmurs, grave like Whisper to her absent ghosts.

We pass a glance between us. *Dead*, his eyes say. I shiver.

"Walk careful," is all Jack says.

We walk careful.

We go through the washrooms, red-cracked-tiled with their green basins stained and scummed with sour water. We go through the dormitories; we know them by the stacks of beds, the ripped drawings hanging on the walls, fluttering by one good corner and bleached too naked to see. The offices Whisper ducks away from, veering to the far side of the plaster-dusted hallways so I have to veer with her or lose the line. She's moving funny: hands opening and closing on her skirts like they're looking for matches. She's got no ghosts, I remember, and though I always knew she's so little I grew past her by my eleventh birthday, I see her in reach and speed and strength now, how much she doesn't have; how much she's gone quiet and old.

"Where are we?" I ask her, voice pitched quiet as I can.

"Activity room," she says, cold and choked-up. "They kept clay and crayons, and the clay never got fired into nothing, just mushed up and put back in the bin. . . ."

I might have known it; there's wax tucked in the cracks between floorboards, little smooth blobs that catch slanted bits of daylight far away. A half-burned stack of cards huddles in an ashy trash can in the corner, wrapped with dirty blankets and guarded by a solemn duty of bottles and cans. I squint, not wanting to put my face near the smell of fire though it's months dead at the very least, and snatch a card out. It's lined, hatched; filled with numbers. *Charts*, I remember Atticus mentioning. Charts where they kept your medication numbers, the measure of everything that made you Freak.

"Jack," I call, and wave it careful between thumb and forefinger.

"Bingo," Jack says, looking over my shoulder. I fish another out. "No, the game. They're game cards."

"Oh." Its flakes cling against my skin even after I drop it. Ashy, and still damp. Unclean.

My foot catches in the blankets when I stand: They're dirty, worn, old. Good for brands. "Watch my back," I say, like it needs saying, and tear one apart into long, tattered strips. I knot them tight 'round the end of my brand, layers worth, each so rotten the knots barely hold. The cloth won't burn long, if it needs to burn, but it'll burn truer than wood.

Jack turns when I'm done, hefts his crowbar thoughtful. "This smells wrong. The people-marks are too new."

"What're you thinking now?" Whisper says, harsh in a way that tells me without asking just whose idea it was to sneak into Lakeshore Psychiatric.

He jogs the bar hand to hand. "Where's the hardest place to reach in here? Where'd they be able to defend best?"

"Isolation," she says, suddenly fumbling.

Isolation.

Jack flashes me one of his dark-wise lightning looks, *you better watch out,* and takes Whisper by the elbow like an old-fashioned gentleman. He leans down to her ear like he's asking to dance. "Come on. You show me where."

The hallway to Isolation don't have footprints. We make 'em as we shuffle forward in the dust, long smearing things to hide the size of our shoes. The windows are blown out all through, cracked and spattered somewhere in the browning grass below. The sunlight comes in dim and bloody.

Whisper puts her hand almost to a blue window frame, halfway between the steps and any room that's got a door for opening. Her face is years and years away. "Where we climbed," she says, fingers hovering. "We went out here. They moved General Population after that." She chuckles, and there's nothing funny in it.

I glance at it, passing by: two stories down to the ground, drowned in weeds. "How'd you land clean?"

"Ghosts caught us." Her voice is muffled. I don't look into the cracked glass for even a glimpse of her face.

Jack sticks with Whisper until we get to the double-metal door and stop. "Here," she says, and draws her arm from Jack's, shoves her hands in her pocketed skirt like she's slow freezing. Ariel I'd comfort — and *Ariel's safe* I remind myself firm to stop the sudden ache — but Whisper, like this, I'm scared to touch.

Jack studies the door, its double-thick glass window all seamed and spidered with cracks. "Keypad lock," he says brief, and grins mean and tight. He taps his metal bar just so on the scuffed box beside the doorknob, and it shudders with sparks.

The door clicks open slow.

First we hear nothing. Not even wind. The walls are concrete, and the floor despite its cracked-up tiles and colors is concrete beneath, and an empty counter runs along the right side of the doorway into the dark that's a hardship again now that my eyes are all ruined with sunlight. There aren't no windows in Isolation.

The thick cell doors hang open at broken-neck angles, row upon row upon row.

I strike a match and nudge it between the twists and wrappings of my brand until it catches. When I hold it high, Isolation is grey too, and there's no crayon-dust, no crushed-up cans, no ashes. Isolation is empty as a scoured pipe.

Jack pads forward to the nearest cell and pushes it open with one gloved fist. The room inside is smaller than my own little house, nothing but a bed stuck to the wall and a fancy metal bucket for a toilet, the edge of a wall for pacing. He squats down in the center, poking through mouse shit and nothings with the end of his wicked crowbar. "Keep going, Teller," he says grim.

I move out to the second door. Toe it open with one foot.

The fourth cell still has a mattress, and I lift it away with my bouncing right shoe, checking careful for shadows like I'd do for bugs back home. Nothing 'gainst the wall, nothing behind the mattress —

Except when it moves, bleeding stuffing and smell, there's a rustle beneath like pigeon wings.

I lean in careful, making sure it's not the sound of something that'll bite. Nudge the mattress off its shelf. Dead center, pressed like a flower between the stained old mattress and rusty springs, is a file.

It's ripped and dark-stained and falling apart, nibbled at the edges by time and bad deeds. I ground the brand clumsy between two springs, open it careful and flip through. It's notes and notes, written in a neat hand — *Whitecoat hand* — covering each side of the paper. I spread it on the mattress and press nose to paper to read.

Malignant osteosarcoma, it says. *Phantom limb syndrome. Post-traumatic stress.* Farther down: *experimental treatment to halt rejection of prosthetic limb.*

Whitecoat words. Words that twist. But I know enough to read the Tale they're twisting. I know that Tale back and front, carved onto my good front door as well as my hands and my heart, because nobody else ever heard it told true and I repeated it every night before bed for a full month afterward to guard it 'gainst forgetting.

I gather the file up careful, touching the soft yellow paper only on the edges, where there's no words for my sweaty fingertips to stain. Take it out into the ward.

There's a flicker of something behind me; a change in the dark. I turn with my brand out, knees bent, ready, but the air lies flat, still.

Just the firelight moving, I tell myself, and walk in my own footprints back to Whisper.

She's sitting slumped on the tall counter, her legs dangling loose like a kid's. "Look at this," I say, and she sits up. Her eyes are red and much too big, a trembling big that makes me want to look away. I hold the file out. Maybe she's just teary from dust. Maybe it's a sneeze.

Jack intercepts it with one thick hand, peeks over clumsy fingers at the worn-down paper beneath. It's not a minute before he gives up on the bad light and the long Whitecoat words and passes it to Whisper. "Corner's?"

"This ain't Corner's." My hand's shaking. The touch of the paper's like a touch of stain; it stays on your skin long after you've put it down, stays your own trouble forever.

"No," Whisper says, and the skin around her lips is a very sickly white. "It's Atticus."

That's why we're not ready when the shadows come.

Narasimha's child, they don't say. Nor: *Teller*, nor *Matthew* in their hiss-echo voices that mix and muddle 'round corners like a river 'round a silty block. They pour out of the cell I could have sworn was dead empty with hands outstretched, blacking out the floor tiles and smudging away the doors. By the time Whisper's up on her feet they're on top of us, wailing, snarling: *Give him BACK* —

"Fuck!" Jack spits, hoarse and furious, and for a second I'm back there again in the ruin of Sanctuary Night, legs and eyes burning as Jack calls out fire and the Pactbridge down. I put my brand high, in a fighter's grip. "Keep back," I hiss at the shadows, hands trembling. My heart beats like the stamp of shadow-feet, shaking my chest down to pieces.

They ran from me before, I tell myself for courage. They ran from my words and my fire.

But they're nothing at all like running now: They hiss back at us, furious; send Whisper fleeing back through the hard double doors. And I can't tell if it's the light or if their chests are thicker, their necks rounder, their black teeth surer and less jaggedy broken. *Don't you don't you touch touch touch* — they rustle through creased lips, my fire lighting every line, and then they leap.

I'm ready for the first hit. I'm ready for the second, the thin-veined black fist swinging a breath from my belly while a wide-open mouth howls wild. But there's a shadow in every corner niche wall cranny and there's only goddamned one of me, and the third takes me right in the nose.

Light explodes behind my eyes. I stumble back, blink them clear, and I've barely time to bury my torch through the shadow's too-fat chest before the pain in my nose turns to chill. It's cold like my first night Above; cold that nearly burns. *Shadow-touch*, I think as the cold seeps down my cheekbones, my mouth. It tastes like fear and endless dragging time, a flicker of *peas-medication-roast beef*, and none of those are things I know, things I've ever had up against my tongue.

My brand falters. I open my mouth, close it. Lick my lips, numb.

"Give him back," comes out of my mouth, weak and whispery, and the shadows all around me, about me, *in* me, raise their heads and howl their horrible grief.

I drop the fire. I drop the fire and my hands go to my lips. The brand hits with a soft *whump* of dust rising.

"Teller!" Jack shouts, and scoops up the brand. He whirls it with his bad hand like a man gone berserk. "Back," he orders, breathing like a furnace run hot too long. "Behind me, *now*!"

I scramble back, stumble 'til I'm through the double-metal doors into the hallway, where Whisper's hugging the file to her chest like Ariel with her scuffed black book. My fingers bend stiff, strange, at the sight of it. They flex, and I swear I didn't make them move.

I yank the other hand off my mouth fast, but it's too late: The chill's slipped into my hands from clamped-down lips. The chill moves my hands toward that creased brown paper, fills them with a terrible urge to grab: cardboard, paper, living flesh —

Oh no no no.

"Don't touch him," slips out, and this time I don't mind it because I can't talk for myself, can't warn, and Whisper and Jack need to stay as far back from me as they can.

"Teller!" Whisper cries, big-eyed and short-armed and easy to snap in two. I snatch my hands away just before she takes them, shake my head as fast as I can.

"S'got my tongue," I manage before the cold comes back in, wails *give him back give him BACK* through my own fumbling lips in a voice I halfway know and never wanted to. The cold roots in deeper, down my jaw, through my chin. I feel the first touch of shadow-fingers along my cold-scraped neck.

Oh god it'll touch my heart.

I think about Ariel's hands on my back, rough and numb through the scales under Bea's old grey blanket. I'm glad she never saw this happen.

Whisper bats my hand away and puts rough little fingers on my lips, her eyes narrow and hard. "Come out coax out get free go clean —"

"Whis, *back up* —" Jack shouts from the doorway. The cold won't let me turn my neck. It won't let me see what's happening to him.

"Come out I draw you out —" Whisper goes, and eye-glinting, puts her other hand on Atticus's old browned-out file.

Something inside me *moves*. My throat twitches like a backward swallow.

All the shadow pours from my icehouse throat into the file in Whisper's hand.

She shrieks, quick and thin, and drops it to the floor. The brown cardboard of the file goes midnight black and cold, so cold it puts off winter into the whole room and turns our choking breath to frost. The shadows' stomping, shrieking, kicking stops. Whisper and I both stumble back against the peel-paint wall in an ear-popping quiet.

Deep inside the file there's a terrible, terrible *rip*.

Jack abandons the doorway in three long strides and plunges his brand into its heart.

The shadows yelp and Jack raises the brand again, but the dark is on the move, fading soft and smoke-thin grey, lengthening out into one soft-edge mocking of legs and head and arms; all the edges of a real person with nothing true or living underneath. It scoots back against the wall like water running downhill and I blink to clear my eyes, to separate out the dark that's living and moving from the normal dark just lying still.

When I get it sorted there's but one shadow on the creaking wood floor, short-limbed and curled forward, holding Atticus's papers to its breast.

"Teller!" Jack throws me the brand. I let it fall to the floor, snatch it up by the handle, and shove the fire hard up beside the face of the last shadow.

"Don't run."

The shadow whimpers, and the mad furnace-roaring in my belly turns cold and sick. That's not a right sound.

That's not a sound a monster makes.

Whisper's prim mouth is back from her teeth, wrinkles all contracted into vicious yellowed points. "What are you?" Nothing. *"Who?"*

Hesitating, hesitant, I push the fire closer.

The shadow keens, high and hurting like a lost little baby. *Who told you that you might gather my roses?* it murmurs. The sound rushes overlapping from corner to corner. It's so close I can see its hair, long and flopping over a small brow, fine cheekbones. *That's what it said, the Beast, the Beast, and her papa he had no good answer.*

I squint. It's not my imagining. This shadow's fuller than they were in the sewers, in the streets. It's the difference between a fed man and a starving one, and something here is very wrong.

Monsters don't weep.

Send me a child, then, he said, the Beast, and they sent it into the big house with no windows and locked doors, it sniffles. *Then you say: No. That's not how it goes. It's us that are the Beasts.*

"Speak clean," Jack says beside me. "Whisper, make it speak."

"I can't make it speak. Shadows aren't ghosts," Whisper snaps.

— *and no little girl's gonna save us*, it gasps.

I draw the fire back, guttering low and thin. A tear-drop smudge of darkness works down one of its cheeks, then the other, and this is not at all the same creature that swiped the Sanctuary Night dinner off the shelves and laughed as the glass broke into our blood.

"What are you?" I whisper. My mouth doesn't taste like peas or roast beef or — I shiver — medication no more; it tastes like my own blood. I hold it in, scared to spit and feed what ghost- or shadow-mouth'd come gaping out of the floor. But my back's curved, my shoulders down, my hands smooth and slow and unsudden: all the things that make a Telling, and from nothing else but habit, the habit of hearing something lost and in pain.

"What are you?" Jack booms at it, and the shadow *changes*. Its limbs grow darker, thicker, strong. It pours together like water coming down the drain and I can see pupils, lashes, the fold of a loose shirt made of dark. It narrows into waist and widens to hips, and the boards creak underneath it as its weight settles in.

I'll be your rose, it says suddenly, clear. Fifty voices collapsing into one, and it's one like a bell, boy-girl clean, touched with the most terrible yearning. *I'll be your Beast. Just take me away from here.*

Whisper steps back, and she's the color of dead things by torchlight. "Corner?"

Don't call me that, the shadow whispers, soft and plaintive. *I don't like it when they call me that name.* It leans toward my torch like a cupped loving hand. The first bit of flame nibbles at the cheekbone, the chin. I yank it back, and it leans farther. A little hole burns into the delicate curve of shadow-jaw.

"What then?" I ask, frantic. *Ask something. Ask anything.* "What's your name?"

Angel, it says, and the flames lick at its face, reach from brand to shadow-skin and catch the edge of that soft shy smile. I toss the brand right down to the floor, but it's much, much too late. *My mama said I was her little angel, and God loved me like every other —*

The fire takes its mouth first. It doesn't struggle while the fire eats it up, head to tips of the fingers to toes, and finally smolders out on the scorched wood floor. A painting of black ash in the shape of a living body. A stain on the floor like any other.

"We killed it," I manage.

"Nuh-uh," Jack says, hoarse and quiet like funerals. He tucks his gloves back on, face bent to that smear on the floor and not looking away. "It chose."

I spare a good look at Jack, and his eyes are tired like a day-and-night duty in the hot-hate sun. "If it chose, that means it's a thinking thing," I say. "That wasn't a thing from the sewers." He gets it: *That wasn't monsters.* You can tell the Whitecoats by the smoothness 'round their eyes, and you can tell monsters because they never, never weep.

But he doesn't reply, just looks over at Whisper hunched over the floor and pats my shoulder. *Hush,* says that pat, better than any word would. *Between us.*

I hush.

Whisper swears a little on the ground, and when I hurry over, her fingers are trying to piece together the shredded mess of Atticus's file. "It's gone," Whisper says, and her face is fury-bleak.

"Goddamn," Jack sighs, but his heart ain't in it. He's too far away, in the land of *hush.* He lifts her up with an offered hand, still looking half over his shoulder at that smear on the floor. "Wanna check the other cells," he says after a moment.

Whisper gathers up the last tears and pieces of the file in one of her fluttered skirt pockets. "Not leaving anything more of us here," she says, and caresses them through the cloth. I take her hand when she's done. It's cold and tight, not soft no more; tighter yet as we step through the door to Isolation, over the spilled-out and burned-in shadows.

My brand is running down, running out. I shrug the burned-up rags onto the floor and stomp them careful, twisting my shoe on the embers 'til I know they're truly out. I cough at the risen dust, suck in a steady breath.

I let it out slow, and someone lets a breath out after me.

"Someone living," Jack calls low and shrugs off his gloves again, quick-step moving to the last unopened cell. *Shouldn't have put down the fire*, I think, but fire don't do nothing against the living. I loose Whisper's hand and follow Jack in.

When I catch up his back's straight, his fists open; everything in his body saying *nothing threatening*. And it's not: a tumbledown pile of pants and arms, gleam-pale and unmoving. Somewhere underneath it all, a glint of eyes. "Hello?" I try, but it don't move, don't speak. *Dying*, I think, and then the air shifts in the eaves and my nose finds the musty-sweet smell of flowers.

"Violet," falls out of me, horrified, and the broken pile of woman moves.

Whisper shoves past me hard, rushes to the side of the tumbledown blanketed thing. "Vee?" she murmurs, stricken, and carefully lifts her chin to the light.

I don't see the face. But I see Whisper's break into cracks and lines and mess. "Oh, Vee," she chokes, wide-eyed and terrible. "Oh no, oh no, my Violet —"

It takes two of us to haul Violet up to sitting. She doesn't help; she's limp like a dead thing in our hands. Violet stares straight forward without blinking, eyes red and dry from staring so long. Nothing moves, nothing but her fingers *taptaptap* and a little smack of lips so we know for sure it's her. I swallow. Wave a hand in front of her gaze, back and then forth again. She doesn't follow.

"What's wrong with her?" I whisper, throat ache-straining, picturing tunnels and houses and all the corners of Safe stacked full of people unseeing, limp and robbed of everything but breathing.

Nobody answers.

Whisper leans down to the curve of Violet's ear, and her lips move urgent, words that I know aren't made for me. She murmurs and sings and cajoles for too long while I hold Violet's shoulders up from sagging, and when her voice dies down there's something ugly in it, ready to break.

"Whis?" Jack asks, soft, too soft.

"There —" Whisper halts, and her voice is queer and small. "There ain't no ghost in her."

"What's that mean?" *Dead meat*, my hands on her shoulders tell me. *It means she's nothing but dead meat.*

"It means gone," Whisper says, breathless. "Lost her mind."

"She was never Sick —" I choke out, and bite my lip.

"Not Sick," Whisper interrupts, harsh like Atticus scared, and she never interrupts; she speaks ladylike and precise like her mama and papa trained her to do. "Lost her mind."

"Not lost," Jack murmurs, back in the shadows. "Stolen."

We carry Violet out into the hungry green yard. There's no shadows left to follow us.

Violet stumbles. We gotta lift her up good over the grass and potholes, dragging her feet in a way that makes me want to cry, until Jack just swears a long tangle of words I was never, ever supposed to say and lifts her with one arm behind her knees, one under her shoulders; carries her like a child to the chest. A glitter of electricity plays on the metal of her allergy bracelet.

"Whisper," Jack says, and Whisper undoes the bracelet's catch. I think she's gonna pocket it, keep it secret and close and safe, but her fist closes about it tight enough that I feel the dent of metal in my own flesh. She's still for a long moment, two, eyes shut against something she won't yet deign to see.

"Whis?" Jack says again, gentler, and shifts Violet's hanging weight in his short, rough arms.

"I wish this place never was," she says, and opens her eyes to stare a stare so full of grieving I want to fly into her arms.

"Won't be, soon," is all I can say.

"That's *not good enough*," she spits, hair tangled, eyes sparking, and still I'm watching the hand with Violet's bracelet in it closed tight as the Pactbridge door.

My hand in my pocket closes on something else. Something strong for reassurance, folded and sharp. Six matches wide.

"Houses burn," I say to Whisper, and the hand tightens into a fist.

The grass rustles. Falls silent.

"Then burn it," she says, and stalks across the long-grown lawn.

Jack looks at me. I look at him.

I pull the first match and strike a light.

There's no getting the smoke off us.

The smoke of houses burning is more sewer-thing than friend; rank and slippery and foul, following you down the streets, through the alleys where every electric light sputters dark from Jack Flash's passing. The smell sticks; marks you out different for the police who come squalling through the afternoon, too late to save what used to be Lakeshore Psychiatric. Marks you Freak.

When we get back to Doctor Marybeth's, I'm sure she knows what we've done.

But: "Oh lord," she says, not to us but at us, and takes Violet off Jack's failing arms to help her safe indoors.

"Water," she snaps, and lays Violet out on her stuffed red couch. I stare for a second. Violet's still and stiff like Jack's face when he tells the Tale of the lightning. Doctor Marybeth runs one hand through her hair and glares at us. "I need water and my rounds bag, *now*."

Whisper scatters up the stairs for the bag. I hurry into the kitchen and fill a clean glass right up with cool clear water. My fingers leave black smudges on the crystal.

"This 'nuff?" I ask, small, and Doctor Marybeth takes it without a second glance.

She listens to Violet's heart. She listens to her breath, light and choosy as it is. She drips the water down Violet's throat with a tiny glass eyedropper, and all the while we sit in the parlor chairs watching, watching like a violation, too scared to look away.

Violet's chest rises and hitches and sinks all out of tune, and I can't bear to look away in case the breath I miss is the last. At least Ariel isn't here. Safe with Beatrice and probably mad at me — and that gives me a little unfunny twitch of a smile. Burning mad at me and with Beatrice: living, breathing, safe.

Violet stares on at a nothingness. Finally I close my eyes against it, shutting out the bad things, the dark. All I see in my eyelids is that awful stare on Mack, on Scar, on Heather.

After an age and a half Doctor Marybeth sits back, lets her stethoscope slide down onto her belly instead of holding it up high. "She's gotta go to the hospital."

My skin goes cold.

"No," Whisper says somewhere behind me. "No way in *hell*."

"She has to." Doctor Marybeth scrubs her eyes. Her voice is heavy, beat. "She can't eat. She can't sit up. She's *catatonic*."

I don't know catatonic. But Violet doesn't look up, doesn't speak while we talk over her head. Spit gathers in the side of her mouth, brought on by her mouth music, the smacking clasping sounds she always makes. I watch it fill up, overflow, sitting in my chair shivering and forgot.

"No hospitals," Whisper says. Her eyes are full of tears; unlike Jack or Ari or me, she doesn't look away when she's crying. She's not ashamed. "Atticus said no —"

"Atticus is dead," Doctor Marybeth's voice cracks. "And there's no one to take care of her."

"There's us," Whisper keeps on. "Same as it's always been."

"You?" And Doctor Marybeth laughs, not a happy laugh. "Can *you* do it? Can you change her pants and put the spoon down her throat? Can you draw the kind of power it takes to run an ECG?" She takes in a shaky breath, and when I dare to open my eyes, her hands are tight and round on the tops of her knees. "You can't. Because you don't even have downstairs right now, so *fuck* what Atticus said."

Jack stands up. I suck in a breath and hold it, not making one little sound.

But she's crying too. There's wet all over Doctor Marybeth's cheeks and dripping off her chin, and Jack just leans forward and puts one heavy-glove hand on hers, smoothes it down from a tight knobbed fist into flatness, palm down on her slacks.

"Trust *me*," she says, and she's pleading, she's leaned over the coffee table and taken Whisper's hand. "I got you out. I sent you supplies that might've cost me my license, never mind my goddamned job. I've kept this secret for twenty-three years and you still won't trust me to do right."

"It's not you —" Jack starts, rough.

"Oh, it is," she snaps, and pushes herself to her feet. "With your stories. If you can't tell the difference between good medicine and bad after all this time —"

"It's not just stories!" Whisper screams, and everyone else flinches back. "They *did* those things, they happened, and it'll happen again and take a *look* at her, just look!"

Doctor Marybeth shudders in place. "They did those things. Don't you even *think* you have to tell me that."

"You want to give her to a —"

"I want to put her in a hospital," Doctor Marybeth says flat, "'cause otherwise she's going to starve and rot in the dark. And even all the things that happened to you in Lakeshore and all the stories you've blown up so big you can't see what's changed won't stop that from being cruel."

Jack's hands have fallen awkward to his sides. He puts them, then himself between Whisper and Doctor Marybeth, blocks the sight of one from the other. "Nobody's bein' cruel," he says, thick and uncomfortable.

Violet's chest rises, falls. The drapes flutter. They match Doctor Marybeth's sofa.

"You would be," Doctor Marybeth says, and turns her gaze to him, burning. "She'd end up in a little room trapped and hungry, and then *you'd* be the goddamned . . . the *Whitecoats* from all your terror stories."

"They're *my* stories," I whisper, and I wouldn't know that anyone hears except that Doctor Marybeth glances toward me, to my working tangled hands and eyes so big I can feel the strain in them, and her mouth goes tight and sorrowful.

"The things you teach your children," she says half to herself.

"So you don't care about us?" Whisper says, and she's gulping sobs. "So leave us alone. Let me take her home." But she's still sitting down, wringing her hands back and forth. The tears shake down her face in little pipe-falls and spray wild across the table. "You don't want us, *leave us alone.*"

"That's not what I said," Doctor Marybeth says quieter, and takes Whisper's hands in hers.

"You said we were Whitecoats —"

"That's not what I said," again, and her voice is smooth and calm again, a voice that's just as in charge as Atticus ever could be but soft and collected as my mama's. *Her doctor voice*, I realize. The one she uses to keep you still while the needle goes in or the baby comes.

"Anne, Annie," Doctor Marybeth says, and then the tears get in her mouth and make her stop for breath. "I love her too."

Whisper's mouth opens, then shuts, and she snatches her hands away and stuffs them behind her back. "Don't ever call me that," she croaks. "That's not my name anymore," before her voice fails and she bawls like a little baby, like a kid who'd never gone to Atticus and got their first lesson: that big kids are quiet, and big kids are sharp, and if the world cuts you, you never cry out loud.

DOCTOR MARYBETH'S TALE

I don't know Doctor Marybeth's Tale.

I never asked her.

CHAPTER
SIX

There are medical words on the Whitecoat papers Doctor Marybeth writes up to send Violet to the hospital; words I don't know. After our silent supper, a supper Whisper won't come down for, I ask Doctor Marybeth for them.

Jane Doe, she gifts me. That's the name for girls who don't have a name they know Above, like Violet. *Catatonic.* That's when someone won't move, won't talk, won't see. *Supervised care facility.*

That's a Whitecoat hospital.

She stops. "Don't hate me for this," she says, hands fidgeting on the papers, straightening them just so against the wood-grain lines of her polished kitchen table. In the other room, Violet lies hands tucked in her lap, staring at the swirls of white plaster on the ceiling. She don't blink. She don't speak.

Doctor Marybeth pronounced my ma dead when I was but three years old. She clipped the cord from my belly when I was born, and held my hand a long night when I was seven and my throat closed up with fever. "I don't hate you," I tell her.

I'm afraid to take her hand or smooth it down calm from a fist. I'm not Jack. I don't need to decide, though, because she takes mine, squeezes it; holds on too long.

I have to hide in the bathroom when the car comes to take Violet away. Passing or not, the Whitecoats — Doctor Marybeth calls them *paramedics* — will have questions. They'll want to know 'bout Violet's finding, the smell of smoke on her clothes. They'll want to know who the strange boy is. It's easier for her to lie to them if I'm not about.

"Lock the door, Matthew," she tells me as the knock raps on the front door, and I push the little brass button beside the bathroom doorknob three times to make sure it's locked tight. I sit on top of Doctor Marybeth's clean white toilet and stare at patterns on the brown-and-white tiled floor while Whitecoat boots stump down the hall past me. Stop in the parlor, and lay eyes and hands on Violet.

"Need to carry her," says a voice, burnt and thin. "The hall's too narrow for the stretcher."

"Shit," says another: prompt, sharp, sucked dry of anything good. "Help me lift."

I close my eyes, picture it like a Tale: his hands on Violet, taking Violet away. And reach out for a hand that ain't here to hold.

Ari. The idea comes without the asking: Ari carried away by Whitecoats with a grunt and a stomp, kicking, screaming. They'd put a needle in. They wouldn't want her changing while they did it.

Forget shadows. Forget ghosts. I should have gone back for her.

The Whitecoat feet tromp back up the hall, heavier this time, slower. "Bring the stretcher to the doorway," the second voice says, and it's strained from weight; and then muttered low, something nobody's meant to hear: "Don't you worry, now. We'll get you somewhere nice and warm."

The feet fade out, disappearing into the big cold world Above.

The silence is like buildings before they burn.

I get up. Turn the knob. Open the bathroom door a touch, just a handspan, and slide my head through the crack. Look down the hall through Doctor Marybeth's wide-open front door.

Everything outside is white lights. White hands, white as drowned blind mice, are putting Violet on a hard white bed with metal wheels that glimmer and force your eyes away. A white car's coughing stink into the air beside it, and the red-and-white plastic bar atop it glows, throwing that sharp light everywhere.

I watch Doctor Marybeth bend over the wheeled bed half-shadowed, her face closed up smooth and tight as a tunnel grave. She's not crying no more. *Atticus's lesson*, I think; *big kids are quiet, and big kids are sharp,* and I huddle tighter behind the thin, useless bathroom door, shaping words for it in my mouth. Tasting them quiet against the day when I can carve the Tale down on the door with the martyrs.

Doctor Marybeth sees them gone and then stands in the doorway a minute, two, letting hot thick air slide through the open door. I put my hands behind my back, fight the wanting to get up and close it, to draw her crook-elbow back inside.

When she does come back to me, her mouth's drawn small and her face is damp. "Nobody's admitted your others to the hospital," she says after a long moment. "I asked."

I should be relieved. Or terrified: *Hide Heather Mack lost in the dark.* "Oh," is all I say, and she closes the door.

We stand quiet for a long minute.

"That's what it's here for. The medical system," she says finally, soft so Whisper and Jack, locked upstairs in the attic room, won't hear her giving sedition into my ears. "It's to take care of those who can't care for themselves."

"Atticus and Whisper could care for themselves." I look down at the pale pinkish wall between the front window and floor. Doctor Marybeth's painted it for a rosy dawn; or so she told me, waiting for the car to come. I've not seen a dawn Above that was softhearted as that.

"Yeah," she says, and wipes her nose with a tidy pinch. "The problems start when you can't decide who can care for themselves and who can't."

The stubborn rises in me, hard as a grown-in crab claw. "And who says they get to decide anyway?"

We both know who *they* is. Doctor Marybeth looks away. She sits down right in the hallway and leans her head against the wall.

"You take an oath when you become a doctor," she says after a minute. Her hand goes up to her belly, just beneath her heart and breasts and the corner-crux of her ribs. My good clean mad fades away; that's where I keep my oaths too, sworn and private. Where Jack Flash taught me all good oaths stay. "They've changed it a lot. Things change. But you swear not to hurt anyone."

She settles her hands on her knees: rough skin, a lighter brown than my own. "Lakeshore didn't hurt most people. It was the patients who were going to hurt other people, or hurt themselves." She looks up at me, and her eyes are black and tired. "You don't see the worst of how people can end up. The real worst cases never make it down to Safe."

"Reynard made it," I say. "And Heather."

Reynard, who was Teller before me, crawled down to Safe. He near drowned in the sewer pipes, dragging himself by his elbows 'cause his legs didn't work right. My pa found him passed out at the gateway to the old sewers, exhausted, beard choked with filth and teeth bared with anger. Heather, who took Reynard's wheelchair after he died and went into the ground, was carried down. Mercy knew her from the same Whitecoat home built with ramps and lifts and buttons where once she'd been kept locked away. One night she and Mack went up without having a duty, and they carried Heather all the way home.

There were others Mercy wanted out; friends, Sick or Freak or in trouble. But we only had one wheelchair.

"That's not what I mean, worst," Doctor Marybeth says. Her eyes don't even flicker. "I don't mean physically. If the bad cases really did make it down to you, you'd have sent a lot more people out."

Suddenly I get it. She means the screamers. Whisper talks sometimes about them: screamers, cutters, ones who'd trip you in the dinner line and smile dog-tooth smiles. *Sent a lot more people* — I turn full to Doctor Marybeth. "You knew 'bout Corner."

"Yeah," she says, like a kid caught filching paper to doodle.

"What happened?" I ask, and this time I hold her eye, try to push the Tale free just by force of looking. Not a hand on the back, not encouragement gentle and soft. *Tell me a Tale. Tell me true.*

"She wouldn't say the whole," Doctor Marybeth says, quieter than sedition, or shadows, or ghosts. "She came to me half past midnight, and wouldn't let me near." She wraps her arms around herself like restraints, showing me the weight and heft of Corner. "Stayed the night, and all she said was she was never going back."

"You didn't know it was Killer," I say, hushed with the thought of Corner's bloodtouch bloodstain hands wrapped 'round Doctor Marybeth's crockery; Corner's body curled up in the upstairs bed with the big eagle quilt about its shoulders. My arms prickle where they clutched it three nights past.

Doctor Marybeth lowers her arms slowly to her sides. "Matthew," she says, careful and delicate as bad news. "I don't think she killed."

I watch her. Blink once, twice. That can't be telling true.

Yes it can, says my gut and head and heart, thick and smug 'cause they've known it all along. That there were holes and tatters in the Tale taught to me. *Oh, it can.*

"Oh?" I manage, ugly little droplet of sound. Doctor Marybeth nods once, still studying me, watching me as Whisper does: that same look of mingled sadness and care that makes me turn aside. She reaches out a hand and I pull mine away, fingertip-small. Enough to make her rest hers back on the beat-up rug; on the floor.

"They'd fought before, of course," she starts, like it's *of course* to think of Atticus and Corner together, in love, fighting. "Not a lot came of it. Corner would sleep somewhere else, go walking. I caught them in the middle of it once, about turning pages fast enough, of all the little things, and they were both so embarrassed. . . ."

I study the pattern of the carpet: a double-headed bird, all in red. Two beaks open wide, two sets of claws. A Beast.

"She came up that night and I thought something'd happened, someone was ill or the roof had fallen in. But she said everyone else was fine, just . . . she wasn't going back to him." A pause. "That exactly. Wasn't going back to him. And asked me for a place to stay the night.

"You didn't know Corner," she says. "You don't know how much it was for her to ask for anything. They were all that way in the beginning, but her the worst. So I gave her the spare room. And I begged her to stay until I could get to the bottom of it."

"How long?" I ask, hollow-voiced and hushed.

"Three days," and now the guilt's in, the ache of someone else's Tale coming through her voice into her restless hands. She plucks at the fringe of the carpet, braids it, discards it. "On the second day I went down to Safe."

Doctor Marybeth is always sent for. There is always someone with a light to guide her through the new tunnels, the old tunnels, the sewer. "I didn't know you knew the way," I say awkward, knowing that this is real secrets now, the kind that would get people in trouble if Atticus were still living and the world not upside down.

"I remembered the way." She's calm and neutral, watching me just as much as I'm watching her for every little flick and fillip of voice. "One day there was going to be an emergency and there'd be no one to hold my hand. So I —" she pauses. Out the rightmost edge of my eye I catch a sharp, small smile. "— I counted the turns."

I whuff. My papa's snort. Don't underestimate those Above.

"So I went down to Atticus," she says, and the smile sinks back into her cheeks to drown. "They'd taken away her Sanctuary."

I wasn't the Teller when Corner's Sanctuary was took — Reynard was. I was nothing but my papa's little boy with a small gift for the Telling, and I watched the taking-away of Sanctuary from behind his stone-steady legs with a fear I didn't have words for. I remember jostling; I remember Atticus saying the terrible click-sharp words.

I remember what color Atticus's eyes were when he exiled the first Beast from Safe.

I don't remember Doctor Marybeth there. But Papa had his big hand on my head all through, and when it was over he took me back to the house he and I shared once my mama was gone and told me, serious and quiet, what it meant to be Killer. Why it was a thing grave enough that someone would ever have their Sanctuary taken away.

That it wouldn't happen again. That I was Safe.

Last time.

My belly turns with a sudden, sharp little terror. "You didn't see him do it, did you? You weren't there for it all."

The look Doctor Marybeth gives me is sharp and peculiar, and "No," she says. "Not until the end. Not 'til it was over."

I'm shamed at how relieved I am to hear those words.

"I got . . . upset with him," Doctor Marybeth says, in a house Above with hardwood floors and worn-patched carpets, in a place where I have no Sanctuary and nobody cares 'bout the Tales of Safe. "I said things that couldn't be taken back. How he could ever throw her out over one of their spats . . ." She closes her eyes. "And then he showed me Jonah's body."

The knot in my belly hardens. "I thought you said it wasn't Killer."

"She wasn't," Doctor Marybeth says soft. "I got an autopsy later." She glances at me to make sure I know *autopsy* and I do. Another Whitecoat wickedness; the sundering of the dead. "Jonah's heart gave out. That was all. He had one of his seizures in the tunnel and he died."

"That's something Corner could do. With the blood-touch," I argue, like I don't already believe her, like I haven't known the story of Corner's exile was rotten since the day I was first asked not to Tell it no more.

"Maybe if she was still in the tunnel. But not from my top bedroom," Doctor Marybeth says. "And Atticus would've known that, if he'd been thinking past his hurt pride. He would have known it cold." She pauses. "I'm sure he came to regret that after."

We're quiet a long minute. Together. Apart.

"I got back Above and told her. I thought maybe if she let it cool he'd listen to reason, understand she wasn't in the tunnels that night, wasn't hurting anyone. Or Whisper and Violet and Scar would talk sense into him; he was at least listening to the other founders in those days. And if not . . ." She stops, swallows back too hard for regular spit and air. "If not, I'd help her find a new name, a job. Somewhere to live."

"Above," I say soft, so soft.

I barely hear the next part, no matter how strong all my straining. "I said I'd keep her safe," Doctor Marybeth whispers, and leans her head back against her sunshine wall. "Except in the morning, she was gone, and it wasn't back to Safe. And that's when the trouble with the shadows started."

My breath catches. Doctor Marybeth's eyes are shining wet.

"There was no telling him anything after that, you know. After people started to see things in the sewers — even before anyone got hurt. For Atticus, that proved everything: the killing, the motive, all of it. There was no explaining. And —" a shrug. A spill of crying that she doesn't move to wipe away. "That was the end."

"The end," I repeat, hollow. My hand twitches; I should paint this, carve it; it's a Tale of Safe. But I've got no paints, no carving knife, and I don't know if it'd go on the martyrs' door or my own. I put the hand in my jeans pocket and it sits itself still. "Who knows this?"

"You." The corners of her mouth tighten. "Me. Jack."

"Jack?" I ask, startled, remembering his hush-up looks and his *laters* — "Jack doesn't come Above."

"No," she says, and looks me full in the face. "I go down."

Oh.

"What're you going to do?" she says after a minute, still crying midnight silent, chin still lifted high.

"Corner killed Atticus," I murmur, turning it over in my head, my free hand cupped like a ball around something too big to hold on to. "And its shadows . . . they hurt Violet. And Whisper's ghosts, and Mack, and Mercy. And . . . and Seed." My throat gets hard and hot. "And I don't know who else yet."

"You don't know she killed Atticus."

"I saw it with my own two eyes," I snap, and the memory of pressure flickers beneath my right one, where something that knew my name — a shadow, a monster, low-voiced Corner with the bloodtouch in its furious hands — asked me for a Tale. "I don't know what we're gonna do," I admit, and close my hand. "Everything's broken."

There's no sound but the wind.

"It —" she pauses, and then takes a deep breath. "What do you need?"

I bite my lip. Think about monsters and not-monsters, and one lone shadow weeping. 'Bout all the Tales that don't get told no more, and all the things we don't know about Corner.

"We found Atticus's file," I start.

She shakes her head, out at the corner of my sight. "They don't keep files at Lakeshore. When they closed it, they transferred it all."

" 'Phantom limb syndrome. Post-traumatic stress,' " I quote her, and she blinks. "We need —" I pause, wet my bitten sore-chewed lips. "We need Corner's file. We need to know about Corner."

Doctor Marybeth puts a hand on my shoulder. Awkward, like she don't know whether to be a mama or a friend or someone who oughtn't to touch at all. "I know where the records were moved. You'll have them. You'll have them by tomorrow evening."

She's so relieved to give something, to trade something good for Violet and those white, white hands that I feel like dirt, like a crawling thing to smile. To take her hand, say "Thank you, Doctor Marybeth," like a child.

And then to ask, quiet like sedition, "There's another file too."

● ○ ●

When I get upstairs, Whisper's perched in the attic bedroom in a pile of skirts and tumbledown, eyes reddened and living. She looks up at me from the center of a circle of paper scraps that radiates out like a summoning sign. Doctor Marybeth's spare bed's been moved to the side, and underneath it is dust and dust that goes on for half an age.

Dust is old skin, I remember; Atticus's teaching. Could be Corner's dust. I step out of it and wrap my arms around my chest, like Doctor Marybeth did, to hold out the sudden cold.

"It's done," I say low, so to not disturb her ghosts. "I need to go get Ari."

Whisper nods once, face bleak as the night sky Above, before turning back to her pictures.

"Bring that one to the left," she says, and Jack looks up from the circle he's pacing round Whisper's scrap-heap fortress, shifts a flick of paper to where she's pointing.

"What're you doing?" I blurt, all knees and elbows, and Whisper settles another curl of scorched notepaper a precise finger sideways.

"I'm going to call out Atticus," she says simple, and the hard, frowning concentration that's normal Whisper, regular Whisper with a broken pipe or food shortage, is back in her face. "It'll take half an hour. Close the door."

The sun's already going down. Ari'll be mad at me for sure now. Bea might be too; I told her I'd be back before dark for bottles, and Bea I owe Sanctuary and don't want to displease. But I'm sworn to keep Safe. To do my best for Safe.

I'm sworn to be here now.

So, "Why?" I ask.

"Because, Teller," Whisper says, like I've just asked her why rock is hard. She inclines her chin downstairs, touches a finger to her nose. Doctor Marybeth. She doesn't want Doctor Marybeth knowing.

There's a tight seam about her eyes that says more: *Because I need Atticus.*

The frown surfaces before I can turn away. I know she sees it because she draws her shoulders up and looks at me until I close the door behind me. "It's her house," I say. Jack keeps up his pacing. He don't say a word.

"She sent Violet away," Whisper replies, and Jack's frowning now too, but he shakes his head once and lets be. I look over Whisper's head at him. We need to talk, me and Jack. Somewhere we don't need warnings. Somewhere quiet.

But now he stoops down and moves one last finger of paper just so, and Whisper spreads her hands for us to give her a good lot of room. I back right up to the door, feel for the handle — too high, at my side. If Doctor Marybeth comes upstairs, I can warn them, or her. I can get it open quick, or keep it shut.

There's a funny feeling in my belly at the thought of the ghost of Atticus.

"Maybe I should go back down —" I say, and Jack quells it with a look. I know he knows what I really mean: *I don't want to be here.*

"Need you, Teller," he says, rough.

I lean back against the door, and Whisper starts to sing.

There ain't words to this one; not that I can pick. It's low and keening and roundabout like the way Whisper sings at funerals; the songs she makes when we put our people's bodies in the ground. It's a sound that wraps 'round an absence, and the shape of the absence is Atticus, and Whisper sings.

Something answers from the bits and snips and shards of Atticus's file. It comes like a chill, the chill that hangs in the pipes sometimes and in the Cold Pipes all the time, the one I thought once might mean ghosts though until today, there was no way to prove it. It rises from the floor, a seeping brush of cold painted right in a circle, thus to thus.

Whisper squints, leans in, not breaking the stride of her sweet-wail, mumbling song. "Atticus?" slides swift into it, *Atticus-Atticus-Atticus* sibilating into her hum and building, drawing circles 'round her circles of paper and blood. The cold gathers in. The cold shimmers.

"I can see it," Jack says, low and surprised. Nobody ever sees Whisper's ghosts; nobody would believe in them but for the things they tell her that always prove sound and true. We don't ask those kinds of questions in Safe. Not against people who've earned and kept their Sanctuary.

But: "I see it too," I say, and Whisper scrunches up her face even further in scolding us to silence.

The ghost looks like a new carving. Its lines are thin and tentative and it's all washed-out color, scratched on the air so light there's no saying for sure that it's really there. It looks like memory badly kept; a six-foot picture from Whisper's Polaroid, half-developed and wasted. I can't tell when its mouth sets to moving, but I *feel* the air change when it speaks.

"Atticus," Whisper breathes, and falls silent herself to listen.

"What's he say?" Jack says, and I search it for arms, for lamplit, glowing eyes, to see if they're red or sun-golden.

"He —" She stops, sits back on her hands. Her face's gone soft for a moment at the sight of him, the sight that must be so much stronger for her than it is to our stupid, ghostless eyes. And then her voice catches, harsh and broke: "He don't know who we are."

It hits me in the belly where my true oaths live.

"How can he not know us?" Jack asks, and his arms hang loose and useless, his mouth open on other words he don't yet want to say.

"Lost his mind," I choke out. "Stolen."

"No," Whisper breathes. "No. It's not our Atticus," and she leans in listening, seeking. Her hand strays to a shard of paper, smudged with Whitecoat notes. "It's Atticus from Lakeshore. It's Atticus twenty years past."

"But he wasn't *dead* twenty years past," I snap too-loud, half not knowing why 'cept that Atticus is *gone*, real gone and not just dead, and that's the end. We're all alone up here.

"He wants his doctor," Whisper breathes, voice high and cracking. "He thinks he's dreaming. He . . . he wants to go home."

Only then do I look hard, look through the mess of paper and strange-tinged air to the edges, the lines: see how soft the arms, how small the shimmer of claw at the end of them. How skinny and fierce the man is behind them. See the lines, and how they're drawn with darkness.

Whisper smiles that twisted, sad smile, and drops her hands to her lap. "He wants Corner."

"Send him back," Jack snaps.

"Jack —"

"It's *not him*."

Then the bed-dust rustles like a train's coming through, pushing all the wind in the world ahead of it on its metal cheekbones. The dust builds up and up, pulling into a hand, a small nose, a sharp-boned familiar face.

You said you'd love me, it whispers to the sometime-ghost of Atticus, and its voice is boy-girl and broken and clean as a bell.

Jack shrugs his gloves off and drops them to the floor.

The ghost of Atticus opens its mouth, and closes it, and reaches out one yearning hand.

The lights go wild, sparking and flailing and flickering in their sockets. "Jack, no —" I get out before they blaze bright as high daylight and *pop pop pop!* go the lamp and bathroom bulbs as their fire flows into his hands. Jack's fingers spark as he plunges them deep into the heart of the thing that's not our Atticus and burns it from the chill heart out, touches it with lightning from bone to not-there bone.

The dust-shadow watches.

The dust-shadow screams.

The door bursts open behind me and I yell, grabbing for anything that'll keep shadows off, bolsters and pillows and the ruined bedside lamp, not thinking 'bout how shadows aren't big and warm with eyes dark and scared — and then it's Doctor Marybeth standing in the door, and my arm's raised up to strike. I throw myself back, stumbling into Whisper's careful-laid circle, slip on a snip of paper and fall against the bed-mattress hard.

"What's this?" Doctor Marybeth breathes, faint and still piercing, and then there's a rush of light, a rush of dark, and the shadow-thing is kneeling in a midnight puddle at her feet, chill arms wrapped 'round her knee-bones, aching with shadow tears.

Doctor give me something give me poison give me pills I can't bear it, it rolls one word over the other, and buries its face against her, half-solid and strange.

Doctor Marybeth stumbles. "Mare!" Jack yells, and his voice is cold with fear. But the shadow moves with her, fluid and swift, moving not-arm with her leg and not-face with the rest of her, flickering into position knee-bent at her feet. *Give me something to sleep tonight*, it begs, and flecks of midnight tear-dust scatter on the floor.

Doctor Marybeth breathes once, shallow, her face gone sick underneath her skin. "Corner?" she says small, and the shadow looks up.

That's not its name, I almost say, but Doctor Marybeth is shivering, shivering blue as she reaches down to lay a finger on that light-mote, broken face. "Oh, little child," she says, teeth shaking in the way of her words. "Oh, *tsujus*."

"Let it go, Mare," Jack says low, his hands crackling sparks. "It's nothing real."

"It's bewitched her," Whisper says, and the first shadow-finger sinks into Doctor Marybeth's skin.

Whisper's on its back before I draw breath, yanking at its narrow throat before I can yell. Her hands go straight through. Her ghost-talk rises to screaming, the first time I've ever heard it not low, not sweet or quiet, and her arms pass through and through again as four more fingers soak through Doctor Marybeth's slacks. Then an arm, a shoulder.

"Jack, kill it!" Whisper wails, tumbling back on her bottom, panting against the floor.

"I can't, I'll shock her —" he snaps. My hands are in my pockets looking for fire, but I can't do nothing with fire. It'll burn the house and scorch the rugs and take the whole thing down, and we've already burned one house today and it was a house we hated.

"My little *tsujus*," Doctor Marybeth says, her eyes far away, off in another place or time or maybe just dying of shadow's-touch. "I'll go to him. I'll make it right. Let things calm down; you know he won't stay angry —"

I'm scared I'm scared I'm scared I'm scared washes over me like rain, and the shadow's head sinks into Doctor Marybeth's belly.

"I'll take care of you," she whispers. "You stay here where it's warm." Her hand flickers over the shadow-head. Over her own belly.

The hand drops before she drops to the floor.

"Mare!" Jack screams, and scrambles over. I can't see her chest. I can't see if it rises or falls. "Teller! Give me wind!"

Flicks of paper scatter as I kick them out of the way, walk and stumble and crawl to Doctor Marybeth's side. *Airway Breathing Circulation* I remember from way back, Atticus's lesson, though delivered by someone else's hands 'cause Atticus couldn't clasp without pinching. Soft hands, and firm, grown-up hands. On my little-boy nose and chin to show me how.

Corner's hands.

I stutter, latch my left hand on to her nose and tilt her chin with my right, far up. "She's not breathing," Whisper wails, and I put my lips down to Doctor Marybeth's and blow.

There's a rhythm to it. One-two-three up-two-three and then take another breath and blow. I go four times before Doctor Marybeth shivers against my nose-pinch hand and coughs, and I back off fearing she's going to cough up shadow, like my mouth's not already been touching it for four breaths, four silent wind-touched three-counts where nothing else moved but the floorboards. But nothing comes back up. Her eyes flutter open instead, and she sucks in a deep, scraping breath.

"Oh God," Jack says, and collapses back to sitting.

I make it to the bathroom before I sick up. There's a grace in that.

Doctor Marybeth's breathing slow on the floor when I get back, my mouth sour and face damp from the cool water from her sink; from tears, from just reaction. I go back to where Whisper's kneeling, brushing Doctor Marybeth's hair off her forehead, all that mad and hate and mistrusting between them forgotten.

"Can you feel it inside?" she asks, big-eyed with a mama's fear.

Doctor Marybeth shakes her head. Her eyes are closed. She looks three-day-duty tired.

Jack says nothing. He kneels drawn-up next to Whisper, hands clasped tight in front of him like a kid expecting to get scolded; eyes heavy, hard, unknowable. His hands flicker with light. "You livin'?" he asks gruffly.

"Jack —" Doctor Marybeth says, hand outstretched to comfort or to take some, just to make sure he's real.

"Don't touch," he snaps, drawing his hands back. His gloves are still across the room. Doctor Marybeth jerks herself back as their hands get too close and spark.

"Sorry," Jack says, low to the edge of my hearing.

"S'okay," she says back, automatic, and leans eyes-shut against the floor.

"Let's get you into bed," Jack says, and delivers Whisper and me a look you don't gainsay. We take her by the arms, one each, and help her onto the mattress. She's cold, cold enough to prickle my fingers, but not blue-lips chill no more. Still, I tuck the blanket up under her arms, careful not to put her in too tight.

"It's all right," Doctor Marybeth says. It's weak enough that no one believes her.

"Hot tea," Whisper says to me. "Quickly."

I hurdle down the steps two-three at a time, tumble into the quiet kitchen fumbling for the kettle. It bangs too loud on the stove. My hands are shaking.

By the time I get back upstairs, Whisper's got a broom in hand. She's swept all the dust into a crumbling, tiny heap while Jack presses his thick gloves against Doctor Marybeth's forehead. He reaches for the mug without thinking, awkward; I know enough to hold it back until Doctor Marybeth looks up and takes it in her little, precise, Normal hand.

"Wasn't Atticus," Jack says, watching Whisper like he didn't notice my hand and Doctor Marybeth's, the clumsiness of his own. His color's high. I pretend for him too; he's earned a little pretending.

"Was so," Whisper says, and bends down with a dustpan. "It spoke his voice. It knew the way his sentences turned."

"It was a shadow," Jack says just in the same tone of voice, flat and factual and feeling just about nothing. "The shadows put on Corner too, just like real."

We don't look over our shoulders when we say the name no more.

Whisper gathers up all the little dust motes and takes them down the stairs, a quiet creak at each step telling just how careful she's walking. The back door opens when Doctor Marybeth's worked halfway down the mug of tea, and there's a flicker of flame out the high attic window. Dust doesn't burn so good. The flame is slow and dim.

When I look back, Doctor Marybeth's watching me, eyes too steady for almost dying. "Sorry," I mutter.

"Don't be," she says, and my hand starts shaking again, enough that she wraps it around her mug to keep it still as her eyes.

"You're not dead," falls out of my mouth. Or lost. Or blank Violet stolen.

But she doesn't even blink. "I'm not dead," she agrees, and takes another sip. She licks her lips after. They look cracked; little ridges of dead skin rising out of them. "I saw . . ."

I take her hand. Breathe in rhythm with the noise of Whisper's feet coming back up the steps. Put on my best Teller voice. "What did you see?"

She closes her eyes. The better to see it in the dark, maybe. "That last night with Corner." She licks her lips again. Her voice is all throaty and scraped.

"You remembered it," I fill in.

She shakes her head. "No," she says, "I saw it how *she* saw it."

I'm good and careful. My hand doesn't slip and spill hot tea all over the quilt Doctor Marybeth's mama made her.

"I see it," she finishes, and lets out a breath.

I put the tea down. Just to be careful and sure. Jack's at the door arguing with Whisper in a voice that's low, cupped-in, but he's listening, I think. Jack can't do nothing in his life if he can't take in three conversations word for word, strung together, all at once.

"Tell me?" I ask.

She tells me.

Corner's not scared.

Corner's got a cool and even calm that comes over its bones when bad things happen (it says in Doctor Marybeth's voice, through Doctor Marybeth's lips), and it's used enough to bad things that the edges of tonight are familiar. The edges of tonight are shadow-dark and worn, like it's every other bad night away from home.

(Shadow-dark? I ask her, choosing words right careful.

Yes, she whispers, and her eyes go far away again.)

This time, at least it's warm. This time, it's safe as safe can be Above, in Marybeth's attic room, under the quilt Marybeth brought from home in a folded brown-paper parcel after she got out of the Whitecoat school where they dumped all the kids of her kind. Marybeth's got no claw arms or bloodtouch and never cut herself even once, but she knows what it's like to be Freak: how the words on your tongue don't come out quite right to anyone, home or away. Marybeth's Safe.

(— and I watch Doctor Marybeth for wincing as these words fall from her tongue, but there isn't none. Just her far-gone eyes and her still small hands and the spirit of Corner telling me dark things, and true.)

It tells me 'bout cool and even calm, the kid-familiar smell of grass and trees; the smell of *never too late to blend in*, Pass quiet, prove them all wrong and build a life Above that'll last. Be a rocket scientist. Be a doctor.

Make your mama proud.

(And Doctor Marybeth's hand rises, and wipes away the tears.)

So when Marybeth gets back, you're ready. Ready to say *yes* to her and take her spare bed and helping hand, be done with him and Safe and all of it. Until you see the slack pallor of her face. The tight fist-curls of her hands.

Because there was a ceremony (you can see it). Because they burned your last year's offering in a special-made fire. They closed the big door to Safe at the end and it clanged and echoed, blowing out the silence.

Because *he* did. He led them, start to end.

I'll find you something, she says, a hand on your back that's not wanted there no more, breath in your hair where it's not wanted no more. Her hand and breath both shaking with rage. *I'll find you work. You stay with me. We'll get you a life that's real.*

But all you can say is *Doctor give me something give me poison give me pills*, the want to die getting harder and sharper with every breath, sharper than any time before or after Lakeshore. There's tears hot on your cheeks and it's shameful, the height of shame. The end of all your plans. Shut door. Unnamed. The Tale of how you came down never told again, and your name turned into *Killer.*

No no, she whispers. *Be strong. I know you're good and strong.*

You're not. (And here the voice stumbles, the bell-voice, the shadow-voice, tripping over broken-backed regrets.) Atticus is strong for the both of you, and you are —

You're alone.

And now Corner's mad.

And now Corner's scared.

"And she's gonna run away —" and Doctor Marybeth lets out a sob that ain't her own, hardly human and half shadow-talk but all real in its weeping. Whisper rushes over at the sound and takes her hand, brushes me aside not thinking, half-thinking.

"It's okay," she murmurs, smoothing out Doctor Marybeth's hair, running her fingers through its strands. "It's okay, dearie, it's okay."

I get up and snug my shoes on, tug the laces up tight. Check my pockets: matches in one, emergency money in the other, twenty-five dollars still secret, still snug. It's been more than half an hour, and half an hour matters, and I did a wrong thing today and I've gotta go fix it *now*. Before it's too big to take back. Before we're all alone, and I'm alone from my Ariel too.

Where'm I learning running? From Corner, maybe. From the shadow-taint that comes from fighting them, from shadows brushing up against your skin. Maybe from Atticus, passed on in the very air, after he made a mistake too big to take back and ran from it by pushing Corner out of Safe. I slept without my ma or pa for years inside his house, learning his lessons. Carving his histories into our people's good doors.

Atticus leaving. Corner leaving, no good-byes.

Whisper looks up as I get to my feet. "Where you going?" She's long-necked and alarmed, like a deer, a rabbit. Something that's scared that you'll move to hurt.

"To find my Ariel," I say, give her a last, twisted little smile, and go.

PAPA'S TALE

Papa didn't walk until his second birthday, and after that, it wasn't often.

(He told it softer 'cause I was his child. He told it to me long before I was the Teller, once it came clear that maybe one day I would be, and with it he put paper and stub-snapped crayons in my hands to teach me the art of clean straight lines. Whisper told me some when I was the Teller for true, and she told it softer too, running skirt between finger and thumb whenever she left a bad thing out. Reynard was the only one who didn't tell it soft, and he wouldn't tell it to me at all. *A boy can hear his own papa's Tale*, he said, with that quirk of the eyebrow and the jump his hands did to make up for his legs never working, *without going to pester the Teller.*)

(So I don't have the whole of it. I don't have the worst.)

Papa didn't walk until his second birthday, and after that they took him to the specialist to look at his feet.

Even as a baby, Papa's feet were hard like a lion's. The gold fur hadn't yet come in; the tough pads were soft and new from want of walking, and the nails were tiny if they were thick and sharp. It wasn't 'til he grew a little longer that his parents realized he wasn't a baby like their others.

Know this, he'd say: Your dadi and dada loved all their children. Back on the farm in the old country, they would never have minded, so long as I could walk and plant wheat and bring your dada water in the afternoons. I'd have danced in the Jaggo for your aunties' weddings. But here (and he'd stop, and gesture upward, taking in the whole of Above with his one scabbed muscled hand) here there are Whitecoats, and they knew much better than we did at home.

You listened to the Whitecoats. You did what they said.

They broke my papa's feet for the first time when he was three years old, and put them back together before he was four.

He didn't remember the first breaking. What he did remember was before it: a bright small room all glass and mirrors, white light on white walls, white tables. "Stand up," the head Whitecoat said to him, over and over, and took from him his mama's hand; *stand straight* even though the standing hurt him.

The Whitecoats came in and he stood for hours. They got him to stand wide, stand thin, poked at his feet with rods and took pictures, the flashes popping on all sides. The light snapped off the white walls and dazzled his eyes so he could no longer see his mama, standing with her five brown fingers pressed up against the thick glass window. He stood stripped down to his undies until his legs shook and he fell and cried for her, and the Whitecoats frowned at him and called for the breaking of his feet.

(*Maybe they wouldn't have done it if I didn't cry,* he never said, but he had a thin stern frown every time he told it, and by the time I was old enough to understand what that frown meant, he was dead and far past asking.)

There were leg braces (Papa took the grey crayon and drew braces). Every morning Dadi strapped him into the metal and leather and tightened them up, and Papa walked about the house hurting and hurting as the braces bent his feet Normal. "Be brave," his own papa said. Papa was brave.

When he could walk 'round the house ten times without falling they sent him away to school.

Papa watched the other kids run the track in gym class (he explained with a great relief how good it was that there was no such thing in Safe). He followed them around and around in circles from indoors, where he sat with his cane and leg braces, and bit his lip down until nobody could see him wanting. It's a bad thing to be caught wanting, he said. Especially when you could not run.

(*They didn't know what to do with my kind back then*, he'd say with a gentle smile, and I'd ask, *lion's-foot people?* and he'd laugh and laugh, his rich Papa laugh, and go *no no, people from Punjab. Indian people.*

One place Above was much like another for me, especially when I was knee-high to my papa and followed him everywhere except the dark duty shifts Above. *Do they now?* I asked him once, and the smile went away and his eyes looked elsewhere. *No*, he said. *They do not.*

Papa sad was frightening. I didn't ask again.)

They broke my papa's feet for the second time when he was ten years old, and put them back together to heal slow enough that he didn't go to school for three months. Papa didn't mind. He'd overstrained them, learning to run with the metal and buckles in the field behind school on empty summer nights. The other kids in school knew what to do with his kind, he said: shoving and teasing and bitter bite words. It was important to learn how to run. "You can't do this to yourself," his mama said, and she held his hand when they held the mask over his face to drive him asleep.

The braces were bigger. They stayed on longer. Papa had nightmares about walking man's-foot, wrong-foot, until his ankles snapped and the lion in him fled, growling, into the dark.

They broke my papa's feet for the third time when he was sixteen and old enough to really know pain. He screamed and screamed through the shot to take the hurt away, and screamed after when he woke up with his feet in plaster casts to make them grow out Normal. The lion-nails cut at the tight hard plaster. They curled in and cut his flesh, and it took two days of screaming to get them to open the casts at the toes.

Never again, he thought to himself, sharp and tossing in the nights where the pain from walking heel-toe like a man around the house five times, six times, seven, beat him down. Soon he would be a man grown up, and never again would the Whitecoats take hammer and scalpel to his toes.

Papa learned his own kind of walking.

He learned to pad soft and bent-kneed on his flexing lion's feet, and he followed his therapy careful to the letter except for the places it made him walk like a man. Lion's-foot men should walk like a lion. He walked the hunt.

Papa graduated from school three months after his nineteenth birthday. He walked bent-kneed and soft up to the stage to take his diploma and looked down from it, golden-eyed and quiet, upon the children who'd pushed him in the halls, or treated my braced-legs papa like he was stupid, or turned away because he was Punjab people and could not run.

And then he walked sure and careful all the way down to Safe.

(*How did you find it?* I asked, because he was the only person I could have ever put to the asking.

Papa grinned, and he swore me to keep it secret, made me promise on Safe and on my conscience and, the worst, the grave of my departed mama, who I dreamt of every night for a solid month after, rising up in sad disappointment if I dared to lie or tattle.)

How Papa found Safe is he watched. He put his foot in strange footprints, and they all led down and down. Because he didn't know what that meant, he began to hunt them. He followed the footprints back and forth from the sewer caps, down the ladders, along dark tunnels that he could only walk by feel, and all the while watched them, looking for their maker.

One night he hid, soft-foot, in the shadows of an alley when one of those sewer caps rose up. Four people came pouring in reverse out of the darkness, Atticus and Violet and Whisper and Scar, and left behind them, slip-scent quiet, Corner to close the lid.

(*Had Corner come up, I'd've been found out,* he said, smile crooked and funny and sharp. This was before Corner was exiled, before its name became a dirty word.)

Papa followed them, followed their footprints, placed his sharp-flex feet in each one and knew them for his prey. He traced them all the way to the back of a grocery, with its rattletrap door chained and locked to concrete to keep thieves away. Atticus cut the lock like paper with one sharp-edged claw. The other three crept in, and when they carried their crates and bags and boxes of cans down the alley and underground, Papa followed.

"I'm Freak too," he said when he walked in on them, all jumped-up panic to protect their roughed-out cavern. He showed them his feet. He Told them the three-times breaking of them, and he stood wide, stood thin while they ran their hands over the thick gold fur and nails and bone. "If you stay here for safekeeping, I should get to stay."

The first five talked about it for a long long time. Hours. Papa stood. There was no light but a candle. His legs shook.

He didn't cry.

One by one they bent their heads and agreed to it. Atticus and Corner told him to bend his head and gave him Sanctuary, and promised he wouldn't have to stand hard like so ever again. They built the big door and fit it with a lock, to keep intruders trapped outside, and they built the Pactbridge to it, in remembrance of their pact with Papa to let those who'd need their Sanctuary through. Those who could make it, cunning and sharp.

But Papa brought more home. He scoured the streets, pad-hunting, and he found people broken and scared and turned away. He whispered in their ears the right tunnel, the turns, the ways and ways of reaching where you might find Safe. When they arrived he stood off to the side, legs apart, feet bare, and reminded the founders with his presence of the pact they'd sworn to give Sanctuary.

Even I understood, young as young, why such a thing would have to be kept secret.

"Come," he'd said to Hide's pa, and Seed little and strange, and my mama when she wasn't mama but just Lise Marie Tremblay and wore damp scarves wrapped around her throat even on the hottest summer days, to hide the gills that gasped for breathing at the base of her narrow throat.

"Come," he said to them, and took their hands, not planning to let go.

And they ran far.

CHAPTER
SEVEN

This time I don't walk to Bea's brown building on the park. Doctor Marybeth gives me a token, gold and silver and light on the palm, and writes down directions for buses.

I've never been on a bus before. The rules of Passing Above are all about staying inconspicuous, staying out of places where people can have a good stare or rub up close, and that means traveling by foot. But it's been more than half an hour, a whole evening into night, and I've been away from my Ariel too long.

The buses hiss softer than trains in the night, red-striped and lamplit just like the Whitecoat vans, but hum steadier, cleaner than that. I drop in my token and ask for the transfer just like Doctor Marybeth said, and the tall tired brown man driving hands me a slip of paper with numbers, cuts, and triangles all through. I hold it light and careful, trying to keep my sweat off, and take an empty seat.

The moving makes me sick, even sitting down. It's too fast and unsteady: a rockless little tunnel that *moves*.

When the driver calls out hoarse the stop I want, I step back down into the dark on legs I don't trust to hold me.

I recognize the shrubs and the rise of the street, even though it's dark and nothing looks quite the same. It's full night now, full of crawling bugs and creaks and crickets. I tuck away my map and walk careful, heel-toe, down, down the sidewalk to where Bea's building sleeps.

Where my Ariel is.

I can't think what to say to her. It's never been me who's run off and left, just her fleeing something and the silence after, where I don't ask and she's not gonna tell me. Explaining's a new turn for me; explaining how I've done wrong. The thought squeezes my heart like I've been running all night.

"You're a Teller," I scold myself, and pick up my drag-foot-slow pace. "So Tell it."

There are shadows who aren't just Killer, sometimes it starts, and then *Let me tell you a Tale about Corner*, and sometimes just *I should have come back for you and I don't know why I'm so taken with running. Sit with me, hold my hand. We'll whisper it all into the dark.*

I still don't have nothing good to say when I walk into the entryway, boxed in with glass and people-smell and sharp-nose chemical things. I push the button and wait for the ringing; push the button and pretend to be brave.

The "Hello?" comes up from sleep, dense and annoyed, Atticus's eyes when they're tinged with orange and just looking to be mad.

"Hello," I say back, not sure if you have to talk into the speaker, and there's quiet. "It's Matthew," I say, and the door buzzes like a whole twisting city full of bees. I jump back with my hand in my pocket and nothing to throw, and then the sound goes out like candle flame.

"*Open* it," Bea's voice says over the speaker. The buzzing comes again, and this time I pull the sticky metal handle and the door comes open, asking me into the cold and musty lobby.

They're waiting in the doorway when I tromp upstairs, seven flights with my heart drumming double like it's the end of the world. I round the corner and they're all peering out, talking hush-voiced, even husher once they hear my tread on the carpet.

None of them are beautiful, sunshine-golden.

Still mad. I swallow, having known it all along. I stick my hands in my pockets so I can press the nails in and stop myself from just turning around and leaving again in front of every single stupid not-Freak person watching me out that door.

"You missed bottles," Cat says, her mouth scrunched up and blotchy.

"I'm sorry," I say, like someone who don't really mean it. I sound little and mean, not proper like a Teller. I straighten my back, straighten myself out. "I just wanted to come for Ari."

"Oh, come on —" Darren says, and shuts up quick when Beatrice looks him straight in the eye. Looks at me.

"Matthew," Beatrice says, and her hand's too tight on the door. "We thought she went after you."

There's no cold like shadow-cold, the touch of something not-alive and hurting and hating on your skin. But there's cold near it. There's the cold that gets to your skin from the inside coming on out.

My hands start shaking, this time for good.

"Shit!" Bea says, her big strong hands going 'round my arms hard enough to hurt. "Inside," she snaps, and woe to the person who disobeys. I get my feet back, get them moving automatically like they're walking Sentry through the apartment door.

It don't get warmer once the door's safe shut.

"When did you last see her?" Bea asks with me barely in the door. The rest of her people back up a little, retreat to chairs or the kitchen or the bedroom, too wound up to go too far. I fold onto the mattress on the floor. Her hair's still on the blanket, twisted into the pillowcase.

"This morning," I say, thinking that it couldn't possibly be only this morning that I left with Whisper's ghosts on the long walk to Lakeshore. And then she went away. Somewhere. I don't know where. My eyes hurt, sudden; remembering how long since they've last had sleep, and how many ways there are to go Above. "When I went out for my duty."

Bea looks at me strange, and I bite my lip. It's *job* here, not duty. I'm not Passing right.

Oh lord my Ariel's gone.

"I was going to be back by sundown," I say. How many bees are there Above? How many people?

"None of the food's gone," Cat says quiet to Beatrice, like I'm not meant to hear, like I'm not right there.

None of it's gone. She can't be far.

"Where might she go?" Bea asks. "Has she got other friends in town?" *Other*, I repeat gratefully, like it'll make a difference. Bea's pacing like Jack, fingers twitching, hands clasped behind her back. Asking all the right questions I don't got. And she ain't just asking me. She looks 'round the circle, one by one, and a few turn their heads away.

There's a soft closing of the bathroom door. I blink, and count again who's here and who's not.

Darren.

I think about their snapping, their avoiding, their fighting, and everything behind my eyes goes red, like Atticus's.

"To Doctor — to our friend's, maybe," I say, licking my lips to keep the dryness off them, to keep myself from hurling after Darren with hammer-fists, shouting, doing anything I could to shake from him what he knows. I clench my hands under the sheet on the mattress where I'm sitting to keep them good and still.

"What're you doing here if you've got friends?" someone mutters, and nobody says a thing against it. I draw
my arms down looser, automatic, for a fight, even as I
don't care one bit what they think of my friends, me, my
Ariel.

"Do you know your friend's phone number?" Bea
asks. I shake my head — I don't know *phone number*; or
I know it, but not as a thing with good or careful use.
People listen to telephone lines. Whitecoats hear what you
say on them. We don't learn phone numbers down in Safe.

I'm not down in Safe, I realize. For real now. For true.

I press my prickle-palms against my closed eyes to
block out the light.

"Last name?" Bea presses. And I shake my head again.

She lets out a breath, a long, long breath, and when I
dare to look she's watching me, sad and tight and a little
mad all mixed in, and now I care a little what they all
think, now maybe I care, because otherwise I'm all alone
and friendless in the bad hot world Above.

"Well," she says. "Bunk here tonight. She's held her
own before. We sort it in the morning."

There's a grumbling, but Bea shuts it down with a
flashing-eyed look that I'd swear reflects orange from the
windowpanes. The rest straggle back to bed in ones and
twos, stopping for water, for a peek out the window blinds.
Darren gets into the bedroom somewhere in the mix of
them; when I look up, the bathroom door's open. Empty.

I sit on my hands. He's one of their sworn, and they'd defend him. I can't take all of them down.

Not yet.

"Nobody saw her go?" I ask Bea when she's the last in the room, securing the lock tight and brushing stub-fingered the lights. My fists are trembling, and she sees it, and maybe she thinks it's a scared shaking and not the flat hard fury that I'm choking down inside me, 'cause she stops on her way back into the bedroom and gives me a glass-edged smile.

"She always comes back," Bea whispers to me. I swallow my own words and just nod to her.

She don't look like she believes it either.

There's no getting him that night. Too many people about. Too many questions, and Beatrice's sworn are looking at me hard and unhappy, and I won't push. I know what I've done.

I've taken Sanctuary. Taken it when I wasn't in true, hard need. And I'm not half-welcome anymore.

I wake up early. Wake half-shamed for being able to sleep at all, but Mack always taught us that if we get caught in a bad spot, it's best to face it half-rested than not at all. So I wake with the first touch of sun on the blinds and lie still and quiet, still and waiting for anyone to emerge from the bedroom. Bea's place sounds of pipes same as Safe, just quieter and thinner, not the deep rumble of water that marks Safe's daylight hours. The little baby pipes sing with people's getting up; a scrape of furniture; a footstep; cars swishing by on the roadway below. None of it moves me. I watch.

Darren comes out first just like the past morning, opening the bedroom door so it don't creak and walking heel-toe, heel-toe to the bathroom. I drop my eyes half-shut, feel him watch for a second, two, before he opens the bathroom door with a slow squeak that echoes through the floor into my bones.

I'm up before it closes again.

I've slept in my shoes, careful and ready for this, and my bouncing-bottom sneaker squishes hard when I stick it between the door and the door frame. I burst into the bathroom with the door shut tight after and get the lock twisted true before he turns.

He's got no chance to shout. I reach out, wrap fingers in his shirt, scared to touch his skin because then the rage in me might come pouring out and I'd push his thick pink Normal face into the mirror. I'm not big but I get him up against the cold beige plaster wall fast enough that I look it, and the set of my teeth does the rest. He doesn't hit me. Just leans back against the wall and looks down with his eyes hard and snarling and cold.

"The fuck," he says. Fingers curled against the plaster.

"I wanna know what you know about Ari."

He sizes me up, man to man, looking for a straight or dirty fight. "That's not her real name." He spits. It glimmers on the yellowed bathtub and slides down inside.

Ariel's real name.

I feel the touch of wings, fine pale brittle living wings under the slightest part of my fingertip. Iridescent. Delicate as shadows, as sunlight. As a story that's not your own to tell.

I bite back the question. Swallow it down.

"It doesn't matter," I say. "I wanna know what you know."

But he's seen the wing-touch in my eyes. "Or what?" he says, not sneering but soft, soft and calculating and cool.

I didn't bring no knives. Bea's got knives in the kitchen, but when you pull a knife into a fight it gets serious, and bleeding means Whitecoats coming in white trucks, cutting your shirt off, seeing the scales that march up and down your back. Knives can be taken away and used against you, but I've got something else.

He doesn't move when I pull the match and strike it on the beat-up cardboard backing. His eyebrow goes up a little, *whatcha gonna do with that*, and I let it burn halfway down to my fingertips before I reach out and touch it to his chin.

Darren yelps. He fumbles sideways into the bathtub, trips over his own feet and lands sprawling in the damp leftovers of somebody's shower. "You crazy fuck!" he hisses, but not loud. Not so anyone'll open the door. Not so anyone'll see.

I'm little, I realize. He's big. Even with the match tossed floating in the toilet, it wouldn't be my Sanctuary Bea took away.

And he don't got nowhere else to go.

I look him over with my hardest face, my Jack-face, my Atticus-face with eyes bright red with righteous fury and rage and punishment coming down from the heavens.

"I wanna know what you know," I repeat, soft.

He tells me.

Once upon a time (he says, 'cause he don't know no other ways to tell a Tale), Darren and Ari and his cousin Jimmy all lived in the same town. Back when he wasn't runaway.

Before.

Things were off with Ariel (that's how he says it, *off*. *FreakSickBeast*, I translate. I know every way that word's said, every word that hides it). From the time they stopped being kids and went into high school, things were off. She didn't play no more in the neighborhood; looked across her shoulder for things that were never there. But then things were off with Ariel's papa too, big and broad, never smiling and seldom outdoors, who all the kids shied away from and all the grown-ups frowned 'bout whenever his name got mentioned. Ariel did good at school and was quiet and didn't make trouble like Darren did, setting garbage-can fires and smoking out behind the mall, so nobody went asking about her. *Wouldn't like them telling us how to run* our *family*, they said, watching Ari and her papa and her brothers disappear into their dark-shuttered house, and left it all alone.

Everyone 'cept Jimmy.

Jimmy saw Ariel and he wanted her.

(Why? I asked. And Darren shook his head, and said there was no knowing why Jimmy did what he did, just that once he was fixed on something he was methodical about getting it. About keeping it once it was got.

He wouldn't look straight while he said it.)

Jimmy sat with Ari on the front porch in the summer. He stuck himself at her little back table in the cafeteria and wouldn't be turned away. He bought her things or stole them, no knowing which. After a while she went into Jimmy's house in the afternoons instead.

She got skinny, bee-thin, skinnier, and nobody knew from her getting quieter because quiet was always what she was. She and Jimmy didn't show up to school no more. Nobody missed it; it was like a whisper going out. And then one day they were gone, and Darren only heard it third-hand 'cause he wasn't there no more either. He'd gone down to the city to get away from his own shit (and he snapped the word, bit it off so it didn't have an edge to cut him).

(So he was bad to her? I asked, even and cool, trying not to spoil his talking mood. Maybe this was the one, the one I'd made ready for; the one who did her hurt. I dunno, he said, stared down into the toilet. I wasn't much looking.)

He didn't see them again for years.

When he did it was in line for a show, midwinter. They were bee-thin, both of them, bee-thin and meaner in the creases formed 'bout Jimmy's eyes. Darren had stolen a coat the week past, and the deep too-big hood on it covered him to the nose-tip. They didn't see his face, shuffling along behind them in a crowd full of kids. But he saw them together and the bruise on her wrist, and the place where the hand went to hold it.

So when she came to Beatrice's the summer following, dirty-boned and desperate with a hard cast to her chin, he knew what'd gone down. There weren't no histories on the street — no asking, no telling, no Tales — but they had history already, even if it was across a crowded classroom or in a long bar line, passing by.

She kept getting jobs and losing 'em. She never brought nothing home. And she stayed inside the apartment, quiet, making no trouble, and kept shut the blinds.

He came home early one afternoon from six hours of shoveling other people's snow and there were bowls dirty in the sink, dirty clothes spattered everywhere, and his temper snapped in two.

He'd seen her with Jimmy, he told her, pointed-like. He saw her with a place to sleep, and it wasn't no good pretending she didn't have friends and somewhere to go when other people worked daytime and night to keep them all in food and safety. If she wasn't gonna put in, if she wouldn't help, he would go right over there and tell Jimmy to take her back.

That's when the wings came pushing down.

(It was like nothing I ever seen, he said, big-eyed and saying he'd punch me out if I called him crazy or Freak or stupid. I wrapped my hand 'round my matches and he leaned right back against the bathtub tiles.)

It was like nothing he'd ever seen, girl growing wings, going small and diving red murder for his face. He ducked around and couldn't hide from her, tried to get on the other side of the door, and then he got mad, got pissed. He wasn't gonna hide from no goddamned bug, not when there were rolled-up papers and dirty shoes and weapons all around.

He'd got a shoe ready when Bea came in.

We never talk about this again, Bea warned him after the window was open and she was gone, gone, gone, and because she had that crazy look in her eye that made nobody on the whole street fuck with her 'less they were drunk as a skunk or high, he didn't talk about it to nobody.

When Ari didn't come back for a whole week, he found out where Jimmy was living. Stood outside to see if she was there; coming, or going.

(And did you go in? I asked, leaning in, people-noise

stirring on the other side of the door. Did you go in and make sure she was safe?

Nah, he said. Turned his face away. Wasn't none of my business.

Jack says hate's a poison. I feel that true now. I feel it sour up my heart.

Tell me how to get there, I say. The red is thicker now, burning, setting matches to my eyes. I wonder if this is how Atticus always felt angry. If the glow of hating burned him 'til he couldn't bear no light.

He tells me.)

I'm thinking 'bout bus tokens when I stalk out of the bathroom into a crowd of staring people pressed to the door, pressed to every whispered word that worms through wood and rock and cracked walls. Doctor Marybeth gave me three tokens, one for going and two for coming, and I'll need another to get us both back safe. I'll need one more for my Ariel.

They stare at me and it's with fear, and shock, and questions.

I leave without saying nothing —

— *None of my business*, Darren said —

— I got nothing to say to them.

It's morning bright outside, stupid teasing bright, and I flinch under the ache of it but keep myself going down the path to the street, to find Jimmy and teach him right back the making of vulnerable. My hands go to my matches again. I pry 'em right off. You can't make wheels run with fire.

Stop, Matthew. Think.

I got no more tokens to break her out, make her Safe. I reach into my pocket to put the matches lower, and feel twenty-five dollars bent and tired under my crisp-moving fingers. Pull them out. They flutter, faded and special and forbidden, in the wind that's already heating for another bright hard day.

My Ariel is in trouble.

This is an emergency.

There's a little shop at the corner that has a sign with tokens, photographed bigger than in real life, posted in among the cluttered windows. I go spend two-seventy-five on one more, hand it to a man who looks like my papa might've if he'd not died so much younger. He watches me with flat eyes full of much too much attention. I want to stare back until he takes his curious and shoves it down his own throat for dinner.

The token's warm in my hand. I tuck it close in my tightest pocket, jam it down. Losing it now would be worse than anything.

And as if that breaks something, I spend three dollars more on a big thick muffin and a paper cup of tea, pushed from a nozzle of a squat machine that I stare at, head thick and empty, before the shop man shows me how to use it. More of Mack's rules: On enemy ground you stay rested, you stay fed, you stay sharp. I'm not Passing now, not in the slightest, but I'm too full of mad to care; implacable hot mad like a storm waiting.

Corner's kind of mad, I think to myself, and drown the thought in nasty tea.

There are two buses to Jimmy's apartment. Instead of going through the city like the ones to Doctor Marybeth's did, they go down tree-lined streets that get narrow and narrower, old houses and older stores that look like they might crumble for touching. I sip my too-hot tea and feel every burn it lays down on my tongue, feel it make me hot and sharp down low in my belly where Doctor Marybeth keeps her sworn oaths and I keep my rage.

It's early enough morning that nobody much's on the bus. Just one skinny man with wires coming down from his ears, and when he looks at me a second too long, I hold the look like I wanted to in the store and he looks right away.

That's right, I think, toothy, and the words of it are red.

The building's colder and littler and meaner than Beatrice's, just like it should be in my head, just like in a Tale. It's squat brown and small-windowed, and there's no garden on each side to hide the place where the dumpsters are. They rise up, fat and metal, and the birds flutter 'bout the edges like roaches runabout. I pace 'round the building three times looking for escape runs before I come up to the door.

Blinds twitch when I do, somewhere above, in a blank window scummed down with dirt. I snap my head up, searching for her, but it's not. I can't tell if it's not. It might be just the wind.

They're watching. Pass.

So I keep walking slow and careful, heel-toe, like I belong here, up to the door. I take myself into the entry-way — dim-lit and cramped — and run a finger down the list of names, close as loving. Close as touching.

It's not two minutes before someone steps out and I slip inside.

I climb five flights of peeling-tile stairs and pad over rucked-up carpets, hunting dark as my papa, to the door that Darren told me. Five-one-three. Five-one-three stands before me and I stare like it's toothed, hinge-jawed and waiting, a dead hand placed in the sewer run for me to trip over at night.

Dead things, I think, and the hand in my mind is Ariel's. Her small white hand.

I knock.

The first knock is quiet. It's a knock like someone who's little, who don't belong. Who's Freak. *Her dead hand and that's all you can do?*

The quiet laughs like teasing. *Freakfreakfreak.*

Bang bang bang I knock the second time, the echo jumping my heart as it finds every corner of the empty hall. *I am coming*, this echo says, big as a Beast in the dark. *I am here.*

It ain't him who opens the door.

My fists go loose without me telling, and for a minute I can't see, can't see nothing for the bright of her eyes.

"Matthew," she shapes, not even talking, and her face is sour white. Her cheek is sickly purple, bruise rising like a stain, and it wasn't before. She's red and purple and red even through normal eyes, through eyes that aren't stained like Atticus's with rage. Her mouth opens in a surprised little O: *You came back*. And something else. Something broken-backed and scared.

"I'm taking you home," is all I tell her, and then I hear moving somewhere behind.

She looks back over her shoulder, hair whipping to and fro, and for a second the red clears and it's oh god bee's-wings, candle flame, everything good and clean and sweet in the world touching gentle on my eyes and nose and lips. Then she looks back at me with red-lined eyes and a tight-lined face and it's gone, that thing that lights without burning, that thing that makes me want to touch her cheek soft nighttimes. She lowers her chin even more than it's tilted down. Hiding.

She opens her mouth, thin and careful, and I know she's gonna say no.

"I'm taking you home," I say again before she gets the chance, before the sick rattling 'round the door to my heart can find a seam and pry in. I reach out for her hand. She snatches it away and before I think I'm half through the door, ready for the shove, the slam, when the voice comes out from back behind her and says "Who you talkin' to?"

"Nobody," Ariel says, high and scared in a way that tells me *yes, fine, let's go*, but it's too damn late for that. Because the footsteps are coming, the steps are *bang bang* themselves; *in or out, Matthew*. She shrinks back into herself with the ridges of wings just peeking past her elbows. So in it is, into the tiny wreck-strewn apartment, face-to-face with a boy — a man — who's taller and broader and thicker than me, and mad. Just starting 'round the edges to get mad.

"Who's this?" he says, soft and biting, and the wings stretch and curl to surround her.

He doesn't look at them. He looks right at me, as if he doesn't see the sheen of translucence coming in to cover her, to keep her eyes from having to look at either of us. His chin's tucked up tight. His arms are loose and swinging, but I can see the thumbs tucked and ready to make up fists.

The door closes with a click behind me. Uncarved. Unstoried. Blind.

"You Jimmy?" I ask, make it just as soft and just as biting, just as clean and sharp.

"I said *who's this*?" he says, not answering, just staring straight at Ari and leaning close in so neither of us can get the space to breathe.

She's still: dead sharks, dead bees. She doesn't even quiver.

The world's red like burning buildings and Atticus's eyes.

I'm between them before I think. I slide between and nudge her back with an elbow, back so she stumbles into the door, and tilt my chin up to look at him in a way that's just asking to get hit. "And I asked if you're Jimmy," I breathe, hard as Atticus, hard as if I had crab claws where my arms were supposed to be and feared nobody and nothing.

He looks down at me for a second or three or five. His eyes are blue, cold as wintertime Above. "And who the fuck are you?"

"I'm taking her home," I get out, Atticus-snarl. Drawing up. Teeth bared.

No fear.

And he backs off. He backs down. He puts his hands in his dirty shorts pockets and steps back and says all mild, "I don't know what the hell you're on about." But his eyes are still sharp as rusty curling nails and there's not a mild thing in the world I can see inside them.

"You don't know what I mean?" I ask, biting off every word, and she doesn't move, doesn't talk, and I wonder deep, deep down if Darren made the whole thing up; if he drew me away to change the locks, change the blinds, change everybody's minds, and I've made a stupid and terrible mistake.

The wings shudder. Ariel's sunshine head, her big wide eyes peek up and over the edges where they meet.

"It's okay, Matthew," she says, barely speaking, and I catch or imagine the tightening of his lips, the taking of a name.

I look back at him, leaned against a wall now and his face rearranged so it says concern and calm, like nothing sharp or cruel could ever walk across its bones. "This the one that hurt you?" I ask her, soft and snapping, and watch him, not her, for the answer.

The quiet stretches out. She stares at me and stares at him and don't say a thing, and the quiet is as good as a picture.

Yes.

I walk right up to him. Close enough for breathing. "This him?"

Silence.

"This the one?"

"Hey —" he says, and puts a hand on my chest and I smack it aside, collide an open-handed slap with wrist, arm, bone. And still she don't talk, still she hides behind her flown-out wings and won't say a word 'gainst him, a word of truth.

"Tell me," I go, pressing up close to him, getting in his face, pushing right back until he has to back off his wall and I can smell him, old sweat and sour shoving right up my nose. I'm gonna make him scared, gonna *teach* him scared, print every nightmare story of Safe on those bad blue eyes 'til they never again sleep for screaming. "Go on, tell me true. This the one that sent you down to Safe?"

I can't look. I can't take my eyes away from his eyes, his fists. But I hear her give a whimper, like a Beast that's gonna die. "Matthew —" she whispers. Sick, scared. Vulnerable.

I throw the punch.

The hit bursts like fire in my hand, a shudder up my good carving wrist, hurts all the way up to my shoulder and *I do not care*. The skin gives under my knuckle, dents all the way down to muscle and bone, and it's good. It puts spit in my mouth that tastes like metal and blood.

He yells, straightens up with a swear that tells me he *is* the one, he's the one that broke my Ariel, broke her down made her Freak made her scared of sweet words or touching so I had to walk slow and careful, talk soft and always be patient and never just kiss her like I wanted to. Took away her want to be kissed.

"Whitecoat," I say, even though he's no such thing, and bring down my arm again.

There's a rhythm to hitting. It's got a rhythm like a Tale, and you match it to the screams your lover is

223

screaming and the sounds you don't hear from the one you hit, the way your breath rattles in your chest as you yell and yell the Tale of how it's gonna be from now on. *You broke her!* is the Tale I tell. *You broke her you broke her you broke her* and my fists land down and down even though they're skinny and not strong for fighting, not strong for keeping the shadows away from the ones I love, but strong enough now, hurt enough now to hit and hate and bring up the blood from his body.

I broke her, he assents finally, when his body goes weak and down on the floor and his own fists don't rise to fight no more. When he can't talk to disagree.

That's right, I whisper, and shake his blood off my fists.

I straighten up. My hands hurt. I burn and hurt shoulders to wrists.

Ariel's curled up in the corner by the apartment door, knees to chest to forehead to arms, and she's shaking now, moving alive like shark-swim or bee-flight or other things that stay moving 'til they lie down whimpering to die. *Alive*, I think, with a strange and stupid relief, and just watch the lock of her wrists, the tight draw of her legs, the shudder of breath that's trying to be quiet, trying to hide away from bad things, worse things, the very worst; roaring right past you with hurt on their minds.

"I'm taking you home," I say again, and scrub the Whitecoat's blood off my knuckle, onto my knee.

The wings fall out of her back, shrivel-clean, and whisper to the floor.

I pick them up in one hand and tuck them under my arm. I don't know where nobody'd look for them Above — the fat dumpsters, or buried underground — but we can't leave them here. She looks up sharp when I take them, sharp and drawn and frightened, and there's tears rolling out and down her face to stain her pants at the knees.

I don't think she's ever looked at me like that before.

"It's all right," I say, but I can't make my voice soft like I should; I can't unbend it from the rough and foul and screaming. Mad's burning in my belly. The smoke comes out in every word.

I go into the bathroom for a bit. Wash my hands clean of the blood and ripped-up skin before I hold one out for her to take or not take, lift her up off the floor so we can run, run, go. She takes it only the littlest bit, staring past me to his body lying crumpled-up and face-broke on the floor. I can't even tell if there's whimpers no more. I can't tell if he's breathing, if he's going to ghosts.

Can't tell, and don't care.

The blinds hang white in the windows. Somewhere far away, a siren sounds.

Oh, I realize, sudden, clear. *Police*. Wasn't quiet enough, quick or quiet enough. Somebody must have heard him scream.

"We gotta go now," I tell her, and she doesn't gather up no things, just slips out the door in front of me and walks silent as something shadow-possessed down the hall, down the stairs, with me out the back to the dumpsters.

The sirens are getting closer. No time. Gotta go.

I put a foot up on the ridged metal side of the dumpster. It smells like broiling garbage and blood and hate, but there's no time to be picky now; no time to stay clean.

I vault myself up and throw away her wings.

We start walking, fast. It don't matter where; we pick a direction and *go*, walk that street heads down, hands down, as three-no-four police cars rush past us, lights blaring, sound blaring hard and cruel.

One foot before the other, I tell myself. Walk slow. Don't run.

Pass.

The sun beats down harder outside, this time of morning. The smell of garbage and pigeons mingles into the air and slides over the concrete, and the muffin in my belly rises up touched with sour. I keep it down with eyes closed because it's no good to waste food, especially not here, not with three-no-four police cars sniffing about behind us.

When I open them she's watching me careful, like something she can't get the measure of. Wary, drawn. Like a Beast.

"Won't hurt you no more," I say, short, clipped. We must be two blocks away now; not far enough, and I'm trying to reach for some love in me and not finding it, not finding anything but *why did you run from me, why didn't you wait for me?* Burned and hollow. A burned-down house.

Why did you run to him?

"It wasn't that bad," she whispers, and presses a hand to the bruise rising on her red-marked cheek.

I pull it down. I grab her wrist hard as the last crack of my bouncing shoes meeting Jimmy's ribs and yank it away from her face, ignore the little squeak she gives and the buzz underneath it. The way she's suddenly shadowed with wings. "Yes it IS!" I scream at her, suddenly tear-blind, throat still dry and screaming nonetheless, the world all washed in red. "It is that bad! He hit you! He broke you all up! How can you say it's *not that bad*!"

Her mouth moves open-shut and she doesn't give one goddamned answer, got nothing to say for herself. It just makes me madder, every part of me aching through and burning mad, hotter and purer than anything I've ever felt.

"How?" I shout, down in her face, breath on her cheek. "How could you let him do that? Why don't you love yourself good?"

She stares up at me, and there's two bright spots in her cheeks under the bruises, under the hitting he did to her. I breathe hard for a second before I see it coming, see that it's not being scared that's made her face so hot and red. It's worse.

It's being shamed.

The wings spring out like a lit match. The wings spring tall and then she's shrinking into them, going small and yellow-black, dead-eyed and dirtied and ready to run.

"NO YOU DON'T!" I holler, and close my hands around her.

If I thought there was burning inside me, I know I was sorely wrong when her stinger presses to my palm. The hurt blossoms like the bright sun in my hand, pain like nothing, pain like a brand to the throat, hot and sharp and unloving. I jerk my hand away just a little before I *think* and then clamp it shut, clamp it tight, before the burning comes again. It's not letting her run I'm afraid of now, tears coming down, swearing words my papa would be shamed to hear me know. It's closing my hands tight. Closing down on the pain and crushing her small and burning inside my palm.

I count the stings, grit-teeth. Crying, standing still like dead things, like statues, much too close to three-no-four police cars. I count stings like they're steps. "Ariel," I whisper, whimper, moan. "I loved you good. I came for you and came and you didn't wait —"

It's five. It's six and seven and eight and nine and ten before the crawl and flutter of her moving in my hands slows down, before it rests on the bottom of my right palm like a mourning cry, and somewhere in the stupid pain that's hazing the world all colors, I feel her stop hitting.

I'm still holding on when she starts to grow.

When she does I let go, finally can let go, catch on to her wrist and hold on tight as she goes long and soft and into a girl again. Don't and can't let go when her feet hit the ground and she pulls away even though my stung-up hand burns, burns so I want to cut it clean off at the wrist to make the hurting stop.

"Don't run from me," I say hoarse, seeing my free hand gone red and swollen, the marks bright as bruises puckering up on my palm. I stare at it, suddenly scared, and bring it limp and burning toward my chest. "Please don't run."

"Let go," she whispers, still just as pale, eyes big and terrible and dark as cages.

"Just don't go," I get out. The world's moving dizzy. I can feel my heart go.

"No," she says faint, and I don't know if it's no she won't or no, she will forever.

"Swear," I whisper, and her lips move, and she swears.

Finally I let go. Finally I let go loose enough to see how tight my hand's been holding, circling the place where the new bruise is.

Where my hand went to make it.

The red abandons me like a shadow burning down.

"Ari," I choke out after a moment, hands aching, heart aching, and fall down on my knees. "Oh no, shit, Ari, I'm sorry —"

And she's crying. She's weeping full-on frightened tears, and it ain't him she's scared of.

It's me.

She don't talk to me all the way to Doctor Marybeth's house.

I don't ask her to. I sit beside her on one bus, two, and don't touch her hand or wrap my arms 'round her. I can't touch her hair to give some reassurance or say I'm the same old quiet Matthew that brought her in, that held her when she was up all night screaming.

There's still tears on her face, and I can't stop shivering.

My hands are red and lumped and tight, and where they aren't straight burning I can still feel the ache, ten little match heads lit bright and stabbed through me. I sit real still with them in my lap, touching nothing, and try hard to breathe.

"Can you knock?" I ask when we get to the front door, subdued and my mouth scarce moving. My hands are big as Jack's now, tight and red-shot. The dizzy comes every time I even look at them.

She don't look at me. She knocks on Doctor Marybeth's door like she's scared, like she's little, like she's Freak and don't belong.

"Not like that," I say, soft, slow. "Three and two. *Dum-dum-dum dum-dum*." It's signal-knocking, the kind that Jack and Whisper might answer. The kind that they'll know is friends.

She makes the knock. Quiet, watching me with both her eyes and the set of her back, the set that's Ariel ready to move. I count seconds and pray someone comes to the door before her patience breaks, before she runs away to somewhere I'm too burned to reach.

And thank everything the door opens, and Jack looks out from behind it with eyes dark-circled and a hand on his metal bar.

"Teller," he says, surprised a little, and steps back fast to let us in.

I kick the door shut behind us once we're through, and Ariel runs right up the stairs and slaps her knee on the landing and keeps going. The door to Doctor Marybeth's attic room slams a few seconds later. I lean back against the closed door and cover my eyes from the light. They sting. They ache.

"What happened?" Jack says, cautious and soft, the kind of voice that knows it's liable to step on a shadow-trap.

I look up at him. He's haggard and hazy to my hurting eyes.

"Jack, I think I'm Killer," I say, and limp to the sitting-room couch before I fall for good.

They bandage up my hands while I sleep.

I wake with the sun low down in the sky. Both hands are wrapped tight, white-gleam and padded-up in the orange light, stiff and sore and hard to move. There's a plastic bag sealed with water between my palms, water that maybe once was ice, 'cause there's a chill in my hands through the bandages that ain't part of the thick-backed summer heat. I set the bag down on the table, let it list and take its shape, and though my hands hurt in ten prickle points like a deep bruise or heartbreak, they don't burn no more.

The water magnifies the sunset-light, brings up sharp the shape of something pointed and wicked-thin behind it: claw-metal and black and distorted wet white. I get the bag between two fingers, clumsy, and set it aside so I can look.

It's a dish topped with tweezers, old metal sharp-end ones, filled with band-aids and cotton swabs and the smell of medicine left out against the air. Sitting right on top of them all is a withered black stinger, bloody and sharp.

I touch it and it flakes into nothing.

ARIEL'S TALE II

Ariel didn't run. Or she did. But she meant to come back, before she got caught.

It wasn't the first time she'd done running, because her papa was big and broad and never smiling and seldom outdoors. Indoors he trod like a storm cloud grown heft and measure: groan and creak and silence on the loose floor tiles. Ariel stayed in her bedroom and learned to move heel-toe, one foot before the other, without making a sound.

(I know this story. I've been told this story before, in the way Beak's fingers rub together though it's a warm day or Scar's chin tilts down into the shadows. I can recite it to the word.)

Maybe she had a mama and sisters. Maybe she had brothers too scared to stick up for her, or little enough to need their own sticking-up; little enough to shove into your best hiding-place when only the dark was safe. None of that's what counts. What counts is that Ariel got big enough that she couldn't hide herself from her papa no more.

She curled up late nights around bruises and cursed her own stupid self for being anywhere to be seen. She made excuses to be out: out at school, out at jobs, out at things that meant going nowhere but straight to sleep when she set foot through her papa's door.

And it didn't matter. She realized, one night (at fifteen, or sixteen, or seventeen years old) it would never matter. She couldn't stay here and keep herself safe and whole.

It came quick after that (or so they always tell me, faces hot and shamed). Her nerve had been slow and hard in bending, but when it broke it broke quick. She ran into the night and came to rest, huddled up knees-to-chest and arms-to-knees, forehead to them all, in a too-small kid's park playhouse (or a washroom with chipped-paint stalls, or a bank-machine house still warm enough in November to not freeze by midnight). She thought of all the places she might run to. Found nothing.

Found night coming on, and cold.

So Ariel lighted in a place that was only just good enough. She ended up with Jimmy.

Jimmy was big and broad; all the better for keeping her papa away. Jimmy was seldom smiling; well, it mattered more when he smiled just for her. And Jimmy had a place down in the city, lock and key secure between her and the world, and nobody looking in or telling where she'd gone.

This is the way the Tale goes, that it's good for a while. That there's someone to hold you at dusk and a quiet space to stay, someone to careful, careful drag you back from the nightmares and glittering cut-sharp edges of your smashed-up broken nerve.

It's good short of forever.

It gets real bad. It gets bad in ways you know on your skin, and this time you picked it. You didn't look close enough, so this time it's just you to blame. So it's bag on back and shoes in hand to tiptoe late-night out the door, and no time for somewhere to run to; no time to wait for the real thing. There's only time to go.

There's running and running 'til you can't outrun your skin.

But here's the problem, here's the knot:

My Ariel came to me from her papa's house, then Jimmy's house, then Bea's, and in none of those places could she get a Whitecoat bracelet on her wrist.

(She squeezed her eyes tight shut when I picked up the knife. "S'okay," I whispered, took her wrist; laid it palm up, straight and fine, and sliced the white plastic away. "See?" I told her. "We won't hurt you. I won't hurt you.")

This is all guessing. It's the ends of others' Tales wrapped together; the kind you tell 'cause you wish it were true. Nothing.

I made all this up.

This is what I know. This is what I know for true:

Ariel went down to the city and the city wasn't safe. So she went to Bea's Sanctuary and that wasn't safe, so she went flying down to the tunnels all wings and tripping horror, and cried 'cause she wasn't a girl, she was a bee instead, she was Freak and Beast and monsters. And a boy took her by the hand, took her home, hung her wings, and then shadows burst through the walls and that wasn't safe either, that was not safe and he was not safe and there was nowhere to go but back: back to the spit and spite and bite you know. Back to the place that might have been safe to start with if anything Above lasted, didn't rot or break or fall. If anything Above could stay true, and not be a monster.

(She went down to the Cold Pipes, and saw something that scared her bad enough to run and never tell it true.)

What's the moral of the story?

People Above will hurt you. People Above will break you, and devour your heart raw.

And so will I.

EIGHT

Doctor Marybeth's good as her word. She brings Corner's file back after her day-and-night duty — it's *rounds* when you're a doctor — and changes the bandages on my swollen hands. She's skinnier than night before last. Shadowier. But I can't bear to look at her shadow-tinged edges any more than I can take the stairs one by one up to the landing, up to the turn, and call soft Ariel's name 'gainst the locked-up door.

"Shouldn't draw attention like that," is all Doctor Marybeth says, like she's Jack or Atticus or someone who knows from hiding, and pats the back of my hand before she goes. I keep down the mad. Even the slightest hint of mad brings it all back, the feel of his skin and then hers, and then it's hard to breathe or see or think from the haze of stupid misery.

Ariel doesn't come down. Whisper takes her a plate of supper, loaded full of beans and spinach and all the good things we can't get often in Safe, and Whisper don't come down for a bit either. When she does, her mouth is drawn tight as a satchel-bag. She don't say nothing at all.

Look what you've made me be, I want to weep at Ariel's feet, arms clutched to her knees like a shadow. But I've heard enough Tales to know nobody's made me do anything; I pick what's for me to be. I picked to be Killer, and Whitecoat, and Beast.

I know doing those things is wrong. And that makes me even worse.

So I try to look at Doctor Marybeth's files in her sitting room, read the tiny biting hand that talks 'bout medicine and meetings and all the other things Whitecoats do to keep you hushed and swaddled. I go over every word one by one, sound them aloud like I've not had to do since my papa taught me letters by lantern-light. Even then the words just stream through my head, thick as ghosts and just as catchable, until I shove the papers hard at Jack and say "What d'you think?" an inch short of snapping.

Jack looks at me across the scratch-wood coffee table and says nothing either, just takes the file in the folds of his glove and settles in to read.

Doctor Marybeth's also brought a newspaper clipping: fire at the old Lakeshore Psychiatric Hospital. I read it slow to make sure I get every word, every chain-link between every word. They aren't saying it was set, not deliberate like we did. *Electrical failure*, it says. *Known homeless squat. Investigation pending.*

Jack Jack Jack, it says to anyone who knows from Safe.

"Is there anything else in the paper?" I ask. I can't ask it whole, about a boy beaten bloody and crumpled-up wings. I'm scared, I'm shamed to ask.

Doctor Marybeth's lips press together. "On television," she says, tightly. "There's a security video."

I don't know what *video* is, but my stomach hollows out, like the hate and the oaths have destroyed each other inside and left a whole lot of nothing.

"It means they saw you go in the building, Matthew," she says, quiet and patient, and I know now that Jack isn't actually reading, he's listening close, close. "They only saw your back. But they'll be looking for someone your height, your age."

They'll be looking for me. "Is he —?"

Doctor Marybeth gives me a look I can't fathom, and shakes her head. "Comatose," she says. *Catatonic.*

"Is he going to —?" I move my mouth on the last word. Can't quite make it come out.

"He might not. People get better from that," she says, soothing and slow.

Jack turns a page. He's a bad liar.

"What do I do?" I say, and it sounds terrible small.

Doctor Marybeth lets out a short breath. "Stay inside. Unless it's absolutely necessary. Cover your hair if you have to go out." She pauses. "And get back into Safe as soon as you can."

Jack apparently don't have anything to add to that.

239

I watch him with his reading and make Safe in my mind, crawl into it and shut the big door behind me. Hope we can get there in time, before they find my back or my face or shake the truth out of Darren, and the Whitecoats come down with their crooked, grasping fingers.

Hope Safe will still want me, after this.

(*Killer's not a thing that gets Sanctuary*, Atticus said.)

"I think the Whitecoats didn't know much about Corner," Jack says, flipping through the copy-smudged pages of its file too quick to be really looking. He lets down one big leg from the pivot of his knee and lifts up the other, trading them off above the red-flowered cushions of Doctor Marybeth's old stuffed couch. "There's nothing 'bout shadows in here."

"Nobody knew about the shadows when Corner was in Lakeshore," Doctor Marybeth says. "Just the bloodtouch."

"What's the word for bloodtouch in Whitecoat?" I ask just for something to say, something to think about that's not the bitter red glow that still turns and whispers in my gut.

"There is none," she says.

"No," Jack says, "these people don't know from bloodtouch either. It's *gender identity disorder*." He says it like he's reaching for a glass of water to rinse the words away.

"That's Corner being boy-girl," Whisper says, shrouded in the corner chair, not speaking so long that I almost forgot she's there. "They wanted it to be picking," she goes on, looking at all of us with her mouth still tight and grudging. "Boy or girl. No use for something that was both. They'd pick for it if it didn't pick for itself quick, and its quick wasn't quick enough. There was to be an operation."

"That's why they ran. Corner didn't want the operation," Doctor Marybeth says into the silence, hollow and far, far away. "Atticus begged me to open the door." After a second she gets up, straight hands and old thoughts and all, and drifts into the kitchen to be by herself.

"Says that here," Jack assents, once she's gone and it's not a disrespect to be speaking. He sets down the file. His eyes are still on the doorway where she left. "And that's all it says."

I rub my eyes; try to clear them of bad and mad. Of beasts, and memories, and angels.

There's a quiet, not a natural one but one you can feel and touch, and when I look up, Jack is watching me funny. "What're you thinking, Teller?"

I'm not half sure what I'm thinking. I'm thinking 'bout shadows. I'm thinking 'bout the limits to their knowing, and the way they fought and wept while burning, wept over different sins. The way Doctor Marybeth's eyes grew dark and smoky when she told the tale of Corner like it was fingerprinted on her skin, and about the last shadow in Lakeshore, the way it said *that's not my name.* "There anything 'bout *Angel* in there?" I ask.

Jack reads, finger-close, pointing at every word as he goes. His face gets darker and darker until I figure he's found something for sure, something wickeder than any of us could imagine. But finally he just says "I can't read this chicken scratch," and shoves the fluttering papers back at me, into an unready hand.

Atticus would say that Whitecoats have poor writing 'cause they don't want no one knowing 'bout the dirt that makes their deeds, but I'm worn and Whisper and Jack are tired and I don't think now's the time. I take the folder and squinch my eyes close, promise myself that I'll take all my smarts and focus and thought for this and just this. The writing is hard. It's thin and blurry besides, faded out from the copying that Doctor Marybeth did so she wouldn't get in trouble taking the real-life file.

I almost miss it when I see the word *Angel.*

"Here!" I call out, pointing at it with the big taped-together mass of fingers that the bandaging's made of my hands. Whisper comes up from her corner chair and Jack from the couch, and they crowd up behind me to look where I'm pointing. It's a form both set down printwise and written on, yet one more thing I don't know from in Whitecoat language and Above. "What's this?"

Whisper leans over me, traces a finger on the paper. "Admission form," she says quietly, and then even though it's a copy I want to put it down, want to keep its own special cold from traveling up my hands. An admission form is what Whitecoats make you sign to take your life away. A deal with wickedness. The turn of a lock, and the dark.

"Why's Angel on Corner's admission form?" I ask, small.

"'Cause Angel's Corner's name," Jack says, and then I really do put down the file.

Corner can't have been in Isolation for real. Corner can't have trailed us up Above and through Lakeshore and hid itself in shadows, speaking true names to drive us wild. And I must speak aloud because Whisper says, "No, it couldn't," in a funny-odd voice, and looks down at the file, wary and sick.

"I thought Corner was its name," I say, careful, knowing the ground I'm shoeing forward on is dangerous.

Whisper shakes her head. She don't even look up. "Corner was what the Whitecoats called it behind its back," she says, but she doesn't say it right; she draws the word out: *Cor-oh-ner*, and Jack sucks in a breath.

"Whis, tell me that isn't why I think it is," he says.

She tips her chin up at him, tiny, and a very un-Whisperlike grin flashes 'cross her face. "Corner stopped three hearts when it came into Lakeshore. One doctor and two orderlies. The coroner's office didn't ever figure out how it managed that."

Jack whuffs out his breath. Shakes his head. "Whitecoats don't know from bloodtouch," he says.

"No," Whisper says. "And they never found out."

"Why'd it keep a Whitecoat name?" I venture, quick and quiet as I can.

"Atticus liked it," she says, briefly, and the last of that bitten grin fades off her face. "Corner fought back 'gainst the Whitecoats. It made him proud."

Wasn't the only one it made proud, I realize, but she's already nose-deep back in Corner's papers.

If we still told Tales of Corner, I'd have known its Above name. I'd have known the Tale of how it tossed that name aside, and why, and took up the new one. But I don't, and that means no one else does: not in Safe or Above or the whole wide world.

Except shadows.

"So how could shadows know that it was called Angel?" I ask, and the twitch, the discomfort, leaks back into the room.

"It lied to us?" Jack puts forward, but even he don't believe it.

"It claimed itself Corner's name," I say. "It came for us when we took up Atticus's file."

"What're you saying?" Whisper says, quiet.

I squeeze my eyes shut and see Atticus, thin and young and begging, a ghost or shadow or broken piece of memory aching to go home. "That the shadow in Lakeshore was Corner." Not Corner-for-real. But part of Corner. Corner split up.

"Corner twenty years past," Whisper breathes, high-voiced and strange — half her whispering voice, I realize; drawing something down in memory of the not-ghost of Atticus burned asunder two floors up.

"And there was a Corner from ten years ago in the attic," I add, surer, stronger, remembering *give me poison give me something give me pills.* "And more between."

"The shadows," Jack says.

"Old Corners," Whisper replies, and scrubs her face with one small hand.

They look at each other over my head, a dark and grown-up look. "What's a shadow, Whis?" Jack says, simple, quiet.

"What a body casts," she replies, just as small. "A dark-mark where we've been."

And the whole thing comes clean, the whole Tale twists, and I feel the click and sigh in my head as it unknots into something true. "How? And how'd it grab hold of them to send into Safe?"

"Don't matter," Whisper says, still looking at Jack. "Maybe it didn't have to. A shadow of Corner might want what Corner wanted anyways, without having to be told.

It'd feel everything the same. What matters is it's been nothing but Corner all along."

Jack's eye is bright, a mean brightness. Not something I like. "So Corner wouldn't have to twist someone to its side. One shadow touching someone out on a duty just long enough to burn its way in, and there's shadows loose in Safe." Like the shadow in Doctor Marybeth, his eyes say. Like Violet.

Like the shadow that dripped, like medicine, into my mouth and leaped out through my hands.

Lots of people go outside of Safe on a thousand separate duties: supply and exploring and just sneaking out for a little solitary quiet. It might have been anyone. It might be any of the people who told us 'bout seeing dark hands or feet moving in the sewers late at night. The shadows might have been in Safe for years.

The spot under my eye burns like a bruise dealt harshly. I rub it, but the burn won't go away.

"Then they would carry its memories," Whisper says, glancing at the darkened kitchen door; the silence that's Doctor Marybeth bearing a shadow in her skin and someone else's Tales in her head. "Anyone talk of Corner's memories, Teller?"

I close my eyes. I lean like I'm remembering, but what I really do is search every inch of me for a taste or smell of Corner, for that wailing glass-bell voice. For a whisper of Safe, pipes and dim and quiet, that ain't really mine.

Half of everything I know about Safe isn't mine. It's Tales and thoughts and things I see all mashed together as truth. But I remember the telling of most of them; the way the ground felt beneath me or the cool of the thin air when the story came to me.

So: "No," I say, knowing it's so, that nobody told me a word 'bout how Corner lived in Safe and left it, even though it was a founder. Even though it lived beside us as family for thirteen long years. "Nobody talks 'bout Corner."

My voice comes out bitter, and it surprises me to swallow that taste right back down.

Whisper's sigh is a regular one, one more road home frustrated for the time being. But Jack's frown goes all the way to his forehead and rucks up the landscape there to something deeper, something worse. I look at him, a question, and he shakes his head. "Something wrong 'bout all this," he says, and retires up the stairs, *creak creak creak* to the room where Ariel's hiding.

She knew the way the Cold Pipes smell. I shiver.

Whisper don't look at me when he's gone. She sinks her chin onto her knees and balances the file in one wrinkled hand to read, squinting against the afternoon coming down through the windows. Looking for shadows.

I watch her a minute or two and then pick myself up, stretch out my legs, and go into the kitchen to find Doctor Marybeth.

She's still shadow-worn. I can see it in the bend of her head, slight and angled as she looks out her own back window. I can see it in the way her own shadow joins to her heels dark and thick, just out of focus, just out of true. The shadow that's Corner's rustles in the dark, moving at my footsteps. It clings tight to her heels like a baby child.

"Does it hurt?" I ask, not meaning to until it comes out, slipped out in the dark where such questions are easier. Corner's shadows burned cold when they poured down my throat, but they didn't *stay* in me. They didn't curl up inside and dog my sleep.

"Yes," she says, low-voiced, unturning. "It whispers when I step out of the light. It wants me to let it die. And I want to."

She stops; more runs out of voice than stops talking. "Matthew, I don't know that I did the right thing that night."

The shock takes me through and through, like lightning.

"Of course you did," I breathe, wanting to take both her arms in my hands and turn her to see the pure heat of my believing. There was no way to not tell Corner 'bout losing its Sanctuary, and no way to not offer a place to stay. And giving it something to let it die —

"She was hurting," Doctor Marybeth says, small as a little kid. "I should have done it. Then she wouldn't have gone bad somehow."

I think about it: no Corner. No Atticus dead and light-less in his own blood, no Beatrice, no Above. Just Ariel and me down Safe in our wing-house, keeping on with the living we were fighting to do before.

Until she ran away again. Until she turned and went running, and Atticus held her to that very last chance, and she became the second Beast exiled from Safe.

And you, all fool and red-mad, would have followed.

"No," I say, staving off the vision of myself dark in the tunnels, wandering forever from the fear of going Above.

"No?" Doctor Marybeth asks, half-turning; mistaking it for something said to her. But it should be something said to her too, so I don't tell her 'bout last chances and bad dreams, the kind you can still have while waking.

"No," I say again, putting on calm, putting on soft. "You said you swore an oath when you became Doctor. Not to hurt."

"Yeah," she says heavy, and turns all the way and puts her hands on her belly where her swearing's kept. Her hair's in her face. I can't see properly her eyes.

"That would've been hurting."

"*This* was hurting," she snaps back.

"You couldn't know it then," I say soft. And don't think about real hurting, about fists and shoes and elbows smacking over and over into the wall of someone's skin and bones. The kind where there's no might-have-been.

"No," she says finally, quiet and kind of beat-up, and I can't tell if I've talked myself into winning or losing when she lifts up empty, shadow-bleak eyes. "What d'you want, Matthew?"

I shift my feet. I try to slide my wrapped-up hands in my pockets, but the bandage catches and I take them out again. "Doctor Marybeth," I ask, thick and feeling worse for the asking, for the knowing, for everything. "Did you get the other file?"

She pauses. Her mouth crimps. "Bring me my bag."

When I asked for the file, Doctor Marybeth put me questions, like she was the Teller and I had the Tale. She asked me the day and time of Ariel's finding, the color of the clothes and shoes she wore. She bade me draw the letters and pictures on the bracelet I cut dirty from her wrist and explained them to me: numbers, family name. Initial. "I'll see," she said, tucking the paper deep away, "what I can do."

Doctor Marybeth is as good as her word. She peels open a side pocket on her bag with careful fingers. Pulls out, brighter and less creased, another copied-out file. "Let's take this outside," she says, a glance over the shoulder, and opens the back door for me.

We pace out onto the lawn and sit down, cross-legged. She reaches over. Puts it into my hands.

"You found where she was," I say, simple, 'cause putting all I feel into something complicated would tangle it up, draw the knot, and choke me blue and hushed before morning. The file is stiff and tidy. It doesn't feel half as wicked as the wicked I know's inside.

"I did," she says grave. "Queen Street Mental Health." A pause. "The inpatient facility."

I can't hear for the dead quiet in me. Plastic bracelets and Whitecoat words. Isolation bunks. Needles.

I knew it all along, and I didn't want to know it.

"That's like Lakeshore, isn't it," I say, voice shadowed from that choke-thing in my throat.

Doctor Marybeth opens her mouth, then closes it, and I can see the spark of her looking to argue that they don't do things like that no more. "That's like Lakeshore," she says finally, and shuts her mouth tight.

To hell with the Tales people should tell for themselves. I open the file.

"Tell me what this word means?" I say after a moment. She looks to where my finger's pointing and tells me. She tells me that and the next and all of them and holds my hand, tight between both of hers like I'm her little kid. And maybe I am, since she brought me out from my mama's dark into lighter dark with her own two hands years past and long ago.

She holds it while I read Ariel's file, and she don't let go.

There's a name for what she is. It's nothing to do with bee's-wing, and it's only part to do with the hurt other people laid down on her in the Tale I built in my head where it could all be fixed with loving. It's many-lettered like all Whitecoat words. And from Doctor Marybeth's face, the care she takes to talk gentle and hold my hand loose so I can draw it away, I can tell she thinks it's so.

"It's not true," I say, faintly, like someone who's been long Sick themself. "It's just that people hurt her."

"I think people hurt her," Doctor Marybeth says, careful and soft, her eyes nothing but a slow concern. Doctor-face. Doctor-voice. "But I don't think it's just that."

The file says hearing things. It says seeing things. It says raging, and fear, and not knowing all the time what's true.

"What do they do?" I say when I've finished the part called *diagnosis*, past the weight in my throat, the knot drawn thinner that makes it hard to talk.

"Therapy," she says. "Medicine to keep them from hurting themselves. Special houses, sometimes, with people who know how to talk the right way." A stop, a stutter even someone not trained as Teller would hear. "Sometimes electroconvulsive therapy."

"What's that mean?" I ask, head coming up.

"Electricity," she says, smaller. "Shocks."

"Like Jack," I whisper. "Like Jack taking your hand all the time."

Her face closes in for a minute. I wonder how many times she's taken hold of Jack's hand.

"Nobody should do that to my Ariel," I whisper. "I'd kill them." Forgetting for just a second, and then the flush comes slow up my cheeks.

Doctor Marybeth doesn't say *no you wouldn't* or *don't be silly* or think I'm fooling 'round. She looks at me very slow and grave and says: "That wouldn't help you nor your little girl."

"She's just as old as me," I say faint, defensive; so used to defending.

"Older," Doctor Marybeth says. "But some people stay young longer," and I got nothing to say to that.

I read on. I read *treatment*, and I wish to everything I hadn't.

"Why do people do this?" I ask her at the end, when I have to put it away so my tears don't spot the page.

"They just wanted to help her be normal," she says, simple, and cups her hands together, holding on to her own private impossibilities.

I cry it out. Doctor Marybeth lets me, is so gentle and tiptoe and kind that the red hatred comes up and I have to sit still, breathe slow once I can breathe without hitching, to let it down to where I feel nothing at all. The tree-shadows move across the yard. A black squirrel follows one, tail twitching and rustling like it's worse than Sick. I tighten my hands up and try not to think.

"What're you gonna do?" Doctor Marybeth asks eventually.

Burn that file, I think, but no. Burning won't stop the Sick that lives in my Ariel's heart. "I don't know," I say, knowing I'm nothing but an echo, a shadow of the boy who begged to buy Ariel a peach. "Talk to her." If she lets me. "Help her. Try to make her Safe."

It comes out like the rattle of empty cans.

"Matthew," Doctor Marybeth says, clear and distinct, and I turn to look at her already before she takes my face in her hands. "Promise me something."

"What?" I whisper, surprised at her touch. It doesn't chill like shadows but feels warm and regular as always, warm like someone vital, living.

"Before you decide a thing more with your Ariel, you talk to me. And if she can't find her way in Safe, let me take her somewhere she can get well." She lifts her hands off my face and raises one before I can say a word. Her eyes are deadly grave. "Not Whitecoats. Not Lakeshore. Well."

She don't wait for my reply.

She knows I won't refuse her.

Jack comes outside in the evening light, when it's dark enough that he'll go outside even with his bound-up hands. The lights are burning in the neighbors' houses, but inward; the dun light of bedroom lamps or the bright one of dinnertimes, the flicker of the television that Doctor Marybeth barely ever turns on.

I've been sitting most of the evening with the file in my lap.

I look up at him quiet, my own bandaged hands tied loose enough that they're starting to itch. He stops halfway through Doctor Marybeth's yard, his foot just shy of her thick-stemmed garden, and stands in the shadow of a tree, in the darkest dark he has.

"What went on with you and the girl?" he asks, hands in gloves tucked in pockets.

I stick my hands in my own pockets and look at the grass that pricks between my bare toes. At the smudge of spilled-out blood on the knee of my jeans. Jack's known me since I was four and shy and Mamaless. He'll find me out if I go lying.

"She wasn't where I left her," I start, breathing the grass and trees and hot thick evening to brace me 'gainst my own Tale. "She went away before I came back, and I had to hold fire to another one's face so he'd tell me where she'd gone."

"That won't make trouble," he says, flat. Threatening it into being. *This better not make trouble.*

"It won't." And I'm pretty sure that of all things, from the silence Darren kept even when I shook and scared him behind the sealed bathroom door, that won't.

Jack is watching me under his thick old prickle-brows. He nods once: *Go on. Tell on.*

"She went back to the one who hurt her. The one who — who broke her," I stutter, and my hands curl into hurting fists all of their own design. It pulls the skin where they're wounded, and they sweat under the bandages. It's not hot enough, eveningtime, for them to sweat so. I still want to hit him.

I want worse to hit myself.

"And?" he says. A hand on the back. My own tricks used against me.

"And I hit him and I kicked him 'til he half died," I blurt out, and my shoulders hunch down like tunnel-walk, though there aren't no tunnels for hours. "I thought he died," I correct. "There were police. We didn't stay."

"You're not all the way sorry, are you?" he says.

Jack has known me since I was four years old.

I shake my head, tiny slow.

Jack's breath goes out with a huff that shakes me through. But there's no *Killer!* come out on the tail of it. There's no red in his eyes when I dare to look up.

He doesn't send me away.

What he says is: "That's grave, Teller," low as low, not changing one whit except to shift his weight left foot to right. "Grave indeed."

I don't speak up to agree.

"And that's why she won't come out," he says, push push push.

I hate him for a second, right red and complete. *Yes*, I want to say. *Yes, that's why she hates me so hard. Because I took away her bad lover.* And she'd never say different. She'd not raise her voice to give answer. I'm the one who bears the Tales, and the Tales I tell are true.

She'd just run. She'd grow wings and fly away from my lying, and it'd be no more than I deserved for finding ways to leave bruises without touching skin to skin.

So: "There's more," I whisper. "I got mad at her after."

Jack's eyebrow goes up.

"I shouted," and my voice has gone small. It's gone soft from the ache to not be saying this, for no one to hear the words I make it say. "I shouted right in her face, and I scared her. I grabbed her," I say, down to a mutter. "It bruised."

"And she turned," Jack finishes for me, because he's got some mercy in him after all. "And marked up your hands."

"I didn't want her to run no more," I whisper, and there's not red but tears in my eyes, not mad but hurting. "I try to be good with her, talk soft and make Safe, and I told her all the stories so she'd know we wouldn't hurt her. But she just keeps running, and I know I'm not good with this but I just wanted her to stop —"

Jack is good and kind. Jack looks away while I do my crying, and he doesn't say nothing about it from the time my voice goes down and my shoulders start to quiver to when I get my breath back under rein again, swallow up the little gulps.

"I just wanted her to stop running," I finish, like there was never a break in the Tale. "I gotta find the right words."

"No, Teller," Jack says, and it's heavy, heavy like he's walked a long road today and has walking yet to go. "There's never been a thing wrong with how you do your talking."

Four or five days ago I would have dragged out the thread of how he's spoken rough about my Ariel. I would have stomped and fought and told him she was Sick and that kind of talking wasn't right. But the words of Whitecoat files are swimming in my eyes, and I don't know what way's home no more. "It's not enough," I say, strained and too-old. "It's never gonna be enough to make it good."

"No," Jack says, not gentle, but gentle as he ever speaks to anything.

"Doctor Marybeth told you, didn't she?" I ask, finally seeing what's behind that stony sad-faced look. I raise the file, shake it. "She told you 'bout this."

"She did," Jack says, even.

I'm bright-red furious for one long second.

"She's Sick," I say, when I can get back my voice. "She needs us. Me. That's what Safe was made for."

"Teller," Jack says, and he never raises his voice, not once. "You're making yourself reasons."

A light goes off in the house 'cross from us. A dinner-light — people long risen from the table and the dishes cleared, a family made of Mama and Papa and little kids putting themselves to bed for dreams that don't taunt you past morning. New shadows fall across us, a stripe of light put down to bed as well. I wonder if those shadows touch Doctor Marybeth, tied as she is to the shadows that come of touching too deep the world below the tunnels, the old sewers and the new.

"I'll stay with her Above," I say. "I'll get thicker shirts and pluck the scales more. She'll pull them for me. I'll stay and make it good."

It's just foolishness to go 'round wanting not to have a Curse, my pa's voice whispers inside, in the dark.

From that stripe of darkness Jack looks at me measured, measuring, long. "Above's not a place for you, boy," he says in that soft slow way.

"It's not so bad," I say. Taste Ariel's lips on the words, salt like tears: *It wasn't that bad.*

Jack looks at me, long and cool, and the longer he looks the less I feel like he'll ruffle my hair or point me the way that needs going. I open my mouth and there's nothing but silence in it, a silence that grows as if from seed to reach out over the whole of Doctor Marybeth's lawn and hush up the eveningtime birds.

And then Doctor Marybeth's at the door, head poked outside into the shadow-driven night.

"Come in," she says, and opens the door wider. "Violet just woke up."

It's Whisper and me who throw on our shoes and go, go, go for the hospital.

Whisper and me and not Jack or Doctor Marybeth. Jack would spark the bus that takes you there into dying, and Doctor Marybeth needs to stay home in case Ariel comes down — and to pretend like she doesn't know us besides. And there's no keeping Whisper away after hearing those words. Ghostless or not, small and old and soft or not, nobody's even fool enough to suggest it. But they both draw the line at Whisper going into Whitecoat places alone.

So it's a quick wash for me, a change into the jeans and shirt that were bought new only a few days past with Atticus's careful-hoard emergency money. Doctor Marybeth lends me a cap, shows me how to pull it down low to hide my face from cameras and policemen and Whitecoats. It keeps half the world out of my view. Mack would hate it.

"You know where the hospital is?" I ask ten minutes later when I get downstairs to Whisper waiting, tidied and still edgy-frantic, a sharp I recognize: someone you love dearest in danger.

"I know," she says, and takes off down the street, between the streetlamps, to the bus.

I'm an old hand at bus riding now. I'm the best Passer of bus riding in all of wide Above. I get my paper transfer and get up to the seats halfway through. Whisper sits down next to me. Her hands are twitching, and they aren't folded in her lap to keep me looking away.

I don't know what I'm expecting for *hospital*. Something like Lakeshore, all old brick and ratted grass and wooden beams gone dry and hard. But the hospital Whisper leads me to is nothing like that at all. It rises up bright-lit and yellow from a lawn with a circle drive cut through it, and the lawn is a short sharp green as even as a barred window. The white vans that Doctor Marybeth called are parked all through that drive with their lights at rest, the men who work them standing outside and crackling with a watchfulness that makes me know it's a prison.

I stop there. I tell my feet to move and they won't do any more moving.

Hospital. Oh my oh my god.

"C'mon, Teller," Whisper says, hissing quiet from the corner of her mouth.

Your papa's feet were broken nearly four times, I tell myself, *and if he could endure that, you can go in there.* It still takes all my doing to follow her inside.

The hospital is made for getting lost. It curves and twists and dead-ends into walls or doors with *Staff Only* written on them. Whisper walks it eyes half-closed. Angry smells fill up my nose, making the end tingle; I'm scared to sneeze for the thought of Whitecoats descending and declaring me Sick, police seeing my face and locking me up in chains. Either one feeling down to the bitten-off scales on my back.

Whisper's drawn up with hurry, marching down another hall with the same walls, same doors, same tile-colored trail as the ones we've passed. "How do we know where we're going?" I ask quiet as I can.

She nods ahead at something I can't see. "Hospitals are full of ghosts," is all she says, dry and urgent. "And keep your hands in your pockets."

I look down. The bandages flutter like a signal light. I stuff them in my pockets.

I trail Whisper past a green-rimmed desk, hurrying to keep but one step behind. There are four Whitecoats behind it, hidden among racks and racks of files that block off exit from the back way. The files draw my eyes; I can't even count how many people locked away they mean, how many admission forms. They're orange and blue and green and stacked like fresh brands as far up as there is to go, and there's no Doctor Marybeth here to let them all out.

"Hey," someone says, and my hands are 'round my matches before I can tell myself *down!* Whisper stops sharp and turns back 'round, looking up with big innocent eyes at the Whitecoat behind the desk.

Anyone watching well can see the hint of red fire beneath that look.

"We're visiting," Whisper says, smooth as you please, never a flicker that lets you know she doesn't live and breathe Above. She cocks her head; listening. "Room four-thirty-eight," she adds.

"You family?" asks the Whitecoat. A girl Whitecoat, hard-faced and crag-nosed and with a look in her eye that says she's fixing to turn us out the door.

"I'm her nephew," I say, thinking on the move. Nephew's good cover Above. They don't expect you to look nothing like each other, and it's still close enough that you can laugh, weep, hold each other's hands.

She frowns. "There's only one woman in four-thirty-eight, and she's a Jane Doe."

My hands freeze in my pockets 'til I remember the man at the shelter, the sad look in his eye. "We're not sure," I mutter, knees tensed to run. "We — she went missing. We came to find out," I say, and hope.

And: "Oh, honey," the Whitecoat nurse says, melting down to sweet before I can blink, and looks at me with big eyes that I don't right trust. She pats my arm, hot callused hand that smells of chemicals and gag-sweet flowers, and I pull back before I think about Passing.

"Shy," Whisper says, her own hand on my shoulder, and steers me into Violet's hospital room before I can undo all my own good tricks.

I've never been in a hospital room before. And they are different from how they are in Tales. The walls are blue, all blue, not pale sick-up green. They're hung with pictures of houses and flowers, things that go soft and blurry when you look at them too close. There's thin flower curtains on the one short window, scratchy-looking even from ten steps back. And there's four beds cut off by nests of curtain, four restless bodies moving. I take in the sound of breath made echo-loud and strange, the soft slow beepings and the burrows of wire, and then Whisper prompts me through the narrow curtains to the far end, to the window, inside.

"Violet," I say, just like Whisper did when we found her hiding, curled up, fled from the touch of shadows.

There's a machine to breathe for her. It covers her face in a clear strangle-mask like something to pump out your soul. Her fingers tap a little on the side of the bed, made up white against blue walls against the blue of the papery dress she's wearing. It's terrible thin. It wouldn't get you through a fall day without freezing.

(*First*, Atticus says, *they take your clothes.*)

She don't make no sound 'cept her smacking, the lip-curls and shapings she always does. She don't look up and see us. She lies still, stately. Stares.

"Violet," Whisper breathes, and her eyes flick over to us, bright hunted Violet-eyes like I know from my first-born days. Her mouth shapes something that's not just a twitching and I reach forward without thinking to move away the clear and muffling mask.

"Don't," Whisper says, not loud or sharp but still enough to freeze me. "There's an alarm," she adds, quieter. I drop my hand to my side.

"Vee?" Whisper says again, leaning over her, and takes her twitching hand. The hand stills, I think. I don't see it move no more in the grasp of Whisper's smaller, thicker fingers. "Vee, baby, it's Annie. You're all right. We'll be back home in two shakes, and we won't let it hurt you no more."

Violet's voice is a husked-out thing. I don't recognize it proper as a voice for a few moments, and so I lose the first few words of it to the hiss of the breathing machine. "— didn't hurt her," is what I catch, and I mouth it after her.

Violet isn't stuttering, I realize. And: *Didn't hurt* her — *Doctor give me poison give me pills.*

My heart jumps halfway through my rib cage, and I lean in careful, careful, slow.

Violet's eyes are dark-chased with shadow.

"It was Corner," Whisper says, voice low, lips right by Violet's old-woman ear; too close, shadow-close, not seeing it yet. "Corner's shadows. Remember, Vee? In Lakeshore, and then we — then it burned."

"She was cold," Violet rasps, not Violet at all. Her fingers *taptaptap* on the bedside, playing pianos, playing bright music. "She was cold and the light was hurting her. I took her somewhere warm."

"Whisper," I say. Slow and careful, because it's scared things cornered that bite, and if shadows rise up out of Violet in the middle of a Whitecoat hospital, there's none of us here who'll get out alive. Whisper glances at me, and I jerk my chin slow, toward the darkness in her eyes.

Whisper drops the hand.

Her eyes are burning bright. They're bright as Atticus's and harder yet, and even though her fists are small and she told ghosts, long ago, that she wasn't the hitting kind, they're balled up like they could take walls down, rip up the curtains, burn the whole Whitecoat hospital and everyone in it.

"Whisper," I say again, and turn real obvious toward the open hospital room door.

The glare she turns on me is fifty-seven years of dead-ends and dead things and nights spent cold alone. "It took my Violet," she manages. Tears sneak 'round the corners of her eyes.

Violet glances one to the other. Her eyes are thick and confused, three shades too dark. I don't know if she even knows who I am. She ain't Violet no more. Just us four now left to Safe. Us four, and shadows.

— shadows, which tell you true names. Shadows which'll tell you secrets.

We burned all the shadows in Lakeshore, all the marks young-Corner left there, hugging the file of its lost-beloved Atticus, and none of them showed no sign of knowing Violet, of knowing Whisper's face.

This one's from the tunnels. This one *knows* things.

Whitecoats rustle on their Whitecoat business outside the door. In the bed opposite, foot-to-foot across the flower-curtained window, someone who ain't got no Safe to flee to turns over on his side. We've got a chance here.

We don't got much time.

I take a deep breath and bring my shoulders down. I think low and slow and careful things. I think about what makes a person vulnerable, and the avoiding of it. I think about making Safe.

"Corner," I say quiet, like a summoning.

Violet's chin ducks into her skinny collarbone, tangled and tangled in wires. "I hate that name," she slurs, faint and damaged under her plastic mask.

"Angel," I say, watching every fingertip for the reach of fingers not human. "You did right. You kept Violet hid away out of the light."

Whisper sucks in a breath. I hold up a hand, hold off her rage, her hurt. I'm the Teller, and this is the middle of a Tale.

Violet's face under the clear mask twists into a look I've never seen her bearing: a flushed smile, shy. The kind of smile that looks away, that's made by a wounded thing waiting to see if you'll praise or hit.

"Is there anyone else Above?" I ask, eyes half-shut. Pretending it's Ariel, who needs to be handled gentle. "Anyone else you've kept out of the light?"

"They're down below," the shadow whispers, letting out a breath in the gap between Violet's stutters. "I can't let anyone up wandering. That's not keeping Safe," it scolds, Atticus to a first-duty child. Violet's fingers open and close on the sheets.

"Are they still alive?" slips out, and I know it's a bad idea the second I say it.

The beeping of the machines gets faster, more insistent. "It was just *once*, they were Whitecoats and it's been *years*, and you — you can't keep holding that 'gainst me —" the shadow says, tears beading up in Violet's staring eyes. "I *never* hurt no one. I never even *saw* Jonah, and —"

And: "Shh," Whisper murmurs, pushing past me, face a red-eyed mask and tear-streaked. Touching, careful, Violet's hand. "You know we don't blame you for that," she says rough, rough-worn too, like it's a talk had fifteen hundred times, over and over in the dark.

Violet's puppet-nose sniffles. Violet's eyes blink back something else's tears.

"So everyone else's back beyond the Pactbridge," Whisper says, her voice hitching, but no matter 'cause the beeping alarm machine by Violet's bedside's slowing again, turning over to sleep.

"Yeah," Violet's voice says, "'cept Reynard and" — catch — "little Matthew and Narasimha and Jack. I can't find them." The keening eyes look up at me. "You'll find them for me, right?"

It's only that this is a hospital that keeps me from sicking up right then and there.

Whisper leans down urgent, just as I've turned away. "Who else is walking patrol duty?" she asks. "Are you watching anything but the Pactbridge?"

Violet shakes her head. Her tongue makes staccato clicks four times before she can bring it to speaking, and when she does, Violet's face is bitter, twisted, hurt. "I can't watch the tunnels. It's just me. Who else but just me?" Its voice twists in the same way I told Whisper that nobody, no one, ever tells Tales about Corner. "Who ever helps?"

Part of Passing's knowing when to cut your losses. Part of Passing's leaving before they throw you out.

"Is she your girl?" asks the lady Whitecoat when we pass her counter again. She's at the edge where Whitecoat space meets the hallway, hovering near as a raised fist and watching us with her spiky-syrup eyes.

Whisper draws herself up tall, and there's a moment where I'm afraid she's just gonna toss it all, say *yes this is my broken Sick Violet love* and get us both locked in with her. And then she smiles, sad and hard and awful, and goes, "No. She's someone else completely."

Whisper leads me out of the hospital slowly, hand in my hand, fingers 'round my fingers, and it ain't to keep me from Passing false no more.

I hold on.

It's cooled down out of doors, finally cooler than a kitchen stove though the wind's still as wet as sewers. I breathe it on my own and not helped by machines, tasting air that doesn't smell like medicines and dying. Air that smells like things that live, even if they live bad lives rooted down Above.

But that's wrong. It's not just bad lives that spend their days Above. And not just good ones that take root down in Safe.

And Safe is held against us by nothing more than Corner, fetched up alone in the dark.

I quicken my steps, looking for the bus stop. We've got to get this home to Jack: four against one, not four against a thousand. We've got to make plans, careful ones, and soon. But: "No," Whisper says and turns down the street, leading me by her tight-grasp hand.

"Where we going?" I'm near-afraid to ask, afraid of being tangled in another thing I don't want to keep secret. My hands still hurt from the last thing I tried to hold.

"I need some dark, Teller," Whisper says, and doesn't look back. "I need underground."

I walk with her down the street a different way, to a flight of steps set odd into the concrete. We go down them into a dimness that smells familiar, full of metal stands and machines and bright big posters.

The trains, I realize. This is the way to the trains.

Train's normally a danger noise; the worst danger noise of all. It's enough to beat the rustle of biting rats or the whisper of shadows, the moving of things we don't even have names for. Train means people, Normal watching people, and one sight of you caught in one corner of their eyes through the windows can mean work crews and police and Whitecoats come down into Safe. That's why train's the most dangerous. The others can kill you, but they can't kill Safe.

It's hard to forget that as Whisper pays the fare and the train grumbles into the station, pulling all the wind in the world behind it. The beat-up silver doors slide open one after another after another. There's just a few seconds to hurry into the car before they close tight behind us, and then it catches and pulls into the tunnels, the bright tiled platform speeding up and then left behind as the train takes us into darkness.

The dark's familiar and soft and good; I can close my eyes into it without the memory of too-bright things taunting and poking inside my lids. My breath goes out before I think 'bout it. My breath goes in and I breathe damp; faint tunnel-smell, dirt and must and metal and time, the smell of almost-home, the smell that's in my bones and belongs there more than grass and trees.

Tunnels. Pipes. Safe.

The homesickness comes up like any regular kind of sick, strong and dirty and no denying it, but this time I let it come.

Whisper's watching me, but not direct. She's watching me bounced off the window, which shows nothing but dark right now, dark and the ribs of tunnel-supports. "Almost there, Teller," she says, and I nod, wordless for a minute as the homesick cradles me like a child, ebbs slow away.

The train pulls into another stop with a squeak and scratch of wheels; pulls out again before she turns and asks me, quiet, "What're you thinking?"

"Dark true things," I say, unbidden; I always begged her to tell me what the dark true things her ghosts whispered were, but I'm not sure I need to ask anymore.

She chuckles, empty of anything that laughter ought to be: delight or ease or good companionship. "Dark true things," she says, hands in her lap, between the roll of wheels and the hum and clunk of tracks. There's a silence, ten chugs long. In the tunnels you can mark time proper. "You know, I lied," she says, with a soft little smile, staring out the window at my safe ghost-reflection. "It was only ever one dark true thing."

"What was it?" I ask, tired, empty.

"That you can't save them," she says. "You can't save other people. And most times, child, you can't save you either."

The train rattles. I sit still and quiet until it chimes to a stop. Whisper sits like a lady in a Polaroid photo, and all the while she stares out at the dark-reflecting glass, looking at nothing. Looking at ghosts.

VIOLET'S TALE

Violet's Tale is much like every other in Safe. Violet used to be Normal and then it didn't matter no more when she turned up Sick; when her mouth began to sing and she didn't drive the singing. Her lover called the Whitecoats, weeping 'gainst their white hands. They took her away, and she tried in Lakeshore three times to die.

She went, with Whisper and Atticus and Corner and Scar, down to Safe and swore she'd never go back.

After a while, every Tale is like every other.

●　○　●

'Cept Violet came back up from Safe (said the shadow in her body, husked-out and weak behind the plastic-tube mask). She came up running from shadows, running from the burning, eyes scorched by the sight of Atticus dead and the night fading out and so much light, so much terrible strip-naked light.

The wind rattled through the streets of Above, and it shook her flesh and bone.

The shadows boiled up from the sewers after her, red-eyed and spitting, and 'cause her mouth wouldn't let her even scream she ran ran ran, back to the only place she knew, to the last place she'd dropped foot in the whole of Above. Lakeshore was terrible. But it was quiet, and dark, and it would not shake its head at her, sad or unloving.

The shadows ran faster. The shadows were waiting.

And when we finally found her, the people who loved her, who carried her out of Lakeshore a second and final time, we gave her to the Whitecoats, weeping.

Before we left, before the Whitecoats and the hurry and hurt drove us out into the full cool night, Whisper leaned close to Violet's ear and said where I wasn't supposed to hear it: *I will come back for you.*

CHAPTER
NINE

"We move," Jack says, his hands 'round a mug of late-night coffee. His face is just as twisted and acrid and sharp. "Tonight."

Whisper sits at the other side of the table, hands in her lap, and twists her fingers through her many-colored skirts. She's gone past weeping. "We can't tonight. We aren't rested. We've got no hands. No fire."

"Don't need hands," Jack says, and the light in his eyes is forked and splitting. "There's no helpers in Safe. All we got to do is get through the door, take down Corner, and then we don't have to worry 'bout its shadows."

"You sure?" I ask.

Jack's face is thunder-grim. "They want what it wants. If there's no Corner? Corner doesn't want a thing."

"That's all we've got to do?" Whisper looks over to Doctor Marybeth for a back-me-up, a word against Jack's plan, but Doctor Marybeth's shutter-faced and silent, sitting in the fullest swath of light to keep the shadows from between her ears. Jack sees the reminder, and it ain't a kind one.

"All we got to do," he repeats, lower. "We go in and make the door. And two of us hold them off while the third goes through and does for Corner."

He's not counting Ariel. Ariel's stings mark up shadows. With her we're not two and one but three and one, and one who can move quick and quiet through the air and leave no footprints.

I don't say nothing. I don't know if we ought to count Ariel no more.

"Nice plan," Whisper snaps.

"We can hold 'em off long enough," Jack says, and though he doesn't look at me, that gives me no question 'bout who he means to send to put a blade in Corner's heart.

"Don't know 'bout you," Whisper shoots back, "but I mean to live."

Jack won't look at her then, and he still doesn't want to look at me. For the first time in my life I see Jack Flash drop his eyes to the table and then the floor, muttering like a little boy caught out eavesdropping. "There's others down there. Waiting on us. We can't plan selfish," he says.

I know it even though nobody wants to say nothing: That means we can't plan.

I close my eyes, fingering through Tales, thinking and thinking with the whole of my worn-out head. Not even Atticus and Whisper and Violet and Scar and Corner — yes, and Corner — made Safe with but the five of them against the world. They had hands Above to help them. They drew secret money from old friends, begged from strangers, kept secrecy and stashed it away. They saved food from Doctor Marybeth and picked up the boxes she left them to vanish down into the tunnels below.

Their hands from Above. Hands that stayed Above when the building was done.

"It doesn't have to be just the three of us," I say, and they both look at me.

I lick my lips. Doctor Marybeth in particular's watching me peculiar. Flickering shadow-doubt lingers in every place her hands go for a second after they're gone. "What d'you mean?" she asks.

"I know some people," I say. "People who might help."

"Where from?" Jack asks.

"Here," I say, and wait for the shout to come.

"We can't let people Above find the way to Safe," he says, and Doctor Marybeth sits up straighter a little, the shadow-gleam red and angry in her eye.

"Oh, come on," Jack snaps. "You know you're different."

Doctor Marybeth doesn't reply.

"We don't *have* Safe," I say, trying not to snap right back; to be calm and cool like someone not to be ignored or put down as a kid. I've been Teller since I overtook thirteen and it's near five years since then. "We draw the shadows into the tunnels, and our help can burn them out. They don't see Safe. They don't see our ways." I wait a moment. "And then we all live."

All five of us. Me and Whisper and Doctor Marybeth and Jack and my Ariel. Happy ever after in hurt and hate and secrets.

"I got hands," I say, and stand myself up to go. "And I got fire."

This time, Beatrice just lets me in through the buzzing-misery door that keeps the world off their toes. Just three visits, and they're used to my coming at strange hours of the night. Used to me coming to bring them sorrows.

I don't even tell myself to hush up for that as I kick and stumble up the steps to the most important task of my life.

They ain't all waiting at the door this time. I've worn my welcome thin and clear too quick for that, but Beatrice shifts me quick inside and there's no time to think about it.

She looks bad. She looks tireder than tired, and wary. The spiked red of her hair is drooping soft down her stubbly scalp.

"Beatrice," I say, and bow my head to her formal, 'cause she's the founder of this Sanctuary.

"You found her," Beatrice says, and the misery takes me for a full five seconds before I remember what I'm here for.

"Yeah," I say, soft, and she looks away.

"Safe?" she says after seven, eight, nine breaths, and it muddles in my head for a tenth. I've not freed Safe yet. And then I figure out what she means, and "Yeah," I say. Swallow against the prick of hurt that I'm already getting used to at the thought of Ari, of her wrist in my hand. "Safe 'nuff."

I look behind her but I don't see Darren; Darren who'd know about newspapers and beatings and bodies sprawled out on the floor punched to blood, police searches for a boy this high. I shouldn't even be outside, but this is an emergency. This is more of an emergency than twenty-five dollars can fix.

When I look back she's watching my hands, my bandaged-up, taped-together, red-puff hands. "Safe enough," she repeats like she don't believe it, and her eye goes cooler.

"I made it Safe," I say, the truth, and swallow down the sick.

"You did something," she says, flat and hard.

I nod my head. Yes. Yes.

Her face shutters up. Her eyes close, and open, and she's quiet.

"Were you even telling me the truth?" she asks finally. "You don't really come from somewhere else, do you? Just another fucking runaway with a good story." She rubs her scalp like it'll itch clean off. "God knows where she picked you up."

(*I got hands*, I told them. Like it was a certain thing.)

"I spoke true," I say, my voice hitching. "I found her on my second time up, and she was curled up little in a crack in the wall and when I held up the brand to see if she was real it was . . ."

Iridescent. I see it, bright and flicker in my head.

"You found her," Bea repeats.

"She had wings," I say, soft, and look up to meet her eye. "She had wings from her running. You *saw it true*."

And between one blink and the next her eyes widen and go yet harder, 'cause I've found the thing she really no longer believes, the thing that scares her and keeps her turn-toss at night: that maybe she didn't see wings, and maybe the bee was just a bee bumbled in, and all this has been teasing, a terrible mistake.

"Matthew," she says, not turned like Doctor Marybeth but with the same grief, "why are you here?"

I clear my throat. "I need to ask you something," I say pitched clean, every syllable made sharp and careful as to not break the ritual of the thing.

She lifts her head up a little higher. "What're you asking?" Hands out of her pockets, and standing tall like a founder ought to be. The rustle of feet behind her, in the dark at the bedroom door, goes quiet as the nighttime breathing of the boards.

I kneel down. I get down on one knee that digs into the blurred wood floor and strip off my sweat-stuck shirt, pulling scales with it where it's dried to them; sharp little yanks of pain that peel up to my shoulders. Beatrice watches. Keeps quiet and still.

"Beatrice," I say, in my best Telling voice, the voice that makes every sound sweet and clear. "We go down to Safe tomorrow to drive out the shadows. We go down to take back our home. Will you and yours carry our fire?"

She looks down at me, arms crossed across her chest, Normal and regular pink. She's ten fingers, ten toes, eyes, nose, ears. One of those hands flicks down; I feel it pass over the scales on my back, touch them, and I dare look up long enough to see her mouth open a little in fear. Fear of wings. Fear of gills and lion's toes.

Fear and wonder.

"Why should we?" she asks, but her voice trembles. "Why're you asking us?"

"You didn't turn her away," I say, and I'm stammering, I'm stumbling. I can't afford to stumble. "You didn't turn us away, her or me. That's . . . that's what we're 'bout" — (and Ariel looked up at me like a barely alive thing, vibrating, looked up like she was waiting to see what I'd do next). "It's about giving people someplace warm to be."

She's watching me. She's still watching me, and I can't figure out why, or how. Desperate, I think back for what Tales I have about Bea, and it's half-nothing; it's that she came from outside the city, from some northward town, and then just Cat and Darren and the way she's put them all together away from the street-Whitecoats, to make Safe —

Sudden, wild, I add: "She'll never be on the streets again. Not her, not nobody like her. You send them to us. They'll never have to sleep there again."

Beatrice runs a hand through her drooped-down hair, scratches the naked side of her head idly. And then her shoulders go down, and she lets out a breath so heavy with old things, remembered things, that down on my knees I near lose my balance.

"Yeah," she says, shy and rough. "Fine. We got your back."

There's a breath, a sigh, a squeak from the other side of the door. And there's a breath from me, a fall of my back and my chest, 'cause it's done and I might live to see my own house warm again after all.

I feel as old as Atticus. Older.

"Why?" I whisper before I can help it, knowing that deal or not, it's a gift; knowing there's nothing less wise than to question a gift lest it go right back to the giver.

She looks down at me, arms crossed again, but not in the way that shuts a body out. Showing the weight and heft of her, of her people. Of Sanctuary. "S'good to have a home."

Were there lesser light, were there a private place to go where no one listened shadow at the door, time enough and memory to hear it once, again, I would ask Bea her Tale.

I will carve this on the doors of Safe, I promise her, and let out a breath to seal it.

"What do we do?" she asks and steps back, lets me stand, lets me pull the Passing down over myself again and zip it up tight.

"We have to talk to my people," I say, and open the door.

I take her hand and lead her down seven flights of stairs, to the wet-slicked streets of Above.

There's *phoning* before I take her back to Doctor Marybeth's. Phoning with one of my extra quarters, ill-spared and precious, from a black-handled slick dirty phone tucked away between two shopfronts, to make sure it's all right to bring her. They fight for six minutes by my counting before I say: "Can't wait this long," mild and quiet. Doctor Marybeth stops and then says "Come," and hangs up just as Jack and Whisper start to shout again.

We come.

Two buses and rain-damp streets, a walk down the block, and we're there, knocking at Doctor Marybeth's door three-and-two, muffled by the bandages slipping on my right hand. Doctor Marybeth opens up near right away.

"This is your friend?" she asks, her shoulders hunched enough in the yellowy hall light that I know the fighting went on all through those two bus rides and up to the door.

Ariel's friend, I almost correct. But I look over at Bea and think of the trust she's laid down in me, the trust I've returned in her even though it's the highest of fool things in the world to trust Normal people Above.

"Yeah," I say, and smile to show each of them the other's nothing to fear. "Doctor Marybeth, this is Beatrice."

Bea nods her head. Wary. But Doctor Marybeth don't take it as rude.

"They still against it?" I ask.

"Yeah," and Doctor Marybeth straightens a little. "But it's my house." She leads us inside, trailing the door open. I shut it tight behind us.

Bea doesn't shed her shoes like everyone else. Her boots creak soft soft down the tiny tiled hall, and she stops a half step behind me in the door of Doctor Marybeth's kitchen.

"Hey," I say, and Jack and Whisper both turn to me with wicked scowls.

"We didn't say —" Whisper says, and before she can finish I move over and make room. Bea takes the signal and slides thin into the kitchen. She looks half-ready for anything. I dunno that she's ready for Whisper and Jack.

"This is Bea," I say. A silence. "She knew Ariel before."

Ariel is Sick, I remember her saying. She knows Ariel, right and true. Better, maybe, than all of us.

"And she's hands?" Jack says, right over her head.

"She's got a place," I say, ignoring Jack's mouth. "She keeps twelve sworn clean and safe and gives them Sanctuary."

She's Atticus, my eyes say to him, just as hot and spark, and maybe they gleam red just a little bit, because Jack backs off and looks Bea up and down for the first time.

"Got twenty more who owe us favors," Bea says, cool as you please, and she is Atticus indeed, 'cause nothing you ever said to snip back at Atticus ever moved him a step out of place. She walks right in and takes a chair, straddles it crosswise and folds her arms on the back. I near expect to see impatient claws clicking. "Matthew says you want us to help you take your place back," she continues, and tucks her hands in the crooks of her elbows. "And he says you'll help keep our people off the streets in return for it."

I bite my lip. I had no right, promising that.

Whisper and Jack pass a long look at each other, eyebrows raised in mimic on both sides. "Well, he's

Narasimha's kid, all right," Jack finally says, dry and wry, and I only get half of what that means before they turn back to the rest of us.

"We do, and we will," Whisper says. There's a smile on her face I don't know I've ever seen, half-curved and attentive and not at all the sharp-tongued, sharp-mind Whisper I've known the whole of my life.

A Passing smile.

I search for remorse in the first blush of that knowledge: Even if we win, I've opened up the knowing of Safe to people who don't need Safe. We'll go through our lives now with people who'd know us to look at in the streets Above, scavenging for our food, our clothes, our lives. People who might give us up.

Doctor Marybeth never did, I tell myself, and set my jaw tight. Doctor Marybeth didn't, and Bea won't. I won't be sorry. I won't be shamed for this.

It can't all be wickedness, Above.

"Tea?" Doctor Marybeth says mildly into the quiet, her eyes not on Bea's face or tough hands but her feet. Bea falters just a second, flushes faint, and unlaces both her boots.

We're silent for a moment while she carries them to the front hall and comes back, more slippery, in stocking-feet.

"Twenty of us," Beatrice says, talking like Doctor Marybeth didn't shame her but a scant minute ago. "No.

A dozen, a good dozen who won't talk shit around. And you three. And Matthew?"

"Not me," Doctor Marybeth says, and there's a flicker of shadow at her fingers as she turns her face away.

"And Ariel," I add, before Jack can get in a word.

This quiet is harder to break. It stands up to mildness and shuffling and polite shame.

"I don't know, Teller," Whisper says. "She's quite unhappy with all of us."

That brings my head up. "Why you?"

"That's Ariel's way," Whisper says gently, and Jack says nothing so loud it booms.

"I'll talk to her," Bea says, shuffling her stocking-foot against the tile.

"Upstairs," Jack rumbles, and points with the tip of his chin. "Lucky if she listens to a word you say."

There's a noise beneath the table that might be a kick. I look right at the wall and try not to think about it.

"I took her in," Bea says, quieter.

"So did Matthew," Jack says, and she stands up a little faster than she looked to be planning and takes herself up Doctor Marybeth's stairs like it's a call to trial.

We wait.

"You trust them?" Jack asks. Not looking at me slantwise; just asking. Asking to hear the answer.

"Yeah," I say. Ears aching from the need to hear, through the boards and carpets, every little word passed 'bout me and my failings, 'bout Ari and Safe and what might make it all right. "She said she and hers would carry our fire," I add, to not look like I'm listening.

"And she knows what that means," Jack says.

"Yeah," I say, giving him my attention for real now. "She knows Sanctuary."

"And we're to give her people Sanctuary."

"I don't know why I promised that," I admit.

Jack shakes his head, laughs soft. "It's no more than your father did."

We don't talk again 'til Bea's feet sound on the old creak steps, *squeak squeak moan* to the landing. It's only one pair of feet, not two, coming down the stair.

"She won't come down," Bea says, and now her mouth is pressed unsure. The blood comes to my face, but I don't dare look away. "But you might go up. She might hear you."

I don't know what I've got to say for hearing.

"All right," I say, and wipe my hands on the legs of my fade-out Salvation Army jeans. If I got nothing to say for myself, I'll speak for Jack and Whisper. I'll speak like a Teller ought to, and speak for Safe.

I take the stairs one at a time, slow and loud so she'll hear me coming, hear the tread and sigh of my thick-nail feet and not be scared when I turn the knob. I let her make herself ready.

I make Safe.

She's curled up in the chair again when I open the upstairs door; curled up too-studied around her black book with a pencil loose in her hand. Her chin's too high to be drawing. For sure, she heard me. And for sure she's pretending she didn't.

"Ariel," I say, hovering in the doorway. Not moving, and likely to die of it. "Can I come in?"

She don't say nothing.

The quilt on the bed is rumpled bright. The bathroom door is open, and I can see sparkles of shining here and there on the floor. *Chitin*, I think; Atticus taught me the word. The thing that makes insects' armor, when they feel the need to be sealed 'gainst the world.

Her wings, smashed in pieces.

Her wings.

"I won't come in unless you let me," I say, watching them catch the faint yellow light of Doctor Marybeth's surviving lamp. It turns each little prickle of wing sunshine-bright. Golden.

"Okay," she mumbles after a moment, and I don't lose my footing from the relief of it. Instead I walk deliberate and careful, hands out and at my sides, and sit myself on the edge of the big old creaky bed.

She shuts her book and puts it down slow.

"I'm sorry," I whisper.

She don't reply.

"Ari, I'm so sorry," I say, trying to keep my voice low and blowing it, hands gone to fists in my lap. Not mad; or not mad at *her*. Just — all my own stupid, to think I could hit and kick and scare the one what hurt her and that'd make it okay. That kicking would cure Sick.

That it'd make her love me good, like light made soft, unburning.

You're doing this wrong, Teller, says the quiet part of me, the part that ain't still wailing and begging to be loved. *If you got nothing else to say, speak for Safe.*

I shove back the hurt. I shove back the shame. I get down on my knees, knee-to-floor and head bowed, no sudden moving; nothing that'll make her need to fear.

"Ari," I whisper, aching to wrap my arms around her and wail *lover give me something give me poison give me pills*. I don't; I'm not gonna touch her, not 'til she touches me. Not unless I can do it sweeter. "We're going down to Safe tomorrow to take it back. Jack and Whisper and me, and your friend Beatrice" — *my friend Beatrice* — "and her sworn, and what ghosts who'll lend arms that Whisper can muster."

I take a breath. It drags in the back of my mouth. But she's watching.

"It's real dangerous. It's dangerous 'cause the plan's to kill Corner, 'cause the shadows are all its shadow, and that means getting someone in quiet to do it while everyone else holds ground. People —" and I stop. "People are gonna die.

"But you're fast. You're quick and small and when you stung it, you did harm. We need you."

She's silent a second. Then: "Why me?" she asks, and it's a real question, not moaning. She's looking at me small and grave.

I swallow. "You know Safe. You know us. You —" I pause, realizing; how she came careening out of the tunnels through the dark, knew exactly where to land, to sting. "You could see it before. Corner. When I couldn't."

She ducks her head. A tiny nod. "It smells," she says quiet, far away in a deep tunnel in another world that was only one week past. "It's hard to see, hard to touch, but I remembered that smell."

I didn't smell a thing. Not even when Corner's bloodtouch-fingers were jammed up against my eyes. "Where'd you remember it from?"

She shifts. I keep my eyes off her, keep their pressure away.

"The Cold Pipes," she says. The noise that jeans make against chair fabric quiets. "It smells like hospitals," and the stutter-beat of my heart on ribs stops tight.

"You saw something there," I say. Not asking. *She was talking to shadows.*

"I don't know," she whispers.

And now I look up. Her eyes are bruised, but I can't tell if it's shadows, not if it's Corner's or our very own. "How d'you not know?"

She shakes her head so hard her hair smacks 'gainst the chair like a slap. "I keep telling you and you never listen. There's things you don't talk about."

"Or what happens? Ari, I'm listening now. I'm listening. What happens if you talk about it?"

When her voice comes again, it's odd, tiny. Like a bee lost in empty tunnels where flowers don't grow. "They lock you up."

I try to meet her eyes, and she looks aside, away. Color high. Shamed. "Ari," I say real careful.

"That's not my name," she mumbles.

I know it isn't. I know.

"Ari, what happened at the Cold Pipes?"

"Nothing," she says, but the way she shifts in the chair, still won't meet my eye, the way she's so terrible, terrible calm gives her away.

"Ari, it's important," I say, try to make it gentle. "Not just for us, for everyone. Ari, best-love, what did you see?"

"I can't," she whispers, and this isn't the usual hiding, the usual weeping; it's agony. The lines of her body are aching to change, blurring down soft into fine hair and stripes and the hint of a long, pointed sting. "Please don't make me, please —"

I hold out my hands. I offer up the dirtying bandages like a sacrifice and say, soft, "Don't run."

She peeks out at them a long, long moment. Caught by their moving, and held. I unwrap them before her, and she looks at the puffed-up, swollen stings.

"I hurt you," she says, going long again without even thinking, turning into arms and legs and girl and restless fingers plucking at each other.

"I forgive you."

"You won't."

"I do." I swallow. "I hurt you too. We — neither of us meant it. Not for true," I say, and hope to everything that's not lying. "I love you."

"You won't," she repeats, toying with the corner of her notebook. Stubborn and hollow. A dead man's voice.

"I love you," I repeat, and then more promises I might not be able to keep: "I will never turn you away. No matter what, okay?"

She blinks at me, and I have to close my eyes to keep on going. To say it to the end.

"No matter if you don't — if you don't love me no more. No matter what happens with us."

And to hell with your last time, I tell the ghost of dead, stupid Atticus.

When I open them again she's looking at me, measuring, caught and wing-grown and surprised past speaking, and then her chin droops and the wings shrivel, crush against the back of the patched-up chair. "I'm Sick, Matthew," she whispers, two bright red spots on her cheeks.

The weight in my belly gets heavy. It would do no good to tell her about Doctor Marybeth and files. Files lie, and stories are better Told from one's own tongue. "What kind of Sick?" I ask.

Her fingers play a little staccato on her knee: *do re mi.* "I . . . see things. Get mood swings. I hear —" she tightens. "I hear voices when there aren't none there." A swallow. "Here," she says, and shoves her book into my hands, rough and sudden. I barely catch it. "Look."

I almost ask *are you sure?* but she's turned away from me. Turned away like I'm to pull a bandage off, and her watching'll make it just hurt worse. Her notebook is thick and worn in my hands.

I open it.

It's pictures. Ari has a fair hand with them, light and dark shaded in careful in snap-broken pencils. It's pictures of the tunnels, of Safe, and sometimes, between, words. Her handwriting's thin and tiny, not Whitecoat-tiny but close; labeling the pictures. Writing down, with careful sketched-in dates, *real* or *not real.*

"Ari —" I say, not understanding.

"Doctor Wishnevsky said it was a good way of double-checking," she says, low. "You put down what you saw. And if it was consistent, or if someone else verified it, then you knew it was real. Like running a checksum. And then if something came back, you could logically know it wasn't real."

I don't know what a checksum is. I've never heard her speak so even before, so matter-of-fact, so knowing. So shamed. "Doctor?" I ask, to stall.

"My therapist," she says, even lower. "From inpatient."

I can't take it in. I can't take in the look on her face. Instead I look down at the paper, turn the page.

The next page isn't familiar: a fall of rock, packed loose. Heaped junk in the gutter where the sewer water ran. A thin, frail fire, and gaping outflow pipes, pipes that are dry and dead and go nowhere. The stones are each laid down precise and neat; the way of somewhere you've seen a lot; somewhere that's a years-long home, though the date scribbed next to it's only five months past. And etched in, with horrible detail and the thickest line a pencil can give, are the outlines, the limbs of shadows.

"The Cold Pipes," I breathe out. *How often could she have been down there?* And then the panic draws in with the very next breath. "Ari, did they touch you? This is really important — did the shadows touch you?"

She looks up, sudden, anguished. "I didn't know they were real," she says. "I didn't know *you* were real for —"

She doesn't finish. It's good. I don't want to know how long.

"Ari, love. Did they touch you?"

She swallows. Nods, and I'm out of words. Wordless. Undone.

I knew it true from the first.

"No," she protests, stung and absolute. With all my trying to walk soft, talk soft, she's still seen it on my face. "I never."

I think of shadows pouring down my throat, pouring out of my hands into two legs two arms and a nose and head and elbows on the floor of Lakeshore Psychiatric, and realize no shadow ever had to make my Ari open the door to Safe. Atticus was right: Safe wasn't safe no more from the first time she ran. Safe wasn't safe from the day Corner laid shadows 'tween her fingers and they trailed to and fro through the Pactbridge door.

"We won't send you out. We'll keep you safe," I say, even though it's the wrong thing, 'cause it's the only thing I know to offer, the only thing I've been able to give, in its insufficiency, all along.

Her voice is bleak and certain. "You can't."

"Help us try," I beg, and that's all I'm doing here, not asking, not speaking, not telling no Tales but begging. "Help us so we can try." I take a guess, wild and stupid. "Help us so you've got somewhere to go next time."

She's crying when I leave her. She's crying, but she don't turn her face away.

I walk down the steps heavy and scuff-feet, not to warn them 'bout my coming but because I can't bear to lift myself farther off the ground. I go down into the kitchen and stand in the doorway, trying not to touch the door frame with my prickling, gauze-trail hands.

They're looking at me. I know I'm crying too, bare-handed and jaw tight shut so it don't make a sound. I know what they're looking at.

"She'll come," I tell them, "and I know how the shadows got into Safe."

The whole of the next day is tense and still.

There's no going down to the tunnels before dark. No matter how the ground pulls me down harder than yesterday, knowing we'll be set for home so soon, there's enough people on the streets and sidewalks that going into the tunnels can't be done before night. There's a lot of things you can do or say or be Above and everyone will think you're just permitted, but jumping down sewers ain't one of them.

We have nothing to do until dark.

Not nothing: Jack plans. He draws maps and maps, something never before done in the history of Safe and a small blasphemy besides. He sits with Beatrice tracing them, saying *here there's a fall and step careful*, or *here we can draw off their ambush*. Whisper and Doctor Marybeth go out for a wealth of supply: water bottles squeaking clear 'gainst each other in the box, cereal bars and protein bars and rolls of sticky bandages, and hid behind the whole of it a small crate-box that's familiar. I open it while they're stacking it all in the sitting room, careful against the walls.

Matches.

Ari comes down, but she sits in the corner with strong tea, ducked away from our gazes. She grazes through Doctor Marybeth's fridge like it's all ready to go off: strawberries and cream and cheese and all the things we don't see often, things that don't keep good in Safe. She's preparing. In case we die. In case she never gets to have them no more.

In case I keep her down in Safe and never let her back into the light.

I'm out on the back lawn when Jack comes looking: plucking at grass spikes, plucking at stupid thoughts. "You ready, Teller?" he asks me, and there's layers and layers and deeps in that question. I don't even need to look at him to know it.

"No," I say, and pull another stem. Put my hands in my pockets to keep them off Doctor Marybeth's lawn.

They come up with matches.

He doesn't pat my head or nothing. He just asks "You gonna be ready?" and sits down to the side of me when I shake my head. An invitation, from Jack Flash: an open ear, a hand on the back. A Teller for the one person who never gets to tell a Tale.

"We know how to break the shadows," I say, turning my matchbook 'round and 'round in the careful cup of my hands.

"Something you're not saying 'bout that, Teller," Jack rumbles, and he's watching me with lightning-eyes, hot and serious in a way so different from Atticus that it can't but remind me of his hard-face ways all over again.

I have four matches left. Four more and they'll be done, and I can burn no more. "We know how. I'm wondering if we should."

His eyes get no less hot, no less grave, but something in them changes. A tightening. A spark. "Go on," he says, and sits still and listening like into a strong wind.

I flip the matches again. Turn, flip, turn. Matches eat the faces off weeping shadows and light your safe way home. "I don't think we oughta kill Corner."

And I've said it. There.

"You're afraid we'll be named Killer," he says. He's not looking away. My hand closes tight around the matchbook, a proper fist around its rounded, creased-up corners. I'm already named Killer.

"No," I tell him. "There's no one to name us that. It's about how Atticus kept Safe going." I pause, trying to get both hands 'round the thought; pull it through all the holes and tears and silences in every Tale ever given me about Safe. The one big untruth repeated every year, to celebration, on Sanctuary Night. "It's about the lying."

Jack sits precise and watching. He waits.

Some people ain't no help in a Tale.

"Corner was forgot. If it'd been remembered, remembered right and true, that would have broken Safe." I lick my lips, uncomfortable. Atticus is only six days dead. It's not strange after all to feel like speaking ill of him will summon him up to look at us with smoldering orange-mad eyes to punish us for gossip.

It's not strange that I should be a little scared.

"Atticus knew that," I keep going, to spite that fear, to kick it down. "Safe needed to be strong, and if everyone knew he made such a bad mistake with Corner, believing someone Killer and doing exile to them just because of their own fighting . . ."

"It would have broken Safe," Jack agrees, still perfectly still. It makes me ache to fidget even more. "And besides, it would have meant the end of Atticus as founder."

And then Atticus, proud Atticus, would have had no place to go, because he couldn't have stayed among us any more than Ari could tell me in words 'bout the Cold Pipes.

Shame's powerful. Shame's stronger than claws.

"But that's what sent Corner mad," I say, 'cause if Corner's not mad, with all that bleeding and fighting and wanting to die, I'm a — I don't know what I am. "It went mad because of the lying. All of us inside, keeping up this

Tale about how it was Killer, and not letting it back home. We —" and I pause, feeling notebook pages under my fingers. "We said its real wasn't real. We left it out to die."

He watches.

"That's what set the shadows on us," I say faint.

"That won't matter, though," Jack says, and there's something sharp in him, keen as a wire.

"But the shadows are Corner's. They came on because Corner was forgot. What if they don't fade? What if we keep on going just like we did before, keep on telling false, and the shadows don't fade?" My hands hurt. They're dug into themselves in little puffy fists. But not mad. Not for hitting.

Not mad.

"There won't be no more shadows if we kill Corner," Jack says.

"Corner's Sick," I protest, fainter still. "Sick's the same as Freak Above."

There's tears in my eyes. I don't move to touch them, because in Safe's and Atticus's and all of Above's teaching, those tears ain't there if you only don't move your hand to wipe them away, and bad things don't happen if you just don't cry.

"Matthew, Corner's Killer," he says gentle.

"Corner wasn't Killer."

"It is now," he says. "And Killer's a thing you can't give Safe to and make well."

"It's just *wrong*, Jack," I burst out, for once in my life not finding words, not able to fit the sounds to the Tale. "It isn't making Safe."

"To kill Corner."

"To kill Corner and pretend it was all just wickedness," I snap, and look up at him, not sure what storm might come down. "I was there. I saw what color Atticus's eyes were when he exiled the first Beast from Safe."

Jack sits straighter, and turns to me with a look in his eye that's sharp and considering, popping with sparks. "Did you now?" he asks.

I don't flinch away from it. I don't run.

"Yeah," I say. "I did."

Jack gets up.

He gets up and puts himself down on one knee before me, puts his head low to the green prickle lawn. He bares his arms to the elbow so the lightning in his veins plays along every snowflake scar and to his burn-red fingertips. "There's lightning in me," he says, husky, hollow. "It came into me when I was young. I can draw down fire to keep us warm and give us good food to eat. I can give us light. But I can't Pass."

He takes my hand. He lets me feel the lightning.

Jack is asking me Sanctuary.

It stings. I hold tight to his burning hand because my own fingers won't let go and ask: "Why me?"

He unbows his head. He looks right up at me and says: "Because you know what needs forgetting and what ought to be remembered."

I look around, but it's grass, fence, trees. Nobody in the houses 'round is looking out the window; nobody in Doctor Marybeth's kitchen is at the strip-curtained back door. They must be in the sitting room, or upstairs, or out.

Nobody'll save me from this.

"You can't decide this yourself," I say, frantic. "You can't just say who's to be leader in Safe."

"No," Jack rumbles, and even though my teeth are chattering from the ache of his ungloved touch, I see the little glint in his eye. "But where I go, the lights turn on. My word'll carry."

It's true. In all of Safe, there was one man not fearful of Atticus, and it was Jack.

"I'll give you Sanctuary," I whisper, and the lightning kisses me bone to bone as he squeezes and the pact is sealed.

"So what're we gonna do?" I ask him later, after we've stared up at the leaves and the sun and sat awkward, like there wasn't no swearing or giving or deal-making done away from everyone else's eyes.

"Go down. Draw the ambush. Kill Corner," Jack says. "And then tell the Tale true."

Doctor Marybeth comes out for us when the sun touches the tops of the trees. She picks her way across the grass, dodging the shade; moving between bits of sunlight like an anti-shadow. Jack looks up at her and his face is a brief smile, tight; *I don't know if I might see you again.*

I'm sorry.

"We've got everything split into packs," she tells him. Cool and sober, like it's a regular day and this is regular work. "Whisper wants you to take a look."

"Right, Mare," Jack says, mild, and I wonder how it is between them; how they came to teach each other the turns down to Safe and up, and all the things that go unsaid. All the dark true things they tell each other, and how they get around them. How they live.

Jack pads to the door, *crunch crunch* and browning the grass a little. He looks over his shoulder for us, eyebrow up.

"I'll be right there," Doctor Marybeth says, and waits cool as you please 'til he's through the door.

"Ma'am?" I ask, because the look in her eye's a little like Atticus scolding. But she just holds out a hand to lift me to standing and leads me to her glass back door, out of the late afternoon heat.

"When you come back —" she says.

"If."

"When," she insists. "You remember what I told you."

I nod. And look down to give her a chance to walk away, go back inside, busy herself with something safe and quiet and fake. There's birds nesting in one of the trees. I watch the flash of wings that still makes me nervous — quick movement in the tunnels is a thing to fear.

She doesn't walk away. She opens the door and waits for me, waits patient.

I wonder how much she has to wait patient, and where she learned how.

I step into the kitchen, and — the hell with it. I've only got tonight. I've only got two hours or three.

"Doctor Marybeth?" I ask her, back straightened up, formal and clear.

"Yeah?" she says.

I settle my shoulders. I put on my listening face, my listening air. I got no right to this either; I can't put a Tale into my head without Atticus having heard it first, without it being offered up to everyone for Sanctuary and a share in what we are. But Atticus never thought to ask for this Tale, and Atticus is dead, and I've broken every rule there was and ever could be, and maybe it's time to make my own. At least while I'm alive for tonight, with Jack sworn to me and the question of what Sanctuary means on my shoulders.

So: "Doctor Marybeth," I ask, "will you tell me the story of how you came down to Safe?"

It's not the right words for her. We don't have no ritual words for those who came down to Safe and went back up, down and up with less, if not nothing, to fear. But she looks me in the eye and sees the words I *mean*.

"I will," she says, and puts her battered blue kettle on for tea.

Once night falls, we move out.

We move down the street in clumps and batches. Walk the sidewalks like people who belong, signaling back and forth one group to the next. The trees whistle at us with wind and we lean into it, sour-smelling; it tastes thick like sewer and home. We walk the turns down to the sewer cap that runs closest to our tunnels and I bring out from my pockets a set of pins, tools that Whisper's found somewhere in her ceaseless rummaging, to take the sewer cap off quick and clean.

My hands are clumsy-stung. Bandaged and thick. I work slow.

I fiddle clanking quiet for one minute, maybe more, while the whole of the first army of Safe stands around me back to back and watches every shadow for a twitch of movement that's wrong.

And then "Open," I say, remembering this time to speak low instead of whispering.

Down goes Jack, down goes Beatrice, down go Whisper and Bea's black-clad sworn. The first lick of flame puffs down below, orange like something looking to be mad, and my fists loosen at the sight of the signal fire.

"Go on," I say to Ariel, second-last, and she looks at me one fearful moment before firming up her chin and climbing down the long ladder, her lovely hair all bound up in braids and tucked away to keep it out of the fire.

Then it's just me. Empty street, and me, and the wind.

I lean back and take in the surenesses of Above, the memory of match-struck sun burning through my eyelids so everything's orange and there can be no shadows: not in my eyes, not in my heart. The first rule of Above: denying all the dark things that live inside. Sending those who bear shadows, who bear the marks of them down and down, into the hospitals, into the pits so everyone else can live their lie.

That's why they have Asylum and we have Sanctuary. Or that's what Atticus would've said.

I think I say different.

I put my bouncing shoes right, then left on the cold slippery ladder. Right, left. And pull the sewer cap closed above me, and take us into the dark.

DOCTOR MARYBETH'S TALE II

Doctor Marybeth is a Doctor. That is the whole of her Tale.

(*There's got to be more than that*, I said, and she went *hush, let me be done*.)

Doctor Marybeth is a Doctor because she believes in making things well. She grew up in a place across more ground than a person can walk — *more ground than you could imagine, Matthew* — where nothing was well: where the uncles drank and the children were sent away to wicked schools run by white men and the mamas were all bent in despair. She got most of her real language torn away from her, 'til she could only hold a few words and cradle songs. She whispers them to herself every night before bed as proof against forgetting. *Tsujus* is one of her real words. It is the most important, because it means *child*. It's the word her mama bid her remember when they took her away to the school: that no matter what, Marybeth would always be her mama's child.

She escaped from the schools when she turned eighteen. And she went on to be a Doctor, because the only way to fight what was wicked in the world was to work, hands and heart, for what was good and well.

She couldn't make her home well, so she left for the city and made money to send back, to put food in the cupboards for her mama and uncles and help build their own school to teach their own Tales. She couldn't make Lakeshore well, so she left the door slipped for Atticus and Corner — and unknowing, Whisper, Violet, and Scar. She couldn't make Atticus and Corner well, so she went down to one to plead for the other.

She can't make the world well, so she gives to us for Safe, even though her money's sometimes thin and her nieces and nephews draw down trouble that's more time and money in the tending, and there are things in the world she wishes she had, things important to her heart.

And she never went down to Safe for good, because Safe's about hiding, not well.

(*Hey* — I started, and she held up her hand, eyes hot and shadow-tinged. I let her explain.)

Healing's not always natural, she says. Healing's not always the way a body wants to go. Sometimes the body wants to run. Sometimes it can't think of anything but what might stop the pain. And though stopping the pain's important if you want a body healing, it isn't the whole. Sometimes that just keeps you broke.

(*You don't agree with Safe*, I said, shocked out of the rote and memory of taking in a Tale.

That there should be such a place? Yes, she said, hands in her lap. *With the whispering and hiding and teaching your children to fear and hate? No. I don't agree with Safe at all.*)

In Doctor Marybeth's world, Safe's what's called a reservation. It's a place that's yours away from the world, where others won't bother you; where you live your life without being locked in schools and hospitals and chains. But it's its own set of chains, of walls. Doctor Marybeth grew up on a reservation. Her uncles drank and the children left and the mamas cried all day. It made nobody well.

It wasn't Safe; it was Isolation.

So Doctor Marybeth stays Above. She works in the hospital, and she lives alone, but she keeps her guest room ready in case someone Sick needs helping. She sends the rare thing down to Safe, but not too much. Not since she broke with Atticus, because Atticus's way is not going to make healing.

(*Go make Safe*, she said, and patted me on the shoulder. And I knew what she meant for real.

And she left me alone with the sunset, watching, before we moved out to retake what was ours.)

TEN

It is a dark, chill road to the gates of Safe from Above.

Jack takes the front: the most important spot on a duty, supply or sentry or any duty to step outside Safe's doors. The man in front counts the turns, carries the light. The man in front swears an oath without talking: to take the blade or hit or shadowfall of anything that rises up before us, so the duty will be warned and Safe will go on.

I was the man in front the night we found Ariel. I went into her hollow and talked to her soft, and risked her stinging when I took her by the hand.

Whisper takes the back. The back's second most important. If the man in front falls, the one in back has counted the turns too and leads us up and out and away, somewhere snug, somewhere with a wall where we can make a good stand.

I stand middle, and that's important too in its way. The man in the middle's kept safe as Safe, guarded by each body that walks the duty with the whole of their lives. The man in the middle's job is to carry the Tale if everyone else falls, and by wit or stealth or sacrifice, take the word of their dying home to Safe.

I stand middle, and Ari stands with me. I stand middle 'cause I've got the knife.

There wasn't much talk about the killing. Somehow, without speaking, Whisper and Jack agreed that it had to be me. Jack agreed about the forgetting, that the forgetting was wrong, but not about the killing, the scouring of shadow-feet from every bit of ground we'd claimed for our own. *Fine*, he said. *We'll tell it in the Tales. But we gotta fight for our own.*

He gave me the knife. It is small and wide and neat, and it burns cold in the palm of my hand as we walk the dark, chill road to Safe.

Bea was clever about her choosing: She brought only half of her Sanctuary-sworn to the park by Doctor Marybeth's house, and some I've never seen. There's none of those that looked at me slantwise when Ariel fled away. But she brought Darren.

I don't talk to him. He don't talk to me. We go down and down and the tromp of boots and beat-up shoes turns into quiet splashing, a sound I know. An almost-home sound.

"'Ware," Jack whispers as we turn into the old sewers, and *'ware, 'ware, 'ware* mutters down the line like a summons. Whisper sings it like a hunting-call, and if the ghosts she's dredged from the alleys and nooks reply, I don't know how.

The dark things skitter out of our way, rats into their nests and the wicked nothings into the mire, and all of them watch our progress down through the old subway tracks, along the vent that goes to the sewers, past the twist you have to be looking for. To Safe.

"Hold," Jack says, soft, and strikes the match.

The fire passes from hand to hand. The brands are lit and smoking in the thin, sweet air before we reach the Pactbridge. By the time I feel its wood beneath my thin-sole shoes, everyone's holding burning, light that'll blind every last person left in Safe and keep the shadows at bay.

"We hold them off," Whisper says from the back of our column of fire. "We get our man through."

Nobody talks. But everyone nods and a few give me looks full of nerves and that stupid lip-twist sadness, and I wipe my hand on the side of my jeans and grip the knife tighter.

Ari takes my hand. Squeezes it once.

Ari and I tuck ourselves away behind the Pactbridge. There's a tunnel-hill of scree cleared down and smooth to keep Safe from just this kind of ambush. We dig both our bodies into the crack in the wall behind it, a tight little space five feet deep that drips groundwater slow and clicking. Ari goes in first, all legs and short-stepped scramble. I look over my shoulder as she tucks herself tight and climb in after her.

"The door," Jack says, not bothering to whisper no more, and he and Bea grasp the rivet-through handles and bang three times on the door to Safe.

"Corner!" Jack roars louder than anything ever uttered in Safe, rattling the walls and rock-roots and gullies of the dark pathways underground. Every tunnel and curve of Safe sings that forbidden name.

Corner Corner Corner lingers in the cracks and worm-mounds. The torches crackle. The torches burn.

The door opens, and the shadows come.

They come screaming, screaming their awful hissing shadow song. Over the Pactbridge they come, and Jack drops both gloves and takes the fire to them.

Fighting's beautiful in Tales. But the fighting for the doors of Safe is all darkness and sparked burning. I can't see who stands, who falls, without peeking out from our hiding place, and I don't dare. There's flashes of things: a burned shadow howling with a flame-scar on its head. Whisper shouting silent into the fray, skirts swirled about her, her face wide and bare-toothed as her ghosts tease and march. None of it's louder than the blood moving in my ears. I press farther and farther into the wall, farther so I can't see a thing. When I wrap an arm around Ariel and hold her close, not just for her comfort but to still my own shaking, she don't argue.

And then: "Back!" Jack calls, loud enough to reach us even through the stones. And like they're breaking, like this whole thing wasn't planned all along, our people scatter, stumble, run down the tunnels.

The shadows start at their heels. Stare. And with a terrible howl, run after them.

The fight roil-rumbles past us, into the old sewers and fleeing toward the new, fire and shadow-dark and yelling racing along the one bit of wall I can still see. I huddle against Ariel, driven near to weeping by the smell of death and her skin. I close my eyes and count backward from ten down to zero.

When it hits nothing, I force my head out and look around.

The path is empty. There's nothing but silence, footprints, the stubs of smoldering brands still smoking their last. The Pactbridge, decorated with a body I don't dare look to, and the big door to Safe.

Standing open.

"C'mon," I tell Ari, soft and not a whisper, and she melts and twists and shortens, growing faint, growing small.

When I can't smell her no more and her buzzing whispers through the concrete and dirt, we slip back onto the Pactbridge and steal into Safe.

Safe is strange-familiar. Safe is home, and the smell of smoke, the cold of it, the echo-roar of shadows dying stiffens my back like nothing ever did in our travels Above.

It didn't used to be so cold. It didn't used to smell like dust, like old water standing too long. Ari hovers at my shoulder, a faint hum that carries I don't want to think how far. There's no sound but her wingbeats and the slower noise of my breathing as we move heel-toe, crunching and shuffling through a dark we don't dare break.

Safe is a shell.

Nobody's in the kitchen. There's a smell there that makes me half-hungry and sick all at once, thick and oversweet: cream gone sour. Ari lights on my shoulder for a moment, and I draw in a breath and turn away. She can't give language when she's turned like this — I don't think she's ever tried — but she jumps and settles, jumps and bounces like brand-new shoes on my shoulder. I don't need words to translate that: *Hurry up. Come on.*

"Okay," I breathe, and shut my eyes. Carve in my head, in wood and paint, the map of my own Safe.

Safe is not like Above. There are only four ways to go, right-left-front-back. The paths, the common, and then just the walls, and I've walked them since I learned walking, walked them through the words of others in every Tale I've kept.

Safe is a Tale I know.

I walk.

The houses rise in ridges on the other side of the common, Whisper's and Hide's and then dimness. I walk like my papa, lion-foot, with Ari circling like a Curse 'round my hair. *Supply*, I think, cans and tools and sacks of beans kept ever-tidy and stacked. There's brands there, to make a light. I turn a little to the left, skim the kitchen counter with one hand, and reach out five paces forward to the metal supply shelves.

My hand closes on nothing.

I kneel down and feel in the dust, shift tins with my hands. The bags are ripped and the tins dented, beat-up like they've been thrown all about. I count them, like turns, noiseless with my mouth.

It don't look like nobody's eaten for days.

It's killed everyone, says the bad voice that lives in the back of my head: Atticus, or Jimmy, or shadows whispering my given name one over the other over the rest.

I swallow. It can't possibly be so. Killing would mean bodies. Bodies would mean smell.

"Ari," I whisper, and forget the carry of sound, 'cause I'm scared to speak above a whisper in the death-silence of Safe. "Ari, you smell anyone living?"

She bobs a second, circle-search, and bounces slowly down the pathways, around Whisper's silent house into the old crumbling pile that belongs to Scar. I follow, push the door open with my palm. Scar's house was always dark; Scar and Violet both were the ones afraid of light, and so he built its entry turned away from the kitchen where Jack sat with his glove off and drew steady electrical fire into the lamps. There's not even an echo of light to see by in the corner where Scar's house opens, not on the brightest of nights. I reach down to my pocket, strike a match.

It burns my fingers. It burns at my eyes, half-adjusted for darkness as they are, and I duck away from it, blinking. The light catches, steadies. Ari flutters and halts.

I step inside.

Scar's laid out on his bed like a corpse-wake, thin and pale and his scars standing out: bright pinkish smears against the grey shrivel of his skin. Ari lights on the fold of Scar's T-shirt. His hands twitch to swat her, but he don't have the strength to move them; the bones stand out in his wrists and the tendons twitch thick and scared once, twice, before they give up.

The smell in Scar's house is a wicked violence: toilets and tears and fear.

The smell's hospitals.

"Scar?" I say, careful, just as unsure as Whisper taking Violet's limp-laid hand in the hospital room where she's still laid out, mindless and shadow-stained.

He don't answer.

"Scar, talk to me," I say, and my voice is shaking. I take his hand, and with the touching his head turns, snaps over so fast I'm scared his neck might break right in two.

"I'm a Beast," old Scar whispers, tossing like he's caught between both hands of a wicked chill. "Beasts get Sanctuary." And then heart-broke: "Killer's the same as Freak Above."

I drop his fingers to the mattress. From them drips a faint wisp of shadow.

Doctor Marybeth's word comes back to me. *Catatonic.* No-think no-do no-see. Shadow-bound.

I swallow hard, real hard.

Scar curls up, or half-curls, which is all he can do so terrible twitching thin. His knees drag up to his belly and I can't take the sight of it, even as the match burns itself down. I open my water bottle and slip a bit of water into his throat, my free hand holding up his struggling, haunted head. He coughs. Some comes up to his chin. I don't know how much of it goes down right.

Ari hovers near the door, nervous, sharp. *Come on*, I imagine her saying, foot-tap big-eyed nerves. "Okay," I say. "Okay."

Scar watches us sharp as we leave him there. The light of my new match glints off his eyes.

We go from house to house, wasting our time. Chrys and Hide made it to their beds. Mack's just laid out on the floor, tilted at odd angles, broken-up and dirty. Heather's chair is overturned and abandoned behind her and Seed's house. There's blood beneath it. I can't tell if it's hers.

Half of them aren't breathing no more.

You can't tell just by looking. I have to reach down and feel their throats. I have to touch. I try to close their eyes at first, but their eyes don't close proper; they spring right back open, watching me, watching nothing.

I knew all their Tales.

Ari buzzes at my shoulder, and I lift my head up, catatonic. Not catatonic, but not feeling, shut off and hollow. I look down at my fingers, but there's no bleed and play of shadow. Just hurt. Sting-hurt and heart-hurt, and a crunched-up, distant breaking that I don't dare feel if I value my own life.

"Atticus's house," I say, sounding far away and even, and Ari flutters something that might be *yes* or *no*. I set my feet on the path away from the sloped-down wall, to the oldest house in Safe, and douse the light.

The body of Atticus is gone rotten.

The smell comes on when I open the door: thick and sick and horrid, sweet enough on the edges to make your mouth water, and the only thing that saves me from puking is the sight of slim Corner sitting above the body in a speck of vented sewer-light. Its fingers are splayed out on a stretch of crab shell, and its eyes are nothing. Not just nothing Normal, but black pits of shadow. Nothing.

Corner is tall. Corner is thin. Corner's hands stroke the dead shell of Atticus like a lover true, and it watches me in ways I can't know, can't read from the weird, torn-up smile on its face.

Mad, I think, and my knees tremble and my heart aches like a mama's.

"Narasimha's boy," that voice says, that boy-girl clean voice gone raspy from not talking. A whisper in the dark 'cause it don't know how to talk clean no more. "The Teller."

"I'm the Teller," I say, and fix my hand on the knife's handle.

Corner's empty-dark eyes follow the curve of my hand. "Come to kill me," it says, dry and sad and hollow, and a tightness comes on my arms right through the elbow, leaks up into the shoulders, creeps down the byways of chest and ribs and lungs.

For a second I feel it. Years of shadow; years of distance; unwanted and fear-bitten *hungry stained filth and there's no light in the tunnels, none but the light that they bring, fire-borne, smoke-choked, burning out the eyes for days. Pain, bright and noise and laughter and then they shut the door behind them shut you out.*

Dry dark smell for the Cold Pipes. Dry dark smell to keep you whole. Another Safe, dug out with spoons and sticks and fingernails, dry, and dark, and shadowed. But it's not the same when nobody else comes with —

This is what the bloodtouch feels like, I tell myself while my arms go weak and I stumble, and it's familiar: a sharpness beneath the eye, what I thought was an edged fingernail and was worse than unseeing all along. I can't think for thinking, for the cold and hate and endlessness of it all. *Remember this. Remember it for Telling.*

"No," I gasp out, and though it terrifies me to do it, goes against every instinct in muscle and bone, I sit down cross-legged — fall down cross-legged. I'm breathing hard, then trying not to breathe at all, gulping shallow from the mouth as the smell of Atticus's dying curls up on my tongue and makes me weep and spit.

The bloodtouch eases off my heart.

It eases off my head, and I blink: The dark lines of wall, floor, the curve of Atticus's dead claw get solid shape again. I spit one more time, dry, muffled; Corner don't care but I'm still terrified to spit before it, before the corpse of rotten Atticus. I wipe the dribbles of snot on my sleeve.

At least Ari's not here to see this, I think.

And she's not.

My heart tightens up again.

I look around, breathing slow and thin, and try not to look like I'm looking. Maybe Corner's bloodtouch can't see whatever blood moves through long-winged bees. *Please don't have run*, I think to her, out somewhere in the dark where she can't hear; wailing. *You promised not to leave me.*

Corner watches me. The knife sits poky chill against the side of my pants. I put my hands in my lap like Whisper might and try not to move.

Listen for the sound of wings.

"Your papa was good to me," Corner says sudden, its hand playing along the ridges of dead Atticus, whose eyes glow no light at all. One fingertip, then two. Upstroke and down. "He wouldn't leave, but he spoke out in quiet 'gainst the thing Atticus did."

"I didn't know that," I say, careful to talk even, talk like the lightest touch ever given. To remind it that I'm a person too. The ground is cold under me. The knife shifts on my hip. I can't hear no noise but our breathing.

"You wouldn't," it says, and smiles wide and terrible.

I don't look away. Oh god, I don't look away.

"Papa never told me," I answer, trying to keep cool and careful, like the memory of someone who spoke out against Atticus.

"He was gone soon after," Corner replies, diffident, and its nothing eyes blink one, two.

"What happened to him?" I ask past a dry throat, my hand wrapped 'round the knife-grip burning cold, cold.

But Corner just shrugs. "Dunno. Went Above. I never saw him no more."

There's no reading it. No seeing truth in those black pit eyes.

But I bet Corner don't know what happened to Violet either. I bet it don't know what's happened right outside, to Scar and Chrys and Hide. Or to Whisper's Lakeshore ghosts, or what its shadows have wrought and unwrought in the alleys and attics and burned places Above.

All wrapped up in its sorrows, it don't *care*.

Killer, my brain whispers, and I blink the tears off my eyes.

"Why'd you do this?" I ask. "Why'd you take away our Safe?"

And Corner's head comes up and its teeth are bared, its terrible rotted teeth, brown-scarred and broken like a punch in the mouth. "I didn't take no one's Safe. Atticus took my Safe," it spits, and its hand comes down hard on the invincible shell of Atticus.

"You took our Safe," I try to say, gentle, but I can't make my voice so; I can't drive away the thought of shadows leaking from the eyes and hands and smile of the scraped-up, blurry picture that's all I remember of my papa. "You killed Atticus."

"He took my Safe," it mumbles again, weeping slow shadow-things down its dead cheeks.

Outside there's a murmur. Outside the people of Safe toss and shudder in their beds, whispering *Doctor give me something give me poison give me pills.*

I push myself standing from the floor of the house that was Atticus and Corner's together.

It flinches away from me. But *"Tsujus,"* I call it, and whisper and move slow, move like one needs to for making a body not feel vulnerable and hemmed-up inside. I hold out my hand to it and say comforting things, move slow, move like a body making Safe.

Corner stinks when it takes my hand. It stinks of the Cold Pipes and shadow and hate when I wrap my arm around it: Corner Sick-thin, Sick in the head and the heart and the soul.

I don't flinch. Not when it puts its arm back 'round me, like it did when I was a child. And not when I reach down to my belt, to the handle.

The moral of the story is to always keep something up your sleeve. Especially when you don't think you need it.

"Killer's a thing you can't give Safe to and make it well," I say to it like a lullaby, like a good-night Tale, and push.

It's easy. It's small and easy. Corner is small and it goes right in.

The first stab stops short. The first scrapes on something hard, and the second, and whether it's belt or bone or something more terrible I don't know, but the third hits solid and hollow. The third makes the sound of a death-bell ringing.

And then Corner screams, and it's a worse scream than any I could ever bring out my lungs.

Corner screams and the bloodtouch comes.

My back stops working. My back goes weak and a chill sets in, cold like the stars stare down at you Above, and with it come the memories. With it come the shadows.

"Teller," the shadows whisper, and they lay their shadow hands on me and I can't see.

I close my eyes. I work the knife out, aim again, shove it deep into Corner's back. I pretend it's a carving, in some strange wood that moves soft. I pretend I'm setting down a Tale in my door.

Higher, I hear Jack telling me, back years ago when he taught me to use such things. I hit higher, and harder, clumsy, screwup, blind, the shadows numbing my face and then my hands. There's no more world, no more Above, no more Safe. There's just shadow everything, and I'm going to die tossing and screaming, and I keep hitting. I work the knife.

Then there's a buzzing and a shout and a shove, and I can feel again, can feel my hands. Corner's not there but got away, and I fall back onto my bottom and try to stop my breath from fleeing wild.

Seeing comes back slow. I open my eyes to darkness, and everything's coming up blood. Everything's coming up sunburns.

It is blood, I realize. Blood on Atticus. I look up and the first thing I've got for thinking is *Atticus is dead*, blood-covered and slumped, and I know that, I knew that, but for true I know it now.

Corner, though. Corner ain't dead.

Corner's fallen 'gainst the body of Atticus, is bleeding smear on the body of Atticus, and the ringing in my ears isn't the shadows stealing away my hearing. It's the sound of furious honeybees.

"Ari," I breathe as Corner waves its hands again, slams one 'gainst the floor, kicks out and rattles the stinking bones of Atticus so they clack one on the other. *Saved me*, I think fleeting, sight swimming, hands cold and useless as the buzzing wavers and falls and sinks to the floor. Goes quiet.

"Hah —" Corner sighs.

"Ari?" I whisper, and there's no answer.

I go rock-still, scared to put my foot anywhere in the broken bare-walled dark. "Ari?" I call, not caring if Corner hears it, and the buzz of her wings starts feeble, somewhere down on the ground, down and halfway to Corner on the right.

Oh god oh god, I think, looking back and forth between them, between that buzz I can't see and the doubled-over body of Corner.

I have to do it. I strike a match.

The light burns. My shadow-scorched eyes tear up all over again, and Corner flinches in the shadows it suddenly throws, even gaunter and more terrible in firelight than it was in the soft sewer-glow. There's no color to Corner, even washed in fire. The only wash of Corner is grey.

Corner's curled up in Atticus's bedding, curled 'round its belly where I stuck it through and through. It moves a little, weakly, like a bee walloped in the ear. But Corner is bleeding, and when Corner coughs, I know it's dying.

Done, I think, absent, sweaty-handed and cold. Done. All of us, Jack and Whisper and Bea and me, made Killer.

Jack and Whisper and Bea and me and Ari.

"Ari," I whisper, and the buzzing starts again from the far wall, from a mess of books and treasures that only Atticus knew what they held for memory.

A little bee wobbles over to me, crawling weak on its eyelash-legs on the bloody, slippery ground. I reach down and pick her up; hesitate just a second before offering my hand, my bandaged-up lifeline for her to sting and sting and sting. But she crawls in like it's houses, like it's someplace warm to go, and I lift her up close to see if she's still moving. To see if she still lives.

She twitches when I bring her close, my own breath ruffling her broken wing. The match flutters and dies and for a second I can't see nothing, can't even feel her in my hand.

And then her fuzz hovers over my lips. For one breath in, one breath out, and she lands back down in my hand and stutters long, smooth and unlovely and bruised more than a hand could ever do on every bit of skin left uncovered.

Corner sees it when her shattered-up wings fall out. But neither of us care anymore.

"Ari?" I ask, and touch her light. The flesh on her flinches with the pain. Too pale, I think. Too wobbly and pale to be good or well.

"It made you cry," she says, simple, as if I should even dare to ask for explanation. Her eyes flutter as she leans back against the wall of Atticus's broken-up house, and then they close.

My heart takes a silence for a few terrible seconds, but I feel her face and she's warm and breathing. Her heart's still going true, and there's no shadow bleeding through her skin.

Sleeping. Passed out, or sleeping. But living.

I leave her be and stumble across, through the blood, to Corner.

I can tell when it sees me with those terrible eyes of shadow. "You lied," it says, thin and almost hopeless. "You said you weren't come to kill me."

I didn't want to, I start to say, and bite down on it. Yes. Yes I did.

"I said that," I say, and then let out a tight breath. "I'm sorry."

"You're not," it says, and it's not terrible now, just sulky and broke-up like Ariel caught after a night of running. *I hate you. You don't. You're not.*

"Yeah," I say. "I am."

I don't ask it to forgive. To take it back. I came down here with Jack's knife. I chose to be Beast.

"You're not," it whispers. "Nobody is. Not you not the doctors not Atticus."

I choose my next words right careful, knowing they're words to the dying. "I don't know about Atticus," I say. Thinking of what Doctor Marybeth told me. What she didn't tell me 'bout speaking with Atticus, after and alone. What color I saw Atticus's eyes turn, hidden back behind my papa's leg and frozen-up with fear, back before I was the Teller and responsible for keeping straight and clean the Tales, on the night they took Corner's Sanctuary away. "I bet he was sorry indeed."

"He never was." The blood seeps through the squeeze of its belly and stains and stains and spreads.

That ain't true. I've been the hand, knowing and unknowing, that rewrites a Tale enough times to know when the Tale's a falsehood. I've been too long the mouth that told false Tales to let this one stand anymore.

"No," I say, thoughtful, soft. "He cried. Couple times, that we knew. That's what it meant when his eyes went golden."

"We don't know that for sure," Corner hisses, eyes so sharp I remember Atticus's; Corner's eyes bright, and the memory of Atticus's fading as his blood spilled free. "We don't know he ever cried, not for real. We took his word for it that crying's what sun-eyes meant. He could have made that up. He might have lied."

"He didn't lie," I whisper.

Corner's cheek twitches. Its eyes close and hands crumple to cover them, shaking, shamed.

"I know," it croaks, dry of hate like it's dry of water, and I think I hear it weeping.

I sit by it. I listen to it cry, and the breath slowly comes back to me, fouled as it is, stinking from Corner's blood and Ariel's hurt and Atticus's dying. The red goes clean from me. The mad washes away clean.

Corner is dying and I am back in Safe.

I am in Safe and I am the Teller and a once-sworn of Safe is weeping.

"Tell me," I say, as I hear Jack's roar and the Pactbridge clatter and the rumble of living feet tumble and stride into Safe, where the last of Corner's shadows are coughing and dying. I settle it down on the floor and hold its hand.

Its mouth works. It's running out of words, out of talking. There's blood bubbling up on its lips. A wisp of shadow coughs out behind it and wraps itself about my fingers. I yank back without thinking as the bloodtouch crawls up my arm, cold cold, turning my eyes dark and the darkness behind them into pictures, remembering; the smell of someone else's mama and the taste of black coffee and the scratch of a wool dress against legs at the age of four.

A Tale in pictures. A Tale told the only way Corner ever could tell it: from the inside.

"Okay," I whisper, soft, tongue numbing, the world going black and dim. "Tell me how you came to Safe."

CORNER'S TALE

Corner never loved in hir life until sie met Atticus.

Corner was not the kind of person who got loved. When Corner was a baby sie was born with two parts, boy-girl, and hir mama went into hysterics every time the Whitecoats even thought the word *scalpel* around her baby child. Hir mama took hir home. There were dolls and trucks both. There were dresses and sailor shorts, whichever sie'd like. And Corner's mama said, "When you grow up you'll have to choose and I'll buy you that surgery, because the way you are, I fear nobody's gonna love you when I'm gone."

Corner's mama loved hir. Hir eyes lit up at the thought of it. *My mama was a good mama*, sie whispered dying, speaking without speaking as the men and women of Safe roared through the big door and Corner bled out on the floor 'round the blade of my gutting knife. *My mama loved me how I am.*

(I nodded, and held hir hand. I couldn't see. It was hold on or fall forever. *Go on*, I said, and squeezed my eyes shut. *Show me all of it*.)

Corner took school at home. Sie studied math and art and languages, and took the tests distant to keep pace with Normal people in schools. Sie worked until sie was seventeen, and the next year meant a university or a job, and Corner and hir mama carefully did not talk about what would happen when it came time to go out into the world.

Corner's mama had a job. She kept order behind the counter at the community center down the block, and when Corner was young hir mama took hir to work and let hir play behind the wood-and-brick counters if sie would be good and careful and never breathe a word about being boy-girl.

Corner stayed home when sie was older; sie liked books and quiet better than the stares when sie went out, because when you were older people took it bad if they couldn't tell. But the women at the community center still remembered hir, and it was hir they called when the accident came on.

"Your mama's fallen down," they said, tight and scared. It was summertime. The birds were pecking at the grass seeds the landlord had laid down, and the sun, the sun was golden like flowers. "Something's burst up in her brain."

Corner ran the four blocks down to the community center foot-tripping and wild, and got there just as the ambulance was ready to take hir mama away. Sie rode with her to the hospital, holding her hand, and wept as hir mama rustled and gasped underneath tubes and mask.

"I almost have the money," Corner's mama said dying. "Just a little longer," before she bled herself out inside and died.

Corner stared and stared and tried to weep, because that was what you did when your mama died, but the world had tilted sideways like a dream, and so sie just held hir mama's hand until the Whitecoats came with the big black bag to take the body away.

"Do you have someone?" the nurses asked, wanting to call hir *sweetheart* but not sure if they could, 'cause you couldn't say *sweetheart* to boys.

"No," Corner said, watching the cart go. "Just me. Just me and my mama."

The nurses got hir a coffee. They sat hir in a chair. And they brought a man from Child Services, who knelt down to look at hir level with a clipboard in his hand.

(*Is Child Services Whitecoats?* I asked, quiet as I could. There was a crash and a clatter outside, and the whispering of more voices than could rightly fit in Safe hissing up and down and through the walls.

Child Services may as well be, Corner's ringing blood-touch said, and shut hir eyes 'gainst weeping.)

It wasn't a week before they found Corner was boy-girl.

They caught hir pants-down doing what, sie don't remember. But the nice lady they'd sent hir to stay with while the lawyers did their work took one look at hir, face and roundish chest and down, and went hauling hir before the Whitecoats in the examination room.

They poked. They prodded and measured. They stood hir under bright lights (and this part I recognized, this part I knew) and talked about hir and got hir to stand wide, stand thin.

(*There were white walls and mirrors*, I said. *Yes*, replied Corner. Hir lips didn't move with the words no more. *Yes. You know.*)

"It is too late," they said. And: "You are not enough like a girl, and not enough like a boy." And: "Your mama has ruined you for the world," which made Corner clench hir fists and bare hir teeth and jump out snarling at the Whitecoat with the sad, twisted smile.

That was when Corner learned sie had the bloodtouch.

The bloodtouch feels like singing (Corner whispered in my ear from the inside on out, and my very bones shuddered as sie wept). The bloodtouch is sweet music, the very edge of life, the closer-than-close that you can hold someone at night with your fingers in their veins. Corner and hir mama were close, bound-tight close, and Corner didn't know that Normal meant touching just on the skin, or more likely touching not at all and stiff clothes and awkward silences. Corner had suckled from hir mama's breast. Hir mama never thought it odd that her baby child could feel her very heart beating.

The bloodtouch sang, and the Whitecoat fell like an old oak tree, kicking and twitching at the toes.

"My mama didn't ruin me," sie screamed as more Whitecoats hammered their way into the room, grabbed hir hands, left bruises about the wrists. "My mama called me her little angel. She said I was one of God's children."

They put a needle in Corner's arm. It numbed Corner's tongue, took away hir thoughts.

They took hir into the dark.

When Corner woke up sie checked hir private parts first thing, scared that the Whitecoats had taken one or the other away. They were still there and safe, and Corner hugged hirself tight in the corner from the relief and fear, knowing they wouldn't stay safe long. The knowing filled hir up and left no room for thoughts and air and food.

There was also a bracelet on hir wrist, and it said *Lakeshore.*

"Why am I in a crazy hospital?" sie asked the Whitecoat they brought to talk to hir, after they'd held hir down in a chair with straps that tugged and set hir near crying.

"Because you killed your doctor," the Whitecoat said, and the bloodtouch hummed and whistled like the happiest little bird in the world.

There were appointments. There were questions, and the food came through a little slot in the door 'cause the nurses didn't dare open it, and there was tying-down or needles whenever the Whitecoats came. Never a body to talk to, and there were no books.

And it went on, day and night blurred bloody, until they brought Atticus in next door.

Atticus didn't do his banging at first. They came and went with Atticus, drawing blood that Corner could feel moving float-ways through the halls, blood that flickered halfway in hir awareness. Once a week had gone, three appointments and a day when the lunch was turkey and not egg salad, Atticus began to bang.

(There was banging in my ears too. I startled, put a hand to my ear to feel the blood inside my eardrum; Corner echoing the shouts that door-beating Atticus made in his room in the burned-down Isolation ward. But no, it was real banging. It was hands breaking down the doors, the locked-shut doors where the people of Safe had crawled and hid and were dying.)

Atticus's banging drove Corner nervous. It made hir pace the walls. It was more terrible than screaming, 'cause screaming was a thing done when one was already near-broken, and the pounding and shouting and banging of Atticus meant he thought he might someday go free. That he was tough and strong.

He got less tough and weaker with every night that passed down the drains.

It was the way the banging went shorter that broke Corner's heart, not the act of it. It was the terrible wearing away, the way hir short sleep made hir nervous, the knowing sie could never bang like that and bust free and live good. One night the banging went on and on and on and Corner tossed in hir stretcher-bed and wept for hir mama and finally the bloodtouch rose, the bloodtouch beckoned, and it reached out the walls for Atticus's guts and brain and heart and wrapped itself around them.

"*Stop!*" sie shouted, bloodtouch humming 'round his heart, and the banging shut off so quick it might never have been there.

And then: "Who's there?" came into the silence, and it was rasping and carrying and scared.

Sie told him. Sie told him *Angel*, and asked his name, and got it.

"Why're you here?" Atticus asked, low and thin and drawn-scared, a kind of scared that Corner knew because sie had felt it deep in hir belly for so long it was the same as breathing.

"Because I'm Freak," Corner said, and that is how Corner met Atticus.

They were the only of their kind to talk to. They talked all through the nights. They were both woozy and stupid for their Whitecoat appointments during the day, and their therapists frowned and stroked their chins and took down scritch-scratch notes and none could make nothing of it. None could make a thing of it because the person in charge of Isolation in the nighttime was a student, Marybeth with shy glasses and a sour face and bedtime stories she'd tell herself in some strange language. She heard the noises and the whispers and didn't tell a word.

She read to them half-nights, stories and stories that Corner could close hir eyes against and imagine not-walls, not-floor, not-bed, and through the rest of the nights Corner stroked Atticus with the bloodtouch down every limb and in the middle. Through the long nights, locked cold in Isolation, they loved and loved and loved.

(*How's the bloodtouch do that?* I asked, feeling it prickle down my skin. *Is it because you know both girl and boy things?*

I don't know, Corner said. Hir eyes were shut now. Hir lips were blue under the blood. *I think I'm just Freak*.)

Corner's therapist got madder. He got mad at hir silences, hir things unsaid. "You must choose," he said. And Corner trembled in the big chair that was supposed to make hir comfortable, because choosing meant the knife.

Corner told Atticus, and Corner wept.

"Please," Atticus begged, one night when Corner was supposed to be sleeping against the threat of the knife and the choice that came tomorrow, his face pressed to the slot in the door that brought the food in. "I don't care 'bout me. Please do something for hir. Keep hir safe."

Corner lay real still. There was a quiet.

"They're not gonna let you out," Doctor Marybeth said, faint on the other side.

"Yes," replied Atticus, and the taste of sunlight-golden flashed through Corner's bloodtouch and onto hir tongue. "I know."

Doctor Marybeth said nothing. She walked down the hall clack-clack in her Student Doctor shoes and closed the door behind her.

It was only when Atticus swung wide hir cell-room door that Corner knew she'd left them open.

And it lasted good, for years and years, until more came down for shelter and there needed to be ruling of Safe.

(I've heard this Tale before. I could tell it from my skin.)

There are differences in living Safe than living penned-up in Whitecoat hands. *A person's free*, the prickling bloodtouch said; weak, and then weaker. *They don't take you 'way from your mama. But the food don't come cut-up, and it goes bad for you when you don't have hands.*

Atticus's claws were good for cutting, for the shaping and carving of Safe. They weren't good for eating. They weren't good for dressing. They couldn't brush a hair back out of your eyes.

Corner fed him, every meal in secret, so the rest wouldn't see. *Who would believe me*, he said, *that I can lead Safe, when I can't even change my own trousers?* Sie drew his bathwater secret. Sie turned the pages of his books so they wouldn't break snipped-up.

He came to hate hir for it.

And that was the problem in the end, Corner and Atticus, bloodtouch hands and crab-claw arms and awkward, desperate loving. They were both Beasts, and when they were in hurt, they were Beastly to each other.

Corner went walking one day after their fighting, fighting again 'bout all the things sie did for him that broke up his heart and reminded him, shell-sharp, how he'd never, ever be able to do for himself. Corner went walking one day

Above, and when the day was over, there was nothing left that was home.

(*You could have stayed with Doctor Marybeth*, I said, louder than before. It was getting hard to see the pictures before my eyelids; hard to hear hir voiceless whispering over the voices, the shouting, the weeping of Whisper as she tried to wake dead eyes-open bodies and they would not wake.)

No, Corner said. There was nothing for hir Above. There was nothing in a world where everyone looked at hir guessing boy or girl, and where the red mad of hating it could bring the bloodtouch out like spit. There was only Safe.

So Corner tried to make Safe.

There was a place hid behind a fall of rock, packed loose; a waste gutter where the sewer water ran. Four dry outflow pipes that were dead and good for storing things so they wouldn't spoil. The stones were neat and even. There was water nearby.

It was a good place to make Safe. All it wanted for was the people.

Sie went to them in the sewers. Sie went to them hands opened, pleading hir Tale, and they struck fire. Sie whispered bloodtouch in their ears to keep hir skin and hair and bone safe, and they ran. Sie howled at the walls, and nobody listened because Atticus was the one who smiled or scowled at the Tales, and everyone believed his word true. Everyone except for Narasimha, lion-foot, who said "I'm sorry. I have a son to think of," and continued upward, up to the light.

Nobody came.

Corner lived alone in the sewers. Corner lived in the dark with hir memories to feed hir, and when hir sight went it wasn't a trouble, because everything worth seeing had gone shadow-lined and strange, had taken on the edge of memories.

Corner was always partway in Safe. Hir shadows curled into cracks and crannies, listened at the big door, heard the clocks strike the hour twenty-four times a day. Sie pressed them into the hands of a bee-girl, lost and lonely, who sat night after night in hir own hollow home and stared through hir like sie was a ghost. Daytimes they slipped free of the girl's fingers and wings; wandered listening for the voice of hir Atticus love or the sound of hir own name.

Corner waited outside Safe, darkening and darkening, for the day when Atticus might forgive hir.

And then one night in the space between the old tunnels and new sewers, weeping past bearing, something living came down and rested its head. Something Safeborn. A Teller.

What color were Atticus's eyes when he exiled the first Beast from Safe? Corner whispered, and my own mouth said red for hir Atticus's anger, for hate and spite. For everything that wasn't loving or Safe.

Corner went into the sewers and wept in the shadows, and knew nobody would ever love hir again.

People unite against things. People fight when they're scared and threatened, not to change, not for the future. They get it wrong in the other Tales. People don't fight for heroes: They fight for the monsters. For fear of the monsters in the dark.

Safe united against Whitecoats, and when the Whitecoats were too far away to keep Safe together, too quiet a threat to keep the arguments from crackling up, Atticus united Safe against Corner.

Those are the things Corner Told me as sie died and Safe fell.

I held hir hand until sie died, and after. Until my skin became my own again.

They came to get me once the shadows died too. Their tooth-hands and their snarl-tails shriveled up once Corner's heart stopped, once the bloodtouch took the life out of hir own tears scattered through the tunnels and warrens that led up and down to Safe. "Careful," Jack said as Whisper took my hand from Corner's dead one. Of me, he meant, not Corner. I didn't understand why.

They led me off the body, and we counted up our dead.

ARIEL'S TALE III

We buried the dead down in the caverns, in a place where the dirt was soft.

The *catatonic* left most with the shadows' dying; it drew out of them, leaving them dark and dark-haunted, tinged with Corner's remembering like Doctor Marybeth was. But lots didn't wake up: the old ones. The Sick ones. The ones that couldn't live days and days without eating.

Whisper and Jack counted our dead. I shuddered in the corner of my house, broken, breaking, and they counted up half of Safe.

It wasn't a good idea to bury dead down in the tunnels. They'd get found eventually, by workers or vermin or the carrion things that scuttle through the sewers, hunting scraps. So in regular times we burned our dead, and scattered the ashes somewhere out of the way. It was a simpler thing to gather all the wood, to gather in a place suitable for fire, to hide the scars of the burning in whatever empty star-spit field we chose.

But we'd never had dead so much in quantity before, nights and nights of fires' worth, and so we marked out a burial ground and dug it and piled the finished graves with stones, and hoped that'd be enough to keep the dark things out and away from the remnants of our friends.

There were lots.

There were lots and there was Darren, slick and troublesome, who went down head-crushed on the Pactbridge, trampled down by shadows. Bea held him long and long while I sat by Corner (they told me later), held him against her chest and didn't cry but sighed, lips pressed tight together to keep the red rage in.

"We can help you take him up," I told her in the small hours, when I'd heard the news, when the clocks in Safe were wound again and the sleepers waking and I found her with Darren's bruised-up body.

"I don't know who his people are," Bea said. She looked up at me. I don't know if she hated me that moment or no; there was no telling a thing from her voice. "We'd have to leave him in the street."

"You don't have a place —" I started, and "No," she said. Cut me off with just the word.

I didn't want this don't-care biter buried down deep with my good dead, but Darren had died protecting Safe, and it wasn't about what I wanted.

"We'll bury him here," I said, and she gave me the body, and we put him with our dead in the ground.

We laid them out straight next to each other, washed up in clean clothes. Heather and Seed's little baby, born out of a dying mama and but a day old when it died thirsting, we tucked between them, in their arms. The second child born in Safe.

We buried them down in the dirt.

We buried them and Ariel stood beside me, and while she didn't take up my hand, she didn't look away from me when I said her name, when I stood half-close, when the time came for me to pass her the shovel and her to take a turn filling the graves.

I looked at her bracelet when I came back to our house, dug it out from the box where it was hidden away.

S-C-H-I-Z- it started to say, and then I couldn't look no more for the tears.

I went walking after. I went walking through the sewers to the place near the Cold Pipes, the place where Corner haunted. It was late afternoon when she came for me in a hum that started up in my dreams, whisper-snap dreams of walking so far there's no way back under the pipes and gullies and trains.

"Found me," I said when she'd set herself down, changed back to a shape where she could be talking. It echoed through the busted-up drained-out pipe. *Found found found.* The opposite of lost. The opposite of lost ain't Safe.

"Yeah," she said, and sat down next to me veiled and shrouded in her wings.

It was quiet between us for a bit. Not a quiet that needed filling.

Then: "You're sad," she said, slow and guarded. I looked over at her, half-surprised, and the look on her face was a stubborn wary thing that made me almost think she was spoiling for an argument, but then I settled myself down and took a breath and thought *Atticus-thought. That's the thing Atticus would say.*

Look closer.

Ariel gets bad when she's scared. That's when she stings; that's what stings, scared things cornered. And she gets scared when she thinks someone might hurt her.

I let my hands sit loose so she knew I wouldn't push her away.

"I'm sad," I said, and something in her uncoiled. Something of the scared and bad.

"Why?" she asked, simple. Waiting.

My throat choked up dry and slow; I looked down at my hands, hands that weren't now blood and dirt, blood and mad, that didn't smell anymore like Atticus's dying. "I hurt you," I whispered. "I'm twice Killer: once for *him* and once for Corner." I didn't have to say that the first thing was worse by far than the two that followed. She knew what I meant: She was clear-eyed and ungrieving for the first time in so long, head-tilted and watching like a Teller. "I — I told a Tale for years and years that I knew wasn't true, even if everyone wanted it so." My hands trembled. I flattened them on my knees. "I don't know that I belong in Safe," I finished, lame and thick. Not knowing 'til I said it that it was true.

Killer's not something you can fix with Safe.

"Someone said something?"

She didn't know *named you Killer*, or the words for a Teller that lies.

"No," I said. "But I did."

She rubbed her wrists. The bruises were near gone. Not all. There was a quiet.

"You'll come up with me?" she said, carefuller even than before.

I turned my head to look at her. The line of her face was jumpy and quick, and she half-turned away before she forced herself to meet my eye, but under the nerves and scared was something else. Was serious.

"I need it here," I said. "The dark. The quiet." A pause. "The sunlight drove me near mad."

"I'd be your dark," Ariel said.

I felt something like the bloodtouch burst inside. Except it was warm; warmer. It was warm like the sunshine ought to be; it was light and heat without burning. And the tears it brought on weren't for sad, or for grieving. They were iridescent.

"You don't mean that," I whispered, finally, scared at the thought that she didn't. Scared at the thought that she did.

She looked at me a long minute — a tunnel minute, a guess, in the place where there's no clocks — and licked her puffy lips. "I dunno. If I could, I mean." She looked away. "But I'd try."

"Doctor Marybeth said you're Sick," I said quietly.

"Yeah," she said. And then she looked down. "Won't get better." *Won't get well.*

"Not here," I agreed, and it wasn't 'til she looked at me, looked and saw me freely crying, that she knew for true what I meant.

Ariel was a hero. She was the best hero Safe ever had, and she was Sick.

Sick may be like Freak Above, but we weren't Above no more. We were in Safe. And Safe could make it easier to be a Freak, to be Beast, but there was nothing we knew to do about healing up those ones who were Sick.

We don't have fancy machines. We can't keep pilltimes and talk out ways to tell real from not. We weren't Whitecoats. But we ain't Doctors either.

And there wasn't no shame in healing.

Ariel was a hero and I loved her. So I was gonna try.

I bought her peaches. A whole basket. Not stolen either, but bought proper, and every single one fat and sweet and kitten-soft against your mouth before you bit down. We went out into the old sewers and found a corner that was almost fallen in, where two could huddle in close and warm without being spotted. And we ate every single one.

It didn't cost twenty-five dollars. Barely five.

They tasted like Atticus's gaze gone sun-golden. I almost lost the first mouthful from gasping, from the sweet and soft and *iridescent* shimmering in my mouth. "You've never had a peach before," Ariel said, and I shook my head, and she put a finger onto my lips where they tingled from too much sweet and smiled, just a little.

Smiled not clean or free. I don't know if Ariel could ever smile clean or free, stuck-over with her own shadows as she was. So not clean. But halfway to forgiving.

We washed our hands on a clean pipefall, and I held her halfway as the day wore down: not full, not holding her in one place, but my hands draped on her shoulders, my chin at rest on her crown. Breathing in and out the smell of girl, of hair, of Ariel.

I ran breath-soft fingers across her shoulders, touched the blades of bone where they might become wings. The skin was all healed up, red at the edges. There hadn't been no reason to fly as a bee since Corner went in the ground.

"D'you want to —?" she asked, small like a little kid, fingers plaited one between the other. *Do you want to touch them?* She looked over her shoulder at me, and her eyes were scrunched and uncertain. Like the old Ariel. Like the girl I fell in love with.

"No," I said, soft and edgeless and sweet as she'd let me be. "Just be you."

She let out a breath, and the edge of wings that had peeked out sank away.

We were just us 'til night came on, and the pipes began singing Above.

I told her I'd be her sky and her sea, and then I put her hand in Doctor Marybeth's, and Doctor Marybeth took her away.

EPILOGUE

After Ariel went Above, I carved the big door top to bottom.

Safe was always built on the bones of its martyrs. But now there were more martyrs, old and young and those we hadn't even known would uphold us. We had to put them all into memory, and my memory is wide and sure and trained to its edges, but not wide enough to hold so much gone, so much death. I carved them first thing while the arguing went on over who would lead Safe in Atticus's place, while wood still felt strange under my blade and every time I picked it up I trembled, remembering the way flesh gave, flesh carved so much different. When they were done I had the rough of it on the door. Not the all, but enough to look at and remember. Enough so I'd finish it right.

The argument went four days and it would have gone twenty, but for lack of food and lack of fire and the hurt that everyone felt like a shadow-stain sunk deep. They wanted Jack; I know they did, and it was nothing but

Jack's straight refusal that brought them 'round and 'round, slow-spiral and late nights, to me.

On the fourth day the whole of Safe came to the big door where I was working sketch-and-cut, and Jack asked: "Teller, will you give Sanctuary for Safe?"

I breathed it in. I breathed in the smell of wood and damp and earth and old, dead fear before I answered.

"All right," I said, uneven, and the first of them knelt to me and lifted his wrists to show the scars. "But I gotta finish being the Teller first."

I carved Doctor Marybeth, and the chain of half-Sick or Passing or just plain tired that she led before me, each of them saying *we want to go up. We want to have a life.* She watched me cool and even while they each bent down and pled their case, and I know she saw Atticus's eyes, Atticus's head shaking no, no, no as I listened to each one. "It wouldn't be right away," she said, mild, when they were done. "The attic room only holds one or two."

We needed their hands. We needed to rebuild, and to mend, and to not lose anyone no more, to not keep looking for yet more missing faces around corners and in the midnight duty light.

But I couldn't say no. Right away or later, I couldn't force no one to stay.

"We'll draw up a schedule," I said. And: "You can come back. Come back if it's not good. Come back if it is." Most of them were young: Beak and Flick and Santamaria and others whose Tales I knew but did not count friends.

The oldest was Whisper.

Whisper I just held on to long and long, and tried not to show how the parting of her from Safe tore me. She had to go care for Violet, she said. The shadows had gone out of Violet, and so Violet was coming out from the hospital. She still couldn't speak without her stutters, and her hands still shook, and she needed someone to stand surety for her and turn the pages of her books the way Whisper had turned them for Atticus after Corner went broken-backed out of Safe. And Whisper, Whisper had sworn to come back for her Violet love.

Doctor Marybeth had promised them the first use of her yellow-paint attic room.

There were so few of us now. We were so small. But I was in charge now. I couldn't kick the walls and go screaming. I held on to Whisper and shuddered instead.

"Even Atticus cried," she said to me, right in my ear, sun-golden, and then my back loosened and my chin and in front of all my people who'd watched me grow, I wept.

So I carved Whisper.

I carved Ariel, golden-haired. Golden-haloed. Resplendent in the shadow of massive bee-wings that took layers and layers and scratches and swears to get right, to make so the light caught them just so on the change of sentry duty: *iridescent*.

I carved her in green. Her favorite color is green.

I carved Corner, and I carved hir thousand black-hand shadows.

I carved me killing Corner.

The color I gave my eyes was the brightest red I could scrounge up, the red of Atticus astride the rocks of Safe when he looked over its founding. My eyes burned as I took the life of Corner and it was not proud, for around us the shadows were weeping, and so was the Teller, knife in hand.

I wasn't no martyr of Safe. I had no place on that door. But the story needed Telling, and Telling every day.

Come Sanctuary Night, I told the story. I told the shadows, and I told the deaths, and I told the founding and refounding of Safe.

I told the stories of Doctor Marybeth and Beatrice and those who swore to her, whose fire and boots and words took back Safe. I told the stories of Ariel and Corner, the ones who were not there.

Then I gave Sanctuary.

I'm writing to you as myself. Atticus said that writers of memoirs shouldn't talk about themselves in the first person, but it's not myself that mattered here, not in the end. It's the people who aren't for speaking: the dead, the banished. The ones who we can't know what they have to say for themselves, but it's important to make our best try.

That's what's meant by Telling. That's why we keep the Tales.

I know what there is to say about me.

I was born here. My ma had scaly gills down the sides of her neck and my pa had the feet of a lion. When I was three, my ma died of a cold that didn't get better. When I was ten, my pa went up on his supply shift and didn't come back, and I was given as foster to Atticus.

I don't have lion-feet, though they're big and have claws instead of nails. I can't breathe underwater. I have scales down my back that shine *iridescent*, and I likely won't get children or live long as Atticus, forty-seven years before we put him in the ground with a wailing and singing that wasn't made small by the things we knew he did, the hurt he sowed on Corner and on Safe.

I was Teller, and I am Killer, and I keep the Sanctuary of Safe, even as I betrayed its every reason when I sent my one beloved up to be well. I am every bit as capable of breaking a body, breaking a heart, as Atticus and the Whitecoats ever were.

I can Tell, and I can Pass. And maybe, I can change.

Because when Corner asked me, bloodtouch-thumb, shadow-thumb to my soft hot eye, *what color were Atticus's eyes when he exiled the first Beast from Safe?* I did not answer true.

Oh, I told truth as we kept it in the Tales, and truth as we kept it in Safe, for nobody dared speak different and half of everyone had forgotten. I told truth as the histories held it, and keeping history is as much about knowing what's to be forgotten.

When Corner asked me, I did not answer true.

And here's the lie, and here, I'll say it:

When Atticus exiled Corner, his eyes weren't red or hot. They were sun-golden.

ACKNOWLEDGMENTS

It's a bit of a stereotype to say that the work and care of a lot of people go into making a first novel. It's also true in ways that I never realized until I tried to make one myself, and found out exactly why all those other novel acknowledgment pages sound like they do: So many pairs of hands go into making a first novelist that it's impossible to count them all, and deeply humbling to try. Here are a few.

Thanks to Elizabeth Bear, Liz Bourke, Amanda Downum, Cathy Freeze, Kelly Jones, Jaime Lee Moyer, David Nickle, Michelle Sagara, Marsha Sisolak, Karina Sumner-Smith, Chris Szego, and Sarah Trick, who all read drafts or chapters or snippets and told me what sang right and what didn't make sense. Chris Coen, Jodi Meadows, and Sarah Prineas graciously looked over supporting materials, the query and synopsis, and were incredibly generous with their thoughts, tips, suggestions, and confidence. They are all the sharpest readers a person could ask for.

Thanks to everyone on the Online Writing Workshop for Science Fiction, Fantasy, and Horror for providing nine years of friendship, learning, recipes, silliness, and ripping each other's work to pieces to find out how it ticks.

Thanks to everyone at Bakka-Phoenix Books for four years that weren't just gainful employment, but one of the best educations in publishing around.

Thanks to Michael Cook of Vanishing Point and Agatha Barc of The Former Lakeshore Psychiatric Hospital Project/Asylum By the Lake for the reference photos that helped build Safe and my (heavily fictionalized) Lakeshore Psychiatric. I am bad at sneaking into storm drains and former asylums, and worse at photography, and the work they do to document Toronto's geographic and social history is invaluable.

Thanks to kaigou, for the Livejournal post on what it's really like to live on the street as a teen and how fiction gets that wrong, which helped create Beatrice and her little world.

Thanks to Eli Clare and his book *Exile and Pride* for the image that sent me rushing to the keyboard, and to Cherie Dimaline and her book *Red Rooms* for the perspective on being a First Nations person in the city.

Thanks to the Toronto Arts Council, whose writers' grant both kept a roof over my head for two rounds of revisions and gave me the confidence to not give up or settle for good enough, but to do the job right.

Thanks to my agent, Caitlin Blasdell, for her sharp

editorial eye, terrifying confidence in both the manuscript and me, and unerring sense of where this book belonged.

Thanks to my editor, Cheryl Klein, for just generally being the smartest, for the rigor and care and excitement she put into every line of this thing, and for not just liking this book but *getting* it, really and truly.

And finally, to my parents, Esther and Nigel Bobet, for the steady supply of both novels and blank notebooks while I was growing up, and for telling me I could do anything I put my mind to when I was young enough to believe it wholeheartedly. I'm sorry I kept stealing your books. Here's one back.

THIS BOOK WAS EDITED

BY CHERYL KLEIN

AND DESIGNED BY

CHRISTOPHER STENGEL.

THE TEXT WAS SET IN SABON,

WITH DISPLAY TYPE SET IN TRAJAN.

THIS BOOK WAS PRINTED

AND BOUND AT R. R. DONNELLEY

IN CRAWFORDSVILLE, INDIANA.

THE PRODUCTION WAS SUPERVISED

BY CHERYL WEISMAN.

THE MANUFACTURING WAS

SUPERVISED BY ADAM CRUZ.